Praise for *BADGER BOY*

Praise for *THE BUCKSKIN LINE*

W9-BGG-544

Forge Books by Elmer Kelton

Badger Boy
Bitter Trail
The Buckskin Line
Buffalo Wagons
Cloudy in the West
Hot Iron
Jericho's Road
The Pumpkin Rollers
Ranger's Trail
The Smiling Country
Texas Rifles
Texas Vendetta
The Way of the Coyote

Lone Star Rising: The Texas Rangers Trilogy
(comprising *The Buckskin Line,*
Badger Boy, and *The Way of the Coyote*)

Sons of Texas
Sons of Texas: The Raiders

THE WAY OF THE
COYOTE

ELMER KELTON

A TOM DOHERTY ASSOCIATES BOOK
NEW YORK

This is a work of fiction. All the characters and events portrayed in this book are either products of the author's imagination or are used fictitiously.

THE WAY OF THE COYOTE

Copyright © 2001 by Elmer Kelton

A Forge Book
Published by Tom Doherty Associates, LLC
175 Fifth Avenue
New York, NY 10010

www.tor.com

Forge® is a registered trademark of Tom Doherty Associates, LLC.

ISBN 0-812-57751-5
EAN 978-0-812-57751-8

First edition: December 2001
First mass market edition: November 2002

Printed in the United States of America

0 9 8 7 6 5 4 3

Dedicated to the memory of Frederic Bean, Tom Lea,
Lawrence Clayton, Terry C. Johnston, and
Norman Zollinger. They all loved the West
and added to our appreciation of it.

PART

Texas Plains, Fall 1865

An old arrow wound in Rusty Shannon's leg had been aching all day, but the sudden appearance of Indians made the pain fall away.

"Them damned Comanches," he declared to the boy. "They don't ever give up."

Sitting on his black horse, Alamo, he squinted anxiously over the edge of a dry ravine toward half a dozen horsemen three hundred yards away. They milled about, studying the tracks marking the way Rusty and young Andy Pickard had come.

An afternoon sun glared upon the summer-curing grass. Open prairie stretched to the uneven horizon like a wind-rippled sea. To run would be futile, for both horses had come a long way and were as tired as their riders. This ravine was the only place to hide, though it seemed more likely to be a trap than a refuge.

"They're comin' on," he said. He drew the rifle from its scabbard beneath his leg.

Dread was in the boy's eyes. "It is for me they come, not you. I go to them."

"Hell no! I didn't bring you this far . . ."

He did not finish, for the boy drummed moccasined heels

against his horse's ribs and put it up out of the ravine before
Rusty could move to stop him. Andy could easily be taken
for an Indian. His hair was braided. He wore a breechcloth
and carried a boy-sized bow. A quiver of arrows lay across
his back, a rawhide strap holding it against his shoulder.
He made no move to bring the bow into use.

He stopped his pony and looked over his shoulder as
Rusty spurred to catch up. The boy said, "You stay back.
They are friends of the one I shot. They want me."

Andy avoided speaking the name of Tonkawa Killer. To
do so might anger the dead man's dark spirit and spur it to
mischief against the living.

Rusty checked the cartridge in the chamber. "Maybe this
rifle can convince them they don't want you all that bad."
He stepped down, putting the horse between him and the
oncoming Indians. He steadied the barrel across the saddle.

The boy's eyes widened. "Don't shoot. They are my people."

"Not if they're out to kill you. They're not your people,
and they sure ain't mine."

Andy Pickard had been taken from a Texas settler family
as a small boy and raised Comanche. Rusty guessed him
to be around ten, too young to carry such a heavy burden
on thin shoulders. His sun-browned skin gave him an Indian appearance, but in close quarters his blue eyes would
give him away. They were deeply troubled as he watched
the warriors move toward him and Rusty.

"They come because I did a bad thing," Andy said.

He had violated a basic tribal taboo; he had killed a Comanche warrior. Now he was subject to retribution in kind
by the dead man's friends and family.

Rusty said, "You had to do it. That evil-eyed Comanche
was set on killin' the both of us." His hand sweated against
the stock of the rifle. Andy might foolishly consent to yield
himself up, but Rusty had no intention of letting him.
"Soon's they come in range, I'll knock down a horse. Show
them we mean business and maybe they'll turn back."

"They not turn back."

As the Indians came close enough, Rusty thumbed the hammer. The click seemed almost as loud as a shot.

Andy said, "Wait. They are not Comanche."

Rusty's lungs burned from holding his breath. He gasped for air. "Are you sure?"

"They are Kiowa."

Rusty wiped a sweaty hand against his trouser leg. "I don't see where that's any improvement." Kiowas shared the Comanches' implacable hostility toward Texans. Rusty had seen people killed by Kiowas. They were no less dead than those who fell to Comanches.

The boy said, "Kiowas no look for me. I go talk."

He did not ask for Rusty's approval. He raised one hand and rode forward. Surprised, the Kiowas paused for council. Rusty quickly remounted and caught up to Andy.

"Damn it, young'un, you're askin' to be killed."

The boy did not respond. Instead, he began moving his hands, talking in sign language. The motions took Rusty by surprise, but they amazed the Indians more . . . a white boy communicating in the silent language common to the plains tribes. Rusty kept a strong but nervous grip on the rifle, careful not to point it directly at the Indians. He was keenly aware that several stared at him with hating eyes that bespoke murder. It would not take much to provoke the thought into the deed.

One Kiowa responded with hand signals. A single thick braid hung down over a shoulder, past his waist, the hair augmented by horsehair and fur. The other side was cut short to show off ear pendants of bear claws and a shining silver coin. Rusty sensed a gradual easing of the Indians' attitude. He saw grudging acceptance, though he perceived that some warriors remained in favor of hanging his scalp from a lodge pole. Red hair was a novelty to them.

He said, "They must think it's strange to see a white Comanche boy."

"There are others. Not just me."

Like Andy, numbers of Texan and Mexican children had been taken captive and raised Comanche. Such forced adoption was one way the tribe offset losses caused by war and accidents of the hunt.

Andy said in a low voice, "I tell them you are my white brother. We been to trade with the Comanche."

"Let's bid them goodbye before their thinkin' changes."

The boy resumed the sign talk. The only part Rusty understood was when he pointed southeastward and indicated that to be their chosen direction. The Kiowas quarreled among themselves. Rusty could tell that a couple of the youngest favored freeing the boy but killing his white brother. Fortunately the older warriors prevailed.

Andy said, "No look back." He set his pony to moving in a walk to demonstrate that he had no fear.

Rusty forced himself to stare ahead and not turn in the saddle. He wished he could be certain the two hotheads were not following. After a couple of hundred yards Andy let his pony move into an easy trot. Rusty sneaked a quick glance. He was relieved to see that the Kiowas were riding westward, all of them.

He wiped his sleeve across his face to take up the cold sweat that stung his eyes. "You sure pulled our bacon out of the fire that time."

"Bacon? We got no bacon." Andy's puzzled look showed that he did not understand. Many expressions went over his head. He had only lately begun hearing the English language again after years of exposure only to Comanche.

Rusty said, "We've still got a ways to go before we can take an easy breath. We'd better ride into the night as far as these horses can travel."

Andy looked back over his shoulder toward the broad prairie and everything he was leaving behind. He appeared about to weep.

Gently Rusty said, "I know it's hard. Go ahead and cry. Ain't nobody around to hear you but me."

Andy squared his shoulders. "I would hear."

*   *   *

The Red River was behind them, but caution prevailed upon Rusty to stop occasionally and survey their back trail. The boy asked, "You think they follow so far?"

Rusty saw no sign of pursuit, yet experience had taught him not to place too much trust in appearances.

"Depends on how bad they want you."

Another long look to the north showed him nothing to arouse anxiety, at least no more than he had carried in the pit of his stomach during the days since he and Andy had hurriedly left the Comanche encampment. They had been two solitary figures on the open plains. The Llano Estacado was a haven to the horseback tribes but remained a forbidding mystery to white Americans, a blank space on their maps. It was a vast country of few landmarks and few tracks. It could swallow up a stranger, lose him in its immensity and doom him to slow starvation. But for several years it had been the only home Andy Pickard could remember. He kept looking behind him.

"Back there . . . I belong."

Rusty understood the boy's painful dilemma. "Them Comanches would kill you in a minute."

The thin voice quavered. "Most are friends."

"It don't take but one enemy to kill you." Rusty had been through this argument several times during their flight. He knew the boy remained strongly tempted to turn about and take his chances. Perhaps at his age he did not fully comprehend the finality of death.

Rusty had seen much of death in his thirty-something years on the Texas frontier. Comanches had killed his own parents and had taken him when he was but three or four years old. From that point his experience had diverged from Andy's, however. Texan fighters had recovered Rusty a few days after his capture. He had been raised by a childless pioneer couple and given their name, Shannon, because he knew no name of his own.

Years later he had followed his foster father's example and attached himself to a frontier company of rangers patrolling the outer line of settlement, guarding against

Comanche and Kiowa incursion. He had remained a ranger volunteer during the four years of civil war. That service had exempted him from joining the Confederate Army and fighting against the United States flag old Daddy Mike Shannon had defended with his blood in conflict against Mexico.

Hardship had robbed Rusty of his youth, giving him the look and bearing of a man ten years older. His hair was the color of rusted metal, untrimmed in weeks and brushing uncombed against a frayed collar. A heavy growth of red-tinged whiskers hid most of his face, causing a deceptively fierce look belied by the gentleness in his voice. "It's tough to turn your back on everything you've known, but you're white. You belong amongst your own kind."

Andy placed his hand against his heart. "Here, inside, I am Comanche."

Another boy might cry, but Andy's Indian-instilled pride would not allow him to give way to that much emotion, not outwardly. Inwardly he could be dying and not show it. Even when Rusty had first found him lying flat on the ground with his leg broken and given up for dead, Andy had not cried.

Rusty said, "You'll feel better when we get to some friendly faces."

Andy clenched his teeth and looked away.

Dusk revealed a campfire several hundred yards ahead. Rusty's first instinct was to circle widely around it, but he reasoned that Indians were unlikely to build so visible a fire this near to settlements.

Andy asked, "The Monahan farm?" That had been Rusty's first announced goal.

"We're not far enough south yet."

If it were still wartime Rusty would suspect that the camp belonged to deserters from the Confederate army or men trying to escape conscription officers. But most of the hide-out brush men had dispersed peacefully when war's end removed any reason for isolating themselves.

He said, "I'd pass them by, but we ain't eaten a fit meal in days. Maybe they even got coffee."

He recognized a chance that these might be outlaws. Defeat of the Confederacy had left legal authority badly diminished at state and local levels. The wartime brush men had grown accustomed to living like coyotes, constantly on the dodge from Confederate authorities. Now a minority had turned to raiding isolated farms and villages, stealing horses and whatever else came easily to hand. The risk of punishment was slight where law enforcement was scattered thin and rendered toothless by lack of funds. The Federal occupation forces appeared more interested in punishing former Confederates than in suppressing the lawless or pursuing hostile Indians.

Rusty made out the shapes of two wagons. These gave him reassurance, for outlaws were not likely to encumber themselves with anything that moved so slowly. He reined up fifty yards short of the fire to shout, "Hello the camp."

Several men cautiously edged away from the firelight. An answer came. "Come on in."

Rusty sensed that several guns were aimed at him. He kept his hands at chest level, away from the pistol at his hip and the rifle in its scabbard. "We're peaceable."

"So are we." The reply came from someone who moved back into the flickering glow of the fire, holding a rifle at arm's length. Once Rusty could see the lanky, hunched-over form and the long unkempt beard, he was reasonably sure he had encountered the man before.

He asked, "Don't I know you from around Fort Belknap?"

The man peered closely at Rusty. "I've freighted goods over that way."

"I was in the ranger company. Served under Captain Whitfield. And before him, Captain Burmeister."

"I remember Whitfield. A good and honest man. But there ain't no rangers since the war ended. What you doin' way off out here in the edge of Indian country?"

"Dodgin' Indians."

"Us too. We're huntin' buffalo. Saltin' humps and tongues to barter back in the settlements." Barter was almost the only method of exchange in Texas since war's end. Spendable money was as scarce as snow in August. The man turned his attention to Andy, his eyes narrowing in suspicion. "What you doin' with that Indian kid?"

"He's not an Indian. They stole him when he was little. Tried makin' him into a Comanche."

"He's got the look of one. I don't know as I'd want to run into him in the dark."

"He's a good kid. Just not quite sure yet who or what he is."

"I'd put some white-boy clothes on him as quick as I could. Else somebody might shoot him for an Indian. Rescued him from the Comanches, did you?"

"It's more like he rescued me. You-all got any coffee? I'd lease my soul to the devil for some fixin's like we had before the war."

"We've got a little coffee cut with parched grain. Best we can do. Mix it with whiskey and it ain't too awful. Got some beans and buffalo hump too. You look kind of slab-sided."

"Much obliged. We're as hollow as a gourd."

Andy had not spoken. He dug into his supper like a starved wolf.

The hunter watched him with interest. "The boy's got the manners of a wild Indian, all right." The comment was matter-of-fact, not judgmental. "You've got a lot to unlearn him before you can make him white again. He some kin to you?"

"No, the only kin we've found is an uncle. He looked Andy over and turned his back on him."

"Probably figured he was too far gone to civilize. You figurin' to finish raisin' him?"

"Somebody's got to."

"I wouldn't want the responsibility. How did he fall into your lap?"

"He came down into the settlements on a horse-stealin' raid."

"That young'un ain't old enough."

"He sneaked off and followed the raidin' party. Didn't let them see him 'til it was too late to send him back. Horse fell on him and broke his leg. That's the way I found him."

"He looks all healed up now."

"We kept him 'til he was, me and some friends of mine. But he was homesick for the Comanches. If I didn't take him back he was fixin' to slip off and go anyway. So, bad as I hated to, I took him."

"What's he doin' here now?"

"A few of the tribe weren't happy to see him back. He had to kill one so we could get away."

The hunter frowned darkly. "Awful young to have blood on his hands. It's hard to wash off."

"Wasn't none of his choosin'."

"If I was you, I'd turn him over to the Yankee army. I've heard they've got schools for Indian boys back east someplace."

"But he's white. Reckon I'll keep him and do the best I can."

"I'm glad it's you and not me."

Rusty explained, "When I look at him I see what I could've been. The Comanches stole me once, just like him. If the Lord hadn't been lookin' my way, I'd be Comanche now myself. Or dead."

Rusty sipped with pleasure the mixture of bad coffee and bad whiskey. "Andy's got a long, twisty road ahead of him. But I want to give him the same chance I had."

The hunter said, "I ain't heard him speak. Has he forgot how to talk English?"

"It's comin' back to him. He just needs time."

"I've known a couple of boys the Indians taken and kept for years. Never could purge all the coyote out of them. They was like a broke horse that has to pitch once in a while no matter how long he's been rode."

"Nothin' comes easy if it's worth anything."

"Just so you don't expect too much. You're dealin' with damaged goods." The hunter started to tip the whiskey jug, then remembered his manners and offered it to Rusty. "You'll probably need a lot of this before you get that boy raised. You got a woman?"

"I'm not married."

"Too bad. Sometimes a woman's influence can help in tamin' a wild one. Got any prospects?"

"The one I wanted married somebody else."

When Rusty and Andy had finished supper, the hunter said, "You-all are welcome to spend the night. Just one thing . . . are them Comanches huntin' for this boy?"

"There's a chance a few still are." Rusty sensed what was on the man's mind. Andy's being here might put the camp in jeopardy. "Maybe it's best we move on a little farther."

"No, you-all stay. We'll double up the guard. If there's any Indians prowlin' about they're apt to give us a try whether the boy is here or not. We won't let him fall back into their hands."

Rusty warmed with gratitude. These men were strangers, yet they were offering an orphan boy their protection. "I'm much obliged."

The hunter shrugged. "We've got the Federals comin' at us from one side and Indians from another. And scallywags that dodged the fightin', pushin' and shovin' now to get onto the Union tit. Us old Texas rebels have got to stick together."

Rusty had never considered himself a rebel. On the contrary, he had harbored a quiet loyalty to the Union all through the war, though it would have been dangerous to make an open display of that loyalty. Hundreds who did so had died at the hands of Confederate zealots. He saw no point in mentioning this now that the war was over. They were all considered Americans again, though many had lost their basic legal rights of citizenship, including the vote.

He said, "I'll stand my share of the guard."

"Figured that. I wouldn't expect no less out of a ranger."

The hunter grunted. "You reckon we'll ever get the rangers back again?"

"Not anytime soon. The Federals have a hard opinion of anything they think smells Confederate. They bristle up at the thought of Texans ridin' in bunches and packin' firearms."

The night passed without incident. Rusty and Andy ate breakfast with the hunters. As Rusty saddled his horse, the leader jerked his head, summoning him to one side.

"You remember me tellin' you about them two boys that came home after years amongst the Indians? One of them eventually went to the bad. Killed a man and tried to run off back to the Comanches. There wasn't no civilizin' him. Posse had to shoot him like a hydrophoby dog."

"It won't be like that with Andy."

"Don't take him for granted. Watch him, or one mornin' you might wake up with your throat cut."

The hunters spared Rusty enough meat and salt to last until he and Andy reached the Monahan family's farm. He intended that to be the first stop on the long trip back to his own place down on the Colorado River. Andy seemed increasingly concerned after they resumed their journey.

"The man say maybe somebody shoot me for Indian."

"Nobody's fixin' to shoot you. Just the same, I'll be glad when we get you into different clothes. And we need to cut that hair."

Andy touched one of the long braids that hung down his shoulders. "Cut? What for?"

"They draw attention. Lots of folks don't trust anybody that looks different." The hunter's warning weighed heavily on Rusty's mind.

"I *am* different. I am not ashamed."

"I'm not sayin' you should be. Ain't your fault the Comanches stole you."

"It was a good life."

"But not the life you were born to. Me and Daddy Mike

and the preacher trailed after the war party that stole you, us and a bunch of volunteers. We never could catch them. It was like the wind picked them up and carried them away. I don't suppose you recollect much about that."

"A little only."

It was well that the boy did not remember much. Rusty remembered more than he wanted about the long pursuit, the shock of first blood when they came upon Andy's kidnapped mother cruelly butchered on the trail. Before that, he had never seen a person dead at Indian hands. In the years since, he had seen many. Back east there had been but one war, between Confederates and the Union. Here on the Texas frontier there had been another, against Comanche and Kiowa. He was grateful the eastern war was over. He could see no end to the one closer at hand.

Through no fault of his own Andy was caught in the middle, whipped about like a leaf in a whirlwind. Rusty had experienced a similar inner conflict, a similar confusion of loyalties during the war between the states.

He said, "It's not like you've got any druthers. At least you know what your real name is. I had to borrow mine."

Andy fingered the braid again. Sternly he said, "I will wear white-man clothes. I will talk white man's talk. But I do not cut my hair."

Rusty heard cattle bawling. The sound told him they were being gathered or driven in a place where he would not expect that to happen. Landmarks indicated he was yet north of the Monahan farm. This was still buffalo range on those occasions when migration drifted the grunting herds across it. They grazed the grass short, their sharp cloven hooves crushing its remnants into the ground, to be revived when the rains came again. It was home to deer in the brushy draws and antelope on the open prairie. Now and then a band of wild horses passed through, led by a blood-bay stallion, ranging free. It also provided forage for scatterings of cattle lost or abandoned during the war years, the offspring unbranded and subject to claim by anyone willing to gather them.

Up to now, few settlers had risked their lives by staking claims this far beyond white neighbors. That would invite a visit by war-painted horsemen from the plains. But more people would be coming soon, Rusty thought. Thousands uprooted by war were seeking new homes and a new beginning. After four years of agonizing conflict between North and South, the frontier would seem a lesser hazard.

Dust swirled over three riders pushing sixty or seventy

cattle toward a line of brush that marked the course of a sometime creek. Rusty first thought the men might be cattle thieves, but reflection dispelled that notion. Cattle were not worth stealing these days. They had multiplied to a point of becoming more nuisance than asset, difficult to sell because few people had money to pay even if they wanted them. They were plentiful enough that anyone needing beef and willing to risk exposure to occasional Indian raiding parties could venture out and get it at no cost beyond the effort expended in the chase.

At sight of Rusty and the boy the riders quickly pulled together in a defensive stance. They eased as the two approaching horsemen drew near enough for recognition. James Monahan rode forward while the other two held the herd together. He was of about Rusty's age, a little to one side or the other of thirty. Like Rusty he could have been taken for forty. The harshness and toil of frontier farm life, compounded by war, had left his face deeply lined, his eyes haunted. He sat soldier-straight in the saddle, however, in an attitude that could be taken for either pride or defiance. Knowing James, Rusty considered it an even mixture.

Rusty was not disappointed by James's noncommittal nod. Their relationship at times had been strained by differing attitudes toward the law. James said, "About decided the Comanches had put you under." His gaze shifted to the boy. "Thought you was takin' Andy back to his Indians."

Rusty rubbed his beard. It had begun to itch. He needed a bath and a shave. "Things came unraveled. Looked for a while like neither one of us was goin' to make it out."

James stared at the boy and grunted. "It was a mistake takin' him back in the first place. He never belonged with the Comanches."

"It was what he wanted."

"A boy his age don't know what's best for him. That's the reason there's mamas and daddies."

"Andy tried to fit into white-man ways, but he'd been with the Indians too long."

"Think it'll be any easier for him now?"

"Maybe not, but the bridges are burned down behind him."

James turned to the sad-faced boy, and sympathy edged into his eyes. "Sorry things didn't work out, Andy. You're welcome to stay with us Monahans as long as you want to. My sisters were considerable taken with you. So was my mother."

Rusty said, "We'll stay a few days to rest our horses, then we'll go on down to my place. The farther I get him away from the Comanches, the better."

"You think they'd come for him?"

"Several of them were itchin' to cut his throat. We had to leave there in a hurry."

"What could a kid like him do to make them that mad? It's not like he would've killed anybody."

"That's the whole trouble. He did."

James blinked, staring hard at the boy.

Rusty said, "He did it to stop one of them from killin' me."

James's expression turned to approval, something Rusty had found that he did not give lightly. "Then I reckon he'll do to keep." He surprised Andy by gripping his hand. "You're not the first who's had to come runnin' to help Rusty Shannon out of a tight spot. He's got a knack for fallin' into holes he can't climb out of by himself."

Rusty said, "I've pulled *you* out of one or two." He nodded in the direction of the herd. "What're you doin' with those cattle? You couldn't swap the whole bunch for a sack of tomcats."

"Not here, but we're figurin' to take them where they *are* worth somethin'. We're gatherin' as many as we can, me and Granddad and Evan Gifford. Come spring I'll get some help and drive them to Missouri. They ought to fetch a bucketful of Yankee silver."

Rusty admired the spirit. Some people were content to sit around and bemoan what the war had cost them. James Monahan was not. Even if the plan did not work out as hoped, it was better to be busy doing something constructive than to idle away the coming winter indulging in self-pity and recriminations.

James said, "The boy's goin' to need a lot of learnin'."

"I'll school him the best I can."

"Teach him all you know. That oughtn't to take long."

"Mainly what I know is rangerin', and I'm a fair hand with a plow. I'll teach him what Daddy Mike taught me."

"You think you can turn an Indian boy into a farmer? I can't see you bein' content to stay on a farm yourself, not for the rest of your life. You've spent too much time on horseback."

"There's no call these days for rangers, so I'll be a farmer."

"The day the call ever comes, you'll drop that plow like it was on fire."

Rusty did not argue the point, but he could not foresee that call coming anytime soon. To the authorities his ranger service branded him a Confederate, though a strong reason for his being in that service had been his loyalty to the Union. To have declared that loyalty at the time could have caused him to be lynched, as James Monahan's Unionist father and brother had been lynched early in the war.

James said, "If you're not in a hurry, you're welcome to ride along with us to the farm. These cattle move slow, so we'll be out another night."

Rusty looked back. He saw no one. "It'll do our horses good to slow down."

"Won't hurt you none either. You look like a hundred miles of washed-out trail." James turned toward the cattle. Rusty and Andy followed.

They came first to Vince Purdy, James's grandfather, a Texan carved out of the old rock of revolution and the Mexican war, bent now from years of labor and hardship but stubbornly refusing to let anything break him. His knotty old hand still took a steely grip that threatened to crack Rusty's knuckles. "I'd given up on you," he said. "Figured the next time I seen you we'd both be playin' a harp."

"I can't even play a fiddle."

Purdy's pale eyes fastened on Andy. "Couldn't you find his people?"

"We found them, but we couldn't stay. It's a long story."

The old man looked southward. "We'll have plenty of time to hear it before we get these cattle home." Several had their forelegs hobbled with rawhide strips so they could not run. "They're wild. They want to turn and go back to where we brought them from."

Like Andy, Rusty thought. "It's a wild country."

"It won't always be. I'd give a lot to be a young man again. . . ." Purdy stared off toward the horizon, his aging eyes reflecting youthful dreams still alive and stirring.

The other man was Evan Gifford, married to James's sister Geneva. Rusty had wanted to marry Geneva himself but had waited too long to ask her. Seeing Gifford always stirred up an aching sense of loss. Still, he would reluctantly admit that her choice had been a good one. Gifford, badly wounded in Confederate service and sent home to Texas to die, had fought his way back to his feet. The Monahan family had come to regard him as one of their own. Like them, he accepted hard work and frontier hazards as challenges to be met head-on. Rusty could understand how Geneva had become attracted to him. In his defiant outlook and unflinching convictions, he reminded Rusty of Geneva's murdered father. James and Evan Gifford could have been brothers instead of brothers-in-law.

Rusty forced the regrets aside and shook hands. "How's the baby, Evan?"

"Stout. You can hear him holler for half a mile." He glanced at Andy, but unlike James and Purdy, he asked no questions. He accepted what his eyes told him. "Geneva was uneasy about you . . . we both were. Preacher Webb and us, we prayed for you and the boy."

Rusty feared Evan could read in his eyes what was in his mind. "I didn't ask James about the rest of the family." It was an oblique way of asking about Geneva without directly mentioning her. Evan had never shown signs of jealousy, and Rusty did not want to stir up any.

"They're fine. We're about finished gatherin' the crops. Gettin' fixed for the winter."

"So now you're puttin' the Monahan brand on these cattle."

"It's better than sittin' around worryin' about the Yankee occupation."

"Maybe you're so far out on the edge that the Yankees won't bother you much." Rusty doubted they would trouble the Monahans anyway. Their loyalty to the Union had been well known during the war. Too well known, for it had killed the father and one son and had driven James into exile west of the settlements. Evan was potentially vulnerable, however, because he had served in the Confederate Army.

A horseman alone could travel forty or fifty miles in a day, depending upon how hard he wanted to push and how much he was willing to punish his horse. A herd of cattle did well, however, to move ten or twelve. The day was well along when Rusty and Andy joined the drive, but James pushed a few more miles before he called a halt.

"If we get them wore-out enough, maybe they won't feel like runnin' tonight," he said. "By tomorrow night we'll have them at home."

Rusty asked, "Once you get them there, what's to keep them from driftin' right back where you found them?"

"Hired a couple of ex-soldiers to see that they don't go far."

"How can you afford to pay anybody?"

"Can't. Times are so hard that some people are glad to work for three meals and a dry place to roll out their blankets. I promised them a share of whatever we get for the cattle next year."

"And if you get nothin'?"

"They won't be any worse off than we are."

James's shirt was a case in point. It had been mended so many times that it was hard to discern which parts were original material and which were patches. "Stupid damned war," James said. "All them fiery speeches, all them bands a-playin'. Look what it brought us to."

Rusty countered, "I was no more in favor of it than you were. I thought Texas already had war enough."

James cast a glance toward Andy, riding beside Vince Purdy on the other side of the herd. The boy and the old man had struck up a friendship during Andy's brief stay at the Monahan farm before going north to seek his adopted people. "How likely are those Comanches to come huntin' for Andy?"

"I think we threw them off of the trail. They'll have no idea where to look."

"You said he killed somebody."

Rusty shifted in the saddle, resting one hip while he placed extra weight on the other. The old arrow wound in his leg often pained him when he became tired. "You remember me tellin' you about the raid he went on with his Indian brother and some others down to the Colorado River country? There was a warrior by the name of Tonkawa Killer. He hated Andy for bein' white. When Andy's horse fell on him and broke his leg, Tonkawa Killer tried to finish him. Thought he had done it.

"In the scatteration after the raid, they couldn't find Andy. Tonkawa Killer told them he had seen the kid turn coward and run away. When Andy showed up with me at the Comanche camp he made Tonkawa Killer out a liar. You never saw a madder Indian. Andy had no choice but to put an arrow in him. Now he's got Comanche blood on his hands. It's like he's been orphaned a second time."

James listened soberly. "He'll feel better after Mother Clemmie fills him up with hot vittles and fresh milk."

"It'll take more than good cookin'. What he really needs is family."

"You can play big brother to him."

"I'll try, but I'm not sure how. I never had a brother before."

James said, "I did." Bitterness pinched his eyes. "The rebels took him away from me."

"Those that did it are gone now."

"Into the hottest fires of hell, I hope. I'd be willin' to go there myself if I could get at them again. I'd keep pokin' them with the devil's pitchfork 'til I knew they were well done."

"Don't rush it any. We'll all get there soon enough. I want to stay around awhile and see what happens to Texas."

One of James's younger sisters opened the corral gates, then moved back toward the main log house to avoid spooking the cattle with her long skirt that flared in the wind. They balked anyway, suspicious of the opening. A brown dog came running through the corral, barking, and almost spilled them all. James shouted at him to go back, and the dog retreated. A young heifer saw him as a wolf and instinctively chased him. The rest of the cattle followed her into the corral. Evan Gifford closed the gate before they realized they were trapped. They milled around the fence, stirring dust, slamming against the logs and looking in vain for a way out. From a safe vantage point, the dog kept barking. The heifer hooked at the fence, trying to reach him.

James growled, "I've got half a mind to kill me a dog. He ain't worth two bits Confederate."

Vince Purdy warned, "If you hurt that dog, Clemmie and the girls will burn the beans for a month."

Rusty's gaze followed Evan Gifford as Evan tied his horse and strode toward an older, smaller log cabin where Geneva waited in the roofed-over dog run between the structure's two sections, holding a baby in her arms. Envy touched him as the couple embraced. The emotion was futile, but he could not help it.

She ought to've been mine, he thought darkly. That baby ought to've been mine.

It would be easy to resent Evan, but he could blame no one. Duty had called upon him to neglect Geneva in favor of his ranger service. Duty had called upon her to tend a badly wounded soldier. Nature had ordained the result.

The girl who had opened the gate started back now that it was closed. She walked at first, then picked up her stride. She called, "Rusty? Is that really you?"

He felt buoyed by the sight of her. Her smile was like sunshine breaking through a cloud. "It's me, Josie."

She seemed unsure whether to laugh or cry. "I couldn't tell for certain, all those whiskers." A tear rolled down a smooth cheek spotted with tiny freckles. She reached up and gripped his left hand in both of her own. "We'd begun worryin' you wasn't comin' back."

"For a time, it looked that way to me too." He found himself compelled to stare at her. Josie was looking more and more like her older sister Geneva, the same bright eyes, the same tilt of her chin.

She glanced toward Andy, riding beside her grandfather. "You brought him back." It was less a statement than a veiled question.

"Things didn't work out for him."

"I'm sorry, and then again I'm not. He's probably better off."

"It's hard to convince him of that."

She asked hopefully, "You stayin' with us awhile?"

"Long enough to rest the horses." He rubbed his face. "And to shave my whiskers. I feel like a bear fresh out of its winter cave."

"You look fine to me. You always look fine to me."

Rusty's face warmed. Josie had a forward manner that disturbed him even as he admitted to himself that he liked it. He said, "These cattle are raisin' a lot of dust. Oughtn't you go back to the house?"

"A little dust won't hurt me. I'm not so fragile. Someday, when we're married, you'll see that."

Rusty's face warmed more. She meant it. He felt a little guilty, wondering if the interest she aroused in him came only because she reminded him of someone else.

A tall man with slightly bent shoulders moved out from the main house, limping a little as if each stride hurt. He stopped beside Josie and extended a wrinkled hand to Rusty.

Rusty said, "Howdy, Preacher. Didn't know if you'd still be here." For all the years Rusty had known him, bachelor Warren Webb had ridden a long and punishing circuit, testifying to his faith and carrying messages of hope wherever scattered settlers had no regular church. He never had accumulated much for himself. He was always giving it away to someone needier. During the war he had remained impartial, serving staunch Confederates and Unionist brush men alike. He had retained the respect of them all, assuring them that heaven still existed despite the hell they found on earth.

The minister smiled. "I live here now. It may surprise you to know that I've married Clemmie Monahan."

Rusty grinned. "Everybody knew it was comin', everybody but you and Clemmie." He grasped the minister's hand again, firmer this time.

Preacher Webb and Daddy Mike Shannon had found Rusty on the Plum Creek battlefield in 1840 after volunteer rangers and militia challenged a huge Comanche raiding party. Rusty had been but a toddler, frightened and confused by the gunfire, the chaos that thundered around him. Over the years he had considered Webb the best friend he had, after Mike and Mother Dora. "I'm pleased for you, Preacher, you and Clemmie both."

Clemmie was the mother of James and Geneva and of the younger sisters Josie and Alice. Rusty could see her standing ramrod-straight in the open dog run between the two main sections of the larger house. She was a small woman tough as rawhide. Though the war's hatreds had cost her a husband and son, she remained unbroken, fiercely defensive of the family that remained to her. Rusty thought it good that she and the minister had married. They were strong-willed people, and together their individual strengths were doubled.

Webb turned his attention toward Andy. "You couldn't find his people?"

"We found them."

Webb's eyes indicated that he guessed much of the story. "At least the boy's among friends here."

"He's feelin' kind of low. He needs you to talk to him the way you talked to me that time at Plum Creek."

"You were younger and easier to comfort. He's been in purgatory longer than you were."

"He never looked at it as purgatory. Livin' the Indian way came natural because he couldn't remember much else. Now he's lost that. He's got no solid ground to plant his feet on."

"You'll be takin' him south with you, I suppose."

"In a few days. He's got kind of used to things down there, and the people. I hope you haven't given his clothes to somebody." Andy had shed his white-boy clothing for breechcloth and moccasins when he had left here to go back to Comanchería.

"They're still here, just like he left them." Webb suggested, "If you'd leave him here the girls would treat him like a younger brother. They'd enjoy teachin' him to read and write. And Clemmie needs somebody like him to help make up for losin' Billy and Lon."

"She's got *you* now. And she's still got one son."

"James is a grown man. He travels his own road. She needs a boy who'll need *her*."

Rusty did not ponder long. "This is too close to Comanche country. It'd be easy for him to take a notion to go back and test his luck. They'd likely kill him."

Webb frowned. "I guess you feel a special kinship to him, seein' what you both have gone through."

"We have a lot in common, and I've got no blood kin anywhere that I know of."

"Maybe it's no accident that he fell to you. The Lord knew you'd understand Andy in ways nobody else would."

"I hope gettin' into regular clothes will help him make the change. But he says he's not cuttin' his hair."

Webb shrugged. "Leave him somethin'. He can't change everything overnight."

Rusty thought back on the buffalo hunter's dark admonitions. "Do you think he can *ever* change it all?"

Among the Comanches, Andy Pickard had earned the name Badger Boy because he had that small animal's fiercely defensive attitude when threatened or abused. He had made it a point to strike back for every blow struck against him. When circumstances did not allow him to do it immediately, he would await his chance to administer punishment. No insult was forgotten or allowed to go unanswered indefinitely. After a time the abuse stopped. Those who would maltreat him learned that retribution was certain, even if occasionally postponed.

He faintly remembered that he had been called Andy long ago, but hearing that name still caught him off guard at times. He had an uneasy feeling of not knowing for certain who he was. His life before capture by the Comanches seemed distant and unreal, like a dream dimly remembered. He could grasp only fragments, while most of it drifted out of his reach.

He was ill at ease among most of these white people who wanted to be his friends. When Rusty was reluctantly taking him north to rejoin The People, they had stopped to rest awhile at the Monahan farm. Andy had perceived a special bond between Rusty and this family, a bond that had to do with the white men's war and the misfortunes it had brought upon them all. In vague ways these people conjured up hazy memories of a white mother and father whose faces Andy could no longer bring into focus but whose voices echoed faintly in his mind.

He could not discern what was memory and what was illusion. The Comanches placed heavy importance upon dreams. Perhaps what he thought he remembered of his Texan family was no more than that, a persistent dream that haunted him like a mischievous spirit. It seemed to offer secrets but dangled them just beyond his grasp.

Memory or dream, it kept coming back while he was with the Monahan family. And sometimes in the middle of the night he woke up in a cold sweat, remembering his Texan mother's screams as she died.

Comanches had killed her. That he knew, yet he held no malice against them. After all, they had taken him in. Buffalo Caller had claimed him as a son, and Steals the Ponies, after resenting him for a time, had accepted him as a brother. The People had become *his* people.

After awakening from a nightmare he would lie with open eyes, mourning over having left them, wondering if somehow he might yet find a way to rejoin them without jeopardizing his life. No way presented itself, but he clutched at the hope.

Andy stayed close to Rusty as much as he could. When Rusty was not available, he turned to Vince Purdy. The Comanches had taught him respect for elders, and Purdy had a gentle nature as well as a wise countenance. Andy felt comfortable in the old man's presence. He wanted to feel the same way about Preacher Webb, for the minister seemed tolerant and understanding. However, when he spoke about religion he left Andy confused. Webb's teachings seemed different in many ways from those of the Comanches. So far as Andy had been able to determine, the two religions had little in common except belief in a central great spirit who oversaw the world.

Clemmie Monahan reminded him in some particulars of

his adoptive mother, Sparrow, widow of Buffalo Caller. She had always been busy, flitting from one task to another like a hummingbird, never settling for long. Clemmie's many attentions to him were well meant but smothering. She treated him like a child, and he did not consider himself a child. He had ridden with older warriors on a raid, though without permission. That should qualify him as grown, or nearly so. Clemmie's daughters were much the same, especially the youngest, the one called Alice. The oldest daughter, Geneva, was kind but did not overwhelm him. She had a husband and a baby who commanded most of her time.

Rusty had spoken little about Geneva, but Andy perceived that there once had been a strong attachment between the two. He saw it in the way Rusty watched her when she was not looking and quickly cut his gaze away if she glanced in his direction.

In this respect he found little difference between white man and Comanche. He had observed Steals the Ponies's disappointment when a young woman he favored had chosen someone else. He saw the same futile longing in Rusty's eyes. Unlike Rusty, Steals the Ponies had put his disappointment aside and sought the favor of another.

As much as possible Andy tried to remain outdoors, away from the attention of the womenfolk. He enjoyed watching the men brand the cattle they had gathered and brought to the farm. A man named Macy, a former soldier for the South, was accomplished with the reata, a long rawhide rope. From horseback he would cast a loop around an animal's hind feet and drag it to a fire. While a couple of men held the struggling creature down, James Monahan would pull a long iron bar from the blazing wood and draw his brand on the bawling animal's side. Rusty said it was the letter M. He promised that once Andy learned all his letters, he would be on his way to reading and understanding the talking leaves of books and newspapers.

Andy understood that when enough cattle had been gathered, James intended to drive them to a faraway place called Missouri and exchange them for money. He could not fathom white men's obsession with money. It was worthless in itself. It could not be eaten. Silver coins could be used as shiny ornaments on necklaces and bracelets and such, but they had no other practical purpose that he could see.

Still, he was told that they could be traded for food, for horses, even for land. It seemed a poor exchange. But white people had strange ways.

He heard James tell Rusty, "You can't do much farmin' from now 'til spring. You and Andy could cow-hunt down yonder this winter like we're doin' here. Come spring, throw your gather in with ours and I'll take them north. The bigger the bunch, the more buyers they ought to draw."

Rusty acknowledged, "I've been thinkin' about it."

That pleased Andy. He had pictured himself wasting the winter days sitting in Rusty's cabin, studying books, learning to read and do ciphers. He would much rather be on horseback chasing wild cattle. Living among The People, he had been considered too young to go on a tribal buffalo hunt. Only grown men were privileged to participate in the excitement. Andy had been compelled to remain with the women and children, watching the action from afar, then moving in to the killing ground for the unpleasant skinning and cutting of meat. Though cattle seemed a less dangerous challenge than buffalo, at least he could share in the pursuit.

Talk in the evenings often turned to politics, which did not hold Andy's attention long. He understood little of it. He could tell that it meant a great deal to Rusty and the Monahans, however.

James said, "I'm hearin' that the military has set up a provisional government for Texas. General Reynolds has appointed his own people to office 'til the state can hold an election."

Evan Gifford said, "But I hear they may not let us old Confederate soldiers vote—me and Macy and Lucas here." He pointed to the men who worked for the Monahans. Lucas bore a jagged battle scar across his arm. Working, Lucas might roll up the other sleeve, but never the one that covered the mark. Andy thought that strange. Such a scar would be regarded as a symbol of honor among Comanche warriors. The more scars, the higher the honor.

James said, "They've been thrashin' the vote question around. One time I hear that everybody can vote if they'll take an oath of allegiance. Next time I hear that soldiers of the Confederacy are disqualified. Just goes to show why there ought to be a law against war. Maybe even a law against laws."

That too gave Andy pause. Among the Comanches, war was highly regarded. Only battle and the hunt gave a young man the chance to gain honor and respect. He had heard older men discuss what a calamity it would be if they killed all their enemies and had no one left to fight.

James declared, "Local sheriffs and judges do the best they can, but nobody knows how much authority they've got under the occupation. Thieves and outlaws run free and nobody does much to stop them."

Rusty nodded. "They need to organize the rangers again."

James said, "No chance. Last thing the Federals want is to give guns and authority to old Confederates."

Andy had heard much talk and wonderment among The People about the war between white men of the North and South. They had taken advantage of the increased opportunity for raiding into the settlements because so many young white men had been drawn away to the distant fighting, weakening the Texan defense.

He had seen a few Yankee soldiers. They looked no different from Texans except for the blue uniforms and that some had black skins. He knew only one black man, a former slave named Shanty who lived near Rusty's farm. He had found that Shanty's color did not rub off like paint, as he had thought it might.

Andy did not understand why Yankees and Texans would fight one another. It was not as if they were different in the way Comanches and Apaches were different. War between those tribes seemed natural because they had so little in common and all wanted to hunt on the same land. So far as he could determine, white men of the North had little interest in coming this far to hunt.

Josie Monahan was trying to teach Andy his letters and to print his name. During his earlier visit she had coached him on the use of English, helping him remember bits of the Texans' language. He still felt awkward, often struggling for a word that seemed determined to hide from him in a far corner of his mind.

She said, "If you'd talk Rusty into stayin' longer, I'd have time to teach you out of the first reader."

He guessed that the first reader must be a book. He wished he could learn to read without having to study so much. Studying made his head hurt.

He suspected that Josie was less interested in teaching him than in keeping Rusty around as long as she could. It was plain that she had strong feelings for him. He was not sure to what extent Rusty shared those feelings, though in his view if Rusty could not have one sister he should be contented with another. They looked much alike, and the younger one was not encumbered with a husband and baby.

He had seen more than one Comanche warrior who was disappointed in his first love but had taken the next youngest sister and found her more than satisfactory.

Josie had taught Andy to recite the alphabet from A to Z. Now she began trying to teach him the look and sound of each letter. She drew one on a slate.

"That's an H," she said. "It makes a 'huh' sound."

It was like no word Andy knew in either English or the Comanche tongue, but he repeated after her to keep her from becoming impatient. "What's it for?" he asked.

"Lots of words start with H, like *harness* and *house* and *horse*. If you use enough imagination you can almost see a horse in that letter. See his body and his legs?"

"His head, his tail, they stand straight up."

"I said you have to use a lot of imagination." She wiped

the slate and made a single vertical mark. "That's the next letter, I."

"Don't look like nothin'."

"I means me, myself. If you use your imagination, you can see your own picture in that letter."

Andy shook his head. "Where my arms and legs?"

She said, "In the picture, you're standin' sideways."

Andy heard Rusty chuckle. Preacher Webb was wrapping a clean cloth around a rope burn on Rusty's right hand after having applied hog grease. Macy had been trying to teach Rusty how to use the reata in catching cattle. Rusty had thrown a loop around a young bull's horns but had made the mistake of letting the rawhide rope play out through his hand.

Andy had learned that Preacher Webb was a medicine man of sorts, though he had none of the feathers and rattles and powders that tribal shamans used. He spoke no incantations beyond a simple "Lord willin', that'll get better. But your hand won't fit a plow handle very good for a while."

"Won't be much plowin' to do anyway with winter comin' on. I expect I'll spend most of my time gatherin' unclaimed cattle like James has been doin'."

Webb glanced toward Andy. "I hope you'll spend some time teachin' Andy to read and write. Josie has made a start."

"I'll do the best I can. When it comes to books, I'm only middlin' myself."

Webb said, "Teach him out of the Bible. That way he'll learn two lessons at one time. I doubt he's studied much religion where he's been."

Rusty replied, "The Comanches have religion. Not the same as you teach, but I guess it fits them all right."

Webb's wrinkles deepened. "Teach him anyhow. When he's old enough, the Lord'll show him what's right."

Andy wondered if that meant going on a vision quest. Among the Comanches, when a boy came of age he went out alone to seek guidance from guardian spirits, usually in a vision. Only when he had experienced such a vision could he be considered truly a man.

James Monahan burst through the front door, his face dark with trouble. "Rusty, we're fixin' to have company. Where's your gun?"

Rusty looked quickly at Andy, then stepped toward his rifle leaning in a corner. "Comanches?"

Andy swallowed. They've come for me, he thought. He could imagine them cutting his throat for what he had done to Tonkawa Killer.

James said, "No, it ain't Comanches. It's the Oldham brothers."

Rusty's worried look told Andy that the name Oldham had a dark connotation. Rusty picked up the rifle, flinching at the pain in his burned hand. He seemed to debate with himself about whether to stand the weapon back in the corner. He said, "Maybe they've come to realize that I was forced into what I did. Maybe if I don't have a gun in my hand this time, I won't need one."

James warned darkly, "I doubt they've realized a damned thing. They're bullheaded, ignorant, and mean as snakes." He lifted his own rifle from its pegs atop the fireplace. "At least step back into the bedroom out of sight 'til I take the measure of their temper." He did not have to check his rifle. He kept it loaded all the time.

Andy could not remember hearing anyone mention the name Oldham before. He looked at Josie, hoping she might explain, but she only stared in silence at the front door, fear in her eyes.

"Who the Oldhams?" he asked.

She shook her head, bidding him to silence. He turned to watch the door. Boots struck heavily on the porch, and a large man entered the room. He had a rough face that reminded Andy of a defiant Apache captive he had seen once. A smaller man followed. He had but one arm, his right sleeve pinned below the shoulder.

The two men stopped. The larger one looked in surprise

at James's rifle. "What's the matter, Monahan? A man'd think we're horse thieves or somethin'."

He carried a pistol in a leather holster high on his right hip. The smaller man wore one on the left side.

James considered before he answered, "I knew who you were when I saw you ride in, Clyde. What I don't know is why you're here."

"Just passin' through the country. Thought we'd sleep in your barn or under your shed tonight. Looks like it figures on rainin'."

James thought again. "Ordinarily we wouldn't turn anybody out to sleep in the rain, but this ain't an ordinary situation. I want you-all to take off them pistols and hand them to my granddaddy."

Clyde Oldham blinked in astonishment, resisting a moment, then giving in. "Never heard of such a thing." He unbuckled his belt and handed the weapon to Vince Purdy. The one-armed man held out until Purdy extended his hand.

Clyde complained, "We've visited better houses than this, and nobody ever told us to hand over our guns."

James said, "We want to head off trouble before it can start. You-all ain't the only guests we've got. Come on out, Rusty."

Rusty stepped from the bedroom. Andy watched the Oldham brothers' faces change, eyes widening in surprise, then narrowing. Clyde exclaimed, "Ranger Shannon!" He stared in disbelief. "I hoped somebody had killed you long before now."

"Been some wanted to. Your brother Buddy-Boy tried as hard as anybody."

Clyde's voice was gritty. "And look what you done to him. He's only got one arm."

"What else could I do? He was fixin' to kill me."

The younger brother's face filled with hatred. "Looks like I'll still have to." He extended his hand toward Purdy. "Give me back my gun, old man."

Purdy stepped away, maintaining a tight grip on the pistol. "I reckon not."

Clemmie Monahan quickly sized up the situation. She said firmly, "There'll be no sheddin' of blood in this house. The war is over."

Andy looked from one face to another in confusion. The tension was tight as a bowstring. He could only guess at the root of it.

James stared fiercely at Clyde Oldham. "I was there at the brush camp when it happened, remember? Your mutton-headed brother took it on himself to declare Rusty a Confederate Army spy and try to shoot him. Damned lucky Buddy-Boy didn't lose more than an arm."

Rusty said, "I don't want any trouble here on my account. It's better if me and Andy go."

Josie protested, "Go? But why? A couple more weeks and I'll have Andy talkin' and readin' pretty good."

Rusty said, "It can't be helped."

Josie argued, "It was wartime when all that happened. We're at peace now."

Rusty said, "Not everybody." He looked at Clemmie. "The war brought too much grief to this place. I don't want to be the cause of any more. We'll leave soon as we can throw our stuff together."

Josie said, "You're not the one in the wrong here. Let *them* leave."

Rusty shook his head. "If they go first, they'll just stop out yonder and lay in wait for us."

Buddy-Boy's eyes reminded Andy of a wolf closing in on a crippled buffalo. "We just might, for a fact."

Rusty shrugged. "You see how it is. So me and Andy will leave. I don't think the Oldhams are Indian enough to trail us."

James said, "We'll take them cow-huntin' with us tomorrow. They can work for their keep."

Clyde protested, "We ain't your slaves."

James lifted the muzzle of the rifle a couple of inches, just enough to get the Oldhams' attention. "You're our guests. We wouldn't think of you-all leavin' before you've wore out your welcome."

Tears glistened in Josie's eyes. "Don't go, Rusty. Please."

Rusty started to reach out to her, then dropped his hands. "We'd figured to leave in a day or two anyhow. This is just a little quicker than we thought."

Clemmie said, "Come into the kitchen, Josie. We'll fix up some vittles for them to take along."

Reluctantly Josie turned away, pausing in the door for a look back.

James said, "You-all can leave at first light."

Rusty shook his head. "No, we'll leave now. No use takin' a chance on somethin' goin' wrong."

Buddy-Boy gave Rusty a look that could wound if not kill. "A rabbit can run far and fast, but a patient wolf always gets him sooner or later."

Rusty's eyes were sad. "It was you and your brother that brought on the trouble. I didn't want any of it. But if you ever bring any more trouble to me, I won't stand still and be a target." He jerked his head. "Come on, Andy."

As he walked out the door Andy heard James say, "Clyde, you and Buddy-Boy set yourselves down. My sisters'll fix you some supper."

Clyde sat in sullen silence. Buddy-Boy said something in an angry voice; Andy could not make out the words. But James's reply was clear. "I'm a damned sight better shot than Rusty is."

Vince Purdy and Preacher Webb came out to the barn to watch Rusty and Andy saddle up. Vince nodded toward lightning flashes in the east. "I'm afraid you're fixin' to get wet."

Rusty said, "That's all right. The country needs rain to make winter grass. Might make our tracks hard to find, too."

Webb said, "Normally I hate to speak ill of anybody, but there's not much good to be said about those Oldhams."

Vince was in a mood for a fight. "You sure you don't want to stay and have it out with them? Leavin' only puts things off to another day."

Webb said gravely, "Killin' is a mean thing in the sight of the Lord, but I believe there's times He knows it needs to be done. God forgive me for sayin' this, Rusty, but it would've been better if you'd killed the both of them that day. You may still have to do it."

"Not if they don't find out where I live."

"Nobody here will tell them anything."

Evan Gifford and Geneva heard the commotion and came out of their cabin. They waited as Rusty and Andy led their horses back toward the main house. Geneva said regretfully, "You're leavin' early."

Rusty could not look at her without a feeling of loss. "Somethin' came up."

Evan said, "The Oldham brothers. I was with James when they rode in. If there's anything I can do—"

"Much obliged. You can help James see that they stay here awhile."

Andy noted that Rusty gave Geneva a long look before he pulled away and moved on toward the main house. Clemmie and the girls came out from the dog run. Josie said, "We've put somethin' together for you and Andy to eat on the way." She handed Rusty a canvas sack and managed to hold on to his hand. He did not immediately pull it away.

Rusty said, "I'm obliged to everybody. I'm sorry we brought trouble to your door."

Clemmie said, "Trouble is no stranger here. You've helped us through the worst there ever was. We'd do anything we can for you."

"You wouldn't do murder. That's what it might take to settle with the Oldhams."

Rusty shook hands with the men, except for James, who remained in the house to watch the brothers. Clemmie and both girls hugged Andy. It made him uncomfortable.

Josie said, "Mind now, Andy, you keep studyin'."

He promised her he would, though he had reservations.

Riding away, Andy turned to look back at the lantern

light in the windows. He said, "That Josie, she likes you. Likes you pretty good."

Rusty did not answer.

Andy said, "Those Oldhams don't. You think they like to hide and kill you?"

"I'd bet my horse and saddle on it."

"Why we don't hide and wait for *them*? Kill them easy."

Rusty gave Andy a look of disbelief. "That's not the way honest men do things."

"It is Comanche way. Kill them, you fix everything."

Rusty grunted. "I've got a lot more to teach you than just how to read."

PART

Colorado River, Texas, 1871

Six years had passed without war, but they had not brought peace. They had brought a reconstruction government but not reconstruction.

The blacksmith rolled the wagon wheel out for Rusty to see. He leaned it against his broad hip and said, "There she is, a few spokes, a new rim, and she's as good as when that wagon first came out of the shop that made it."

The original wheel had buckled when Andy brought the team a little too fast down a rough hillside. He had a youth's weakness for speed. "It'll do fine," Rusty said. He dug into his pocket, wishing he did not have to spend any of the dollars he had received for cattle he sent up the trail with James Monahan. It seemed there were never enough dollars to cover his needs and still pay the heavy taxes imposed by the occupation government.

The blacksmith remarked, "You've taught that Andy boy readin' and writin', but you ain't taught him much about caution. He's whipped most of the young fellers his size around here and some a right smart bigger. Still got a lot of Indian in him."

"Lord knows I've tried. He's got no notion about consequences. Do it now and think about it later, that's his style."

More than once since he had been living with Rusty, Andy had taken a horse, a blanket and very little else and disappeared without offering any explanation. After several weeks he would return thinner, browner, and silent about where he had been. Threats of punishment had no effect.

The responsibility weighed heavily on Rusty's shoulders, like a hundred-pound sack of feed. Sometimes he wondered if he had assumed a load he was not equipped to carry. He observed, "At least Andy makes friends of most of the boys after he's whipped them."

"I've been afraid he'd get hisself killed before you could finish raisin' him. He'd be sixteen, maybe seventeen now, wouldn't he?"

"The best we can guess."

"Ever talk about goin' back to the Comanches?"

"Not anymore, but now and then he gets moody. He stares off to the north, and I can guess what's in his mind." At times Andy would be sitting in a room with Rusty or riding alongside him on horseback but seem to be miles and years away.

The blacksmith said, "He sure needs a woman's influence. You got any prospects?"

Rusty sidestepped the question. "Do you hear somethin'?"

Shouts arose from down toward the mercantile store.

The blacksmith turned his right ear in that direction. "Sounds like a fight. I'd bet you a dollar that Indian of yours is in the middle of it."

Rusty said, "I've got no extra dollar to throw away." He set out down the dirt street in a brisk trot, ignoring pain from the old arrow wound in his leg. He muttered, "Damn it, I can't turn my back for five minutes . . ."

There was hardly a young man living in or around the settlement who had not made his peace with Andy, often after a stern comparison of knuckles. But now and then a new one turned up.

The first face he saw was that of Fowler Gaskin, long-time neighbor, perpetual thorn in the side of Daddy Mike and now of Rusty. Old Fowler called himself a farmer, though he farmed just enough to stave off starvation. Rail-thin and sallow-faced, he was perpetually hungry-looking. For miles around, neighbors dreaded his visits because he seldom left without taking something with him whether it was offered or not. Nothing he borrowed ever seemed to find its way home unless the owner went and fetched it. Half the time it was not to be found, even then. Gaskin would have broken it, sold it or traded it for something else.

Gaskin was shouting, "Git him, Euclid! Git up and show him. We don't let no damned halfway Indian come to town and act like he's as good as a white man." Tobacco juice streamed from Fowler's lips and glistened in his gray-speckled beard.

Though Euclid Summerville was several years older than Andy and forty pounds heavier, he lay pinned on his back. Andy sat astraddle and pounded on him while Summerville waved his hands futilely, trying to ward off the blows.

He was Gaskin's nephew. Rusty used to believe that Texas could never produce specimens of humanity as worthless as Gaskin's late sons, but Summerville had proven him wrong. He was as lazy as his uncle, sharing the old man's bad habits and contributing a few of his own. Rusty had heard speculation that he had been more than friendly with Gaskin's homely daughter. If that was so, he hated to think what manner of offspring the inbreeding might produce.

"How I wear my hair is my business," Andy declared. "Now say you like it just the way it is."

Summerville choked as he tried to answer. "Damn Indian son of a bitch!" He face was red enough to suggest he was about to go into some kind of slobbering fit.

Andy gave Summerville's arm a strong twist. "Say it."

"All right, all right. I'm sayin' it."

Gaskin stepped in closer to protest. "Git up from there and whup him, Euclid. You can do it."

Obviously Summerville could not. His dusty face, already pudgy, was beginning to swell from the punishment. Blood trickled from the corner of his mouth. Andy pushed to his feet and stepped back. Stooping to pick up a pocketknife, he started to close the blade, then reconsidered and broke it off against a hitching post. He pitched the ruined knife to Summerville.

"Next time you try to cut off my hair, I'm liable to cut off somethin' of yours."

Gaskin shouted, "Where's the law when you need it? This damned Comanche needs to be throwed in jail."

A bystander said, "Euclid started it. You'd better tell him to pick on people his own size from now on. The smaller ones can beat the whey out of him." Several onlookers laughed.

For the first time, Gaskin took notice of Rusty. "You Shannons! Damned Unionists and Indian lovers, the lot of you."

Rusty managed to contain his rising temper. "You'd better go home, Fowler, and take Euclid with you. He's liable to pick a fight with some schoolgirl and get beat up again."

Gaskin could see that none of the crowd showed sympathy for his nephew. He muttered to himself and jerked Summerville's arm. Near exhaustion, Summerville almost fell. "Come on," Gaskin said. "We got better things to do than furnish entertainment for the town loafers."

Summerville mumbled some halfhearted excuse, but it was not intelligible. The community did not have a high regard for his mental abilities.

Watching them leave, Andy dusted himself off, then sucked at a bleeding knuckle.

Rusty said crisply, "Haven't you ever seen a fight you could back away from? You're lucky Euclid didn't stick that blade between your ribs."

"He tried to cut off my braids."

"You'd save a lot of trouble if you'd cut them off yourself."

"I've told you before, I won't do that."

Rusty had not pressed that argument much. For most of six years Andy had been resolute against giving up this remaining symbol of his life among the Indians. He wore the same plain clothes as most other farm boys, but the braids and moccasins remained, marking him as someone different.

Turning to leave, Rusty saw a man striding in his direction, his expression stern. The badge on his shirt marked him as a member of the recently organized state police force.

"You two!" the lawman said curtly. "You ain't goin' nowhere 'til I've talked to you."

Rusty bristled but tried not to show it. "Talk. We're listenin'." He regarded the man as having been misled into an exaggerated view of his own importance.

"I heard there was a fight in the street just now." The policeman glared at Andy. "By the looks of you, you was in the middle of it."

Andy held stubbornly silent. Rusty said, "There wasn't much to it, just a little difference of opinion. No blood spilled, hardly."

"It's my job to keep the peace. Looks to me like the war ought to've given you rebels enough fightin' to last you for twenty years."

By that, Rusty guessed the man had not fought for the Confederacy. He had probably either dodged conscription or had gone east and served with the Union, which in the eyes of most old Texans branded him as a scalawag. Since the reconstruction government had organized its own police force it had tried to obtain officers free of Confederate connections. Some were well-meaning and honest citizens. Some were not worth the gunpowder and wadding it would take to send them to Kingdom Come.

Rusty had a gut opinion about this one. He said, "You know how it is when you throw a couple of bull yearlin's together. They've got to see who's the toughest. Wasn't no harm done."

The officer demanded, "Who else was involved?"

"I believe he's already left town. Anyway, he learned his lesson. I doubt he'll pick on Andy Pickard anymore."

The officer scowled at Andy. "Boy, you look old enough to get acquainted with the inside of the jailhouse. Remember that the next time you come to town." He walked away.

Relieved to see him go, Rusty warned, "Next time it's liable to be a troop of soldiers instead of one state policeman. We'd best be gettin' home. I'm lookin' for Len Tanner to come back most any day now."

Rusty and Tanner had ridden together as rangers before and during the war years. They knew enough about one another to earn each a medal or to put them both in jail.

The lanky, freckle-faced Tanner bit the end from a ragged, home-rolled cigar and lifted a tallow candle from the table to light it. His gaze followed Andy Pickard, walking out onto the dog run of Rusty Shannon's log cabin. He said, "I'd swear that boy's grown a foot since last I seen him. Next time I look, he'll be a man."

Rusty argued, "Look again. He just about is. Anyway, you've only been gone a couple of months."

Tanner had ridden to East Texas to visit his kinfolks, which he regarded as duty more than pleasure. "What you feedin' him?"

"Same as what I eat, and I ain't growed a bit. Just get a little older every day."

"How old is Andy now?"

"Old enough to beat the stuffin' out of Euclid Summerville, and him a grown man."

"Grown, maybe, but not much of a man."

Tanner stretched his long legs out in front of him and leaned back in his wooden chair, which squeaked under the strain. Rusty had braced it with rawhide strips because dryness had loosened its joints. "First time you brought Andy here I didn't think you could ever make a white boy out of him. But damned if he don't talk pert near as good as me and you."

"He reads faster than I do, and writes better too."

"That ain't sayin' no hell of a lot." Tanner grinned, enjoying his little joke. Rusty saw no reason to spoil his fun. He knew Tanner did not mean it maliciously.

Having no home of his own and no evident ambition toward acquiring one, Tanner spent much of his time here with Rusty and Andy. He came and went as the whim struck him. He helped with the farm and the cattle enough to earn his keep. He was a good hand when he wanted to be, but he never put his heart into work with plow and cow as he had done while serving as a ranger.

Tanner said, "Wish I'd seen the fight. Looks like there'll always be some Comanche in him."

"I'd like to have a Yankee dollar for every scrap those braids have got him into. Reminds me some of Daddy Mike. He was bad about fightin' too."

"Mike finally got killed."

Rusty sobered. "Yes, he did."

He contemplated that possibility for Andy but rejected the notion. He could not allow such a thing to happen, not so long as he had breath in his body.

Andy came back into the room, visibly disturbed. "Rusty, come look. Somethin's happened to the moon."

"How could anything happen to the moon?"

Andy's voice quavered. "Looks like it's burnin' up. Come see."

Rusty and Tanner exchanged dubious glances, but both arose from their chairs and followed Andy outside. Andy pointed upward. His voice was shaky. "There. See?"

The moon had dulled and turned the color of red clay, all except for a silver rind on one edge.

Andy shivered. "Maybe it's an omen. Another war, or somethin'."

Rusty laid a comforting hand on the youngster's shoulder. "It's just an eclipse."

"What's an eclipse?"

"They say it happens when the earth throws its shadow across the moon. And once in a while the moon passes in front of the sun. I've seen chickens go to roost in the middle of the afternoon. It don't mean anything."

"The medicine men would say—"

"Medicine men see omens in just about anything that's out of the ordinary."

Tanner stared at the moon. He had let his cigar go out. "Looks kind of spooky to me too."

Half the time Rusty could not tell whether Tanner was joking or not. He glared at his friend, wishing he wouldn't reinforce Andy's misgivings. "Maybe the schoolhouse has got a book that tells about things such as that."

Andy argued, "Books can't tell you everything. I remember one night an owl lit on top of Raven Wing's tepee. The medicine man wanted to do a ceremony and take the curse off of him. Raven Wing said he'd have to wait because he needed to go and find a lost horse. Turned out an Apache had it, and he killed Raven Wing. Books don't tell you that about owls." Andy looked at the moon again. "If it burns up, the nights'll be awful dark."

Rusty perceived that the silver edge was growing larger. The shadow was slowly passing from the moon. "Look. It's comin' back."

Tanner said, "You're right. Appears the fire is goin' out."

Rusty started to argue. "There never was any fire. It was just . . ." He realized Tanner was pulling his leg. The skinny former ranger enjoyed a practical joke almost as much as he enjoyed a good meal or a lively fight.

"Someday, Len, the Lord is goin' to smite you hip and thigh."

"The yeller-leg Yankee government has done smote me. Made me pay a tax on my horse and even charged me two dollars just for bein' alive. Poll tax, they called it, and I ain't got to vote even once."

"Two dollars must've come hard for you."

"Too hard. I didn't have it to give them, so they made

me work on the road for two days. I thought they made slavery illegal."

"Not when it's for taxes."

The Federals had imposed their own handpicked government on the state. They had agreed to let most Texas men vote provided they take an oath of allegiance to the Union. But when the election did not go the way they wanted they nullified the results. Now the graft-ridden state government was spending three times more than its predecessor and had raised taxes to an alarming degree.

Texas had three political parties. The Democrats were mostly former Confederates, many still disenfranchised. A group of Union loyalists called themselves Moderate Republicans. They tried to live up to the name through reconciliation with former enemies. However, a larger group known as Radicals dominated state politics, holding the governor's mansion and a majority of the legislature. They were more intent on punishing Confederates than on rebuilding the war-weakened economy. Governor Edmund J. Davis had legal power verging on dictatorship.

Rusty said, "There's too many people on both sides who won't admit the war is over. They've never given up fightin' it."

Tanner agreed. "Neither side trusts me and you very much. One bunch is down on us because we didn't go into the Confederate Army. The other thinks bein' rangers was the same as bein' Confederate soldiers."

"I just try to mind my own business and not mix into quarrels that don't concern me. The mess will straighten itself out sooner or later."

Tanner argued, "How do you mind your own business when people keep tryin' to draw you into a fight? I ran into a bunch of old rebels the other night. They accused me of bein' a Unionist because I didn't go into the army. I had to talk fast to keep them from takin' a whip to me."

"I know. Some Union men stopped here last week. Said they were lookin' for Ku Klux. More than likely they'll come again."

Tanner shook his head. "In some ways it was better when there was an honest-to-God war. At least you had a pretty good idee where people stood. You wasn't bein' whipsawed by politicians and wonderin' when somebody was fixin' to shoot you in the back."

Andy put in, "It's like that with the Comanches. About the only friends we've got are the Kiowas, and we're not always sure about them. Old men say even the Kiowas used to be our enemies."

Rusty caught the *we* and *our*. Andy often let things like that slip without realizing it. "When're you goin' to decide that you're not a Comanche? You never were."

He tried to guess what Andy was thinking. The boy's face was often a mask, revealing little in his eyes or his expression. It worried Rusty that much of the time he had no clue to what was going through Andy's mind.

He had just as well *be* an Indian when it comes to hiding his feelings, Rusty thought.

Andy returned to the dog run to look again at the moon.

Tanner asked, "You ever get to feelin' maybe you done the wrong thing, that you ought to've left him to be a Comanche? Now he's betwixt and between, not quite one and not quite the other. Like me and you."

Rusty could not argue. "Hell of a shape for anybody to be in."

"Hell of a shape for *Texas* to be in."

Rusty reined his mule to a stop and turned loose of the plow, raising a hand to the brim of his hat to help shade his eyes. He was not surprised to see a dozen men riding in from the direction of the settlement. It was safer these days to travel with company. Groups of riders had become commonplace, some on legitimate business, some up to no good. He could tell from a distance that these were white, not Indian. "Stay there," he told the mule, though he knew it would not move a foot without being compelled to.

He walked to a rifle leaning against the rail fence that

protected his cornfield from cattle. He cradled it across his left arm, trying not to appear threatening but letting them know he was of a mind to defend himself.

He recognized one of the riders and growled under his breath. Fowler Gaskin, and behind him his nephew, Euclid Summerville.

Some of the others were known to Rusty, but some were not. They were grim-faced as they rode up to the rails and stopped. Gaskin stared at Rusty with all the malice he could muster. He had hated Daddy Mike, and after Mike's death he had transferred that hatred to Rusty. The old man could not be happy without hating somebody.

Summerville demonstrated less hostility. It took energy to hate properly, and he was not one to put out that much effort without a pressing need.

Gaskin demanded, "Where's that Indian kid that likes to beat up on people?"

Rusty had sent Andy out with Tanner to look for two strayed mares. "You know he's not an Indian, so why don't you stop callin' him one? Anyway, he's not here."

"Damned good thing. He always makes me feel like he's fixin' to put an arrow in my gut."

Rusty said nothing that would dispel the old man's misgivings. Because of Andy, Gaskin seldom came around anymore. Rusty wanted to keep it that way.

A broad-shouldered man edged his horse forward. He was some twenty-five years older than Rusty and looked every day of it. Rusty had encountered Jeremiah Brackett many times in town, though he had never had occasion to visit the man's farm. "Shannon, we heard you had some Unionist visitors the other day. I'd like to know what they wanted and what you told them."

Brackett had been an officer in the Confederate Army and wounded more than once. Not all of his wounds had been physical. It was said around the settlement that no one had seen him laugh since the war.

Rusty said, "They wanted to know if I'm a member of the Ku Klux. I told them I'm not and don't know who is.

They argued amongst theirselves about whether to thank me or shoot me. Then they went on their way."

A couple of the Unionists had not believed him and had advocated burning down his cabin as an object lesson, but the more levelheaded restrained them. Rusty chose not to mention that. It might give some of these yahoos the same notion. Both sides occasionally burned the homes of those with whom they disagreed. It had become an almost-accepted method of expressing political opinion.

A younger man beside Brackett demanded, "Are you sure you didn't tell them anything?" A long scar on one side of his face marked him as Brackett's only surviving son, Farley. It was said he had taken a deep saber cut while riding with Hood's brigade. Like his father, he was reputed to be carrying internal scars as well.

Rusty said, "I didn't know anything to tell. I'm just tryin' to be a farmer and mind my own business."

Fowler Gaskin accused, "Everybody knows you kept a Union flag in your cabin through the war. That's how come you stayed in the rangers, so you wouldn't have to go off and fight like them two poor boys of mine."

Rusty declared, "Daddy Mike brought that flag home from the Mexican war. It had bullet holes in it, and some of them bullets were shot at him."

As for Gaskin's "poor boys," they had been killed in a New Orleans whorehouse fight. Rusty never had decided whether the old man knew the truth and was covering it up or if he actually believed his sons had died on a battlefield. The facts were well known in the community, but perhaps no one had ever felt mean enough to disabuse Gaskin of his illusions.

The elder Brackett said, "A man can't sit on the fence all his life. Sooner or later he has to come down on one side or the other."

Rusty shook his head. "The war's been over for six years. Ought not to be but one side anymore. We're all Americans."

"I have not accepted their damned Yankee oath, and I

do not intend to. The war is not over, it's simply taking a rest. When the south rises again there will be no fence for you to sit on." Brackett started to turn his horse away but paused for a last admonition. "I suggest from now on you be very circumspect in your associations."

Summerville appeared disappointed. He waved a rawhide quirt. "I thought we was goin' to whup up on him a little. And that Indian kid too."

Brackett gave Summerville a look of disgust and turned away. His son and the others followed him, all but Summerville and Gaskin. Rusty had a feeling they had not been invited to join the party; they were not the type Jeremiah Brackett would normally associate with. They had simply tagged along, hoping to participate with the others in what they dared not try alone.

Summerville lamented, "We come a long ways not to do nothin'."

Gaskin spat a stream of tobacco. Much of it fell back into his gray-and-black whiskers and glistened in the sun. "There'll come a better time."

Rusty had been a little apprehensive when the whole bunch sat there facing him. The apprehension was gone now. Neither Gaskin nor Summerville had the nerve to make a move against him without a lot of backing.

Summerville said, "Uncle Fowler, I thought they was goin' over yonder and talk to that nigger Shanty next. They ain't headed that way."

He pointed in the direction of a small farm that a former slave had inherited from his longtime owner. Shanty was well along in years but still managed to put in a good day's work. Quiet and inoffensive, he had tried to avoid trouble from those who objected to seeing a black man own a farm, even a small one like his. To people who had that attitude, a black was fit only to labor for someone white.

Rusty warned, "You leave Shanty alone. If you do anything to hurt him, you'll see more of me than you ever wanted to."

Gaskin said, "The nigger'll keep for another day." His

voice dropped ominously. "Or some dark night."

Rusty raised the rifle a little. "You heard what I said."

"I heard. But I don't put much store in any white man who'll speak up for a darkey. Especially a white man who wouldn't go fight like my boys done."

More than once Rusty had felt a strong temptation to throw the truth in Gaskin's face, and that wish came to him now. But he held his tongue. He said, "You'd better whip up to a lope if you're goin' to catch your friends. You've wore out your welcome here."

Andy and Tanner rode in shortly before sundown, penning the two strayed mares they had gone out to find. Rusty looked the animals over, then bridled one of them.

Tanner said, "It's late to be goin' somewhere. Night's comin' on."

Rusty saddled the mare while he told about the visitors. "Fowler Gaskin let it slip that they're thinkin' of callin' on Shanty. I'll see if he'd like to come over here and stay with us for a spell."

It would not be the first time Shanty had stayed at Rusty's farm. Night riders had threatened him before.

Andy had developed a strong bond with the former slave. He had never understood how anybody could be hostile toward someone who kept to himself and caused no trouble. He asked, "What they got against Shanty? He never hurt anybody."

Rusty tried to explain. "He's not white. There's people who don't think anybody but a white man ought to own property. It makes them nervous to see somebody like Shanty able to do for himself."

"That don't make any sense."

"You're right, but there's no talkin' to folks who feel that way."

"The Comanches been makin' it on their own since the first grandfathers came up out of the earth. And some of the dumbest people I ever saw are white."

Rusty shrugged. "Bein' wrong doesn't keep them from bein' dangerous. Especially to somebody like Shanty, an old man livin' by himself. All his life he's been taught to hunker down like a rabbit and not fight back."

Shanty had been at Rusty's place when Rusty first brought Andy home with a broken leg. His was one of the first friendly faces the confused and frightened boy had seen since being left behind by a Comanche war party. Shanty had remained close while Andy's leg slowly healed. Though unable to read, Shanty had patiently coached Andy in the use of the language, reviving early childhood memories buried during his years with the Indians.

Andy's face twisted. "They'd better not do anything to Shanty. I'll kill them."

Rusty frowned. "You shouldn't talk so free about killin'. Some people might think you mean it."

"I do mean it."

The look in Andy's eyes disturbed Rusty. He *did* mean it.

Len's right, Rusty thought. There's still a streak of Comanche in him. He may never lose it.

Andy said, "I'll go with you."

"No, you stay here. Chances are there won't be any trouble. And if there *is* any, I don't want you in harm's way. Len, you keep him here."

Approaching Shanty's log cabin, Rusty wondered how anyone could begrudge the old fellow this humble home, this modest parcel of farming land. As the only slave of a hard-drinking Indian fighter named Isaac York, he had lived here longer than most people around him. No one had objected to his presence so long as he belonged to a white man. It was only after his dying owner had willed him this little place that objections had arisen. In recent times, as many whites lost their own land to punitive reconstruction measures, those objections had intensified. A widespread feeling had developed that the government favored former slaves, taxing them lightly if at all, while it tried to crush former rebels under the weight of confiscatory levies.

Though darkness approached, Rusty saw the old man still working in his small rail-fenced garden. Shanty grew almost everything he needed for subsistence, even a small plot of scraggly tobacco. He was not often indoors during the daytime except to eat or to get out of the rain. Age had slowed him so that it took longer to finish the work necessary even for a small place like his.

During the time he had spent at Rusty's, he and Rusty

had swapped labor, alternating between the two farms. The main concern had been that someone always be nearby, that Shanty not be left to face potentially hostile visitors alone. For a time, that danger had seemed to pass. Now, like smoldering coals fanned by a rising wind, old animosities had flared anew. Rusty felt that it had less to do with Shanty as an individual than with general unrest stirred up by the seemingly endless Federal occupation that continued years after the cannons had fallen silent. Men feeling oppressed sought to vent their frustrations. Freed slaves became an easy target for their anger.

A brown dog of amalgamated ancestry wriggled through the rail fence and trotted out, barking either a welcome or a warning. Rusty was not certain which until the animal wagged its tail so vigorously that its whole body shook.

Shanty ambled to the gate rather than risk fragile limbs by climbing over the fence. "Hush up, dog. Mr. Rusty," he said by way of greeting, "you're travelin' late." His smile showed a wide row of perfectly white teeth. So far as Rusty could see, he had never lost one.

"Somethin' came up. You been havin' any company?"

"Company? This place ain't on the road to nowheres in particular. Nobody much ever comes by."

"The ones I've got in mind wouldn't come friendly. They travel in packs, like wolves."

"Oh, *them*. I don't count them as company. There was five or six by here a couple nights ago. Mostly wanted to know if I belong to the Freedmen's Bureau. I told them I don't belong to nothin'. I don't hardly ever leave this place."

The Freedmen's Bureau had been organized ostensibly to benefit former slaves. In Rusty's view it had been subverted to the ambitions of white opportunists exploiting the people they claimed to aid.

He pressed, "They didn't hurt you none, or threaten to?"

"A couple of them talked about burnin' down my cabin. The others said wait and see if I was goin' to be a good nigger or not. One of them offered me a hundred dollars in Yankee silver to sell him this farm."

"What did you tell him?"

"I told him I didn't have no other place to go. How much is a hundred dollars, Mr. Rusty?"

"Not near enough. Not even in Yankee silver."

"That's what I figured. I'd probably use it up in a year or so, and then where'd I be?"

"Just another poor soul trampin' around the country. Isaac York didn't mean that to happen, and neither do I. You'd best stay at my place 'til this all blows over."

"But I got my field and my garden—"

"We can come over here every few days and take care of things like we did that other time."

Shanty shook his head. "I don't want to be a burden. I've tried not to be a bother to anybody. Most folks around here seem friendly enough to me."

"You'd be no burden, you'd be a help. Seems like there's always plenty to do."

Shanty patted the dog. "Ol' Rough here, he's used to this farm. I'm afraid if I taken him someplace else he'd up and run off."

"Keep him tied for a couple of days. He'll adjust to the change."

"I'll do some thinkin' on it." Shanty looked westward, where a red sunset was rapidly fading. "Gettin' on toward dark. Late for travelin'. You'd just as well stay all night."

Rusty considered. Given time, perhaps he could convince Shanty that he needed to get away from here. "I'm much obliged."

"Then I'll be fixin' us a little supper. You mind corn bread and sowbelly?"

"Long as somebody else is fixin' it, anything sounds good to me."

For years, Shanty had slept in a shed while his owner slept in the cabin. Now that he owned the farm, Shanty slept indoors. He offered to share the cabin with Rusty, but it was small. They would have to move the table and chairs out into the yard to make room for spreading his blankets on the floor.

Rusty said, "I'll sleep outside. I can hear better if somebody is comin'."

"Whatever suits you is plumb fine with me."

Rusty stayed up until late, sitting on a bench just outside the door, watching, listening.

Shanty came out with an old banjo and played a couple of tunes. Then he lapsed into silence, helping Rusty listen. "Ain't nobody comin'. Don't you reckon you'd ought to be gettin' some sleep?"

"I'm rememberin' another time I stayed here, and night riders came with a notion of runnin' you off."

"You ran *them* off, you and the sheriff."

"But this is a different bunch, and Tom Blessing ain't the sheriff anymore."

"The Lord has always watched over me. He'll keep on watchin'."

"I've seen bad things happen to people who didn't watch out for themselves because they thought the Lord was doin' it for them."

"Well, when the time comes that He wants to call me home, I'm willin' to go. I leave things to Him and don't let worry mess with my sleep."

Rusty found himself smiling. "If Preacher Webb was to ever give up the ministry, you could take up where he left off."

"I can't read the Book."

"You don't have to. You know it by heart."

Rusty lay on the shed's dirt floor. The dog came up and licked his hand. Rusty said, "Go lay down."

The dog circled a couple of times, finding a spot that suited him, then settled with his head on the edge of Rusty's blanket. Rusty doubted that he was of any practical use, like a horse or a mule or a milk cow would be, but he provided company for Shanty. For an old man living alone, that was probably a considerable comfort.

The dog's barking awakened Rusty. For a moment, while he blinked the sleep from his eyes, he thought the dog had probably rousted a varmint come to raid Shanty's chickens. Then he heard hoofbeats. He had slept in his clothes, except for his boots. Hastily he pulled them on and got to his feet, rifle in his hand. He did not know how long he had been asleep, but he doubted that anyone traveling at this time of night was burdened with honorable intentions. He walked out to where the dog had taken a stand.

"Easy, boy." The dog kept barking.

The moon's pale light showed him several riders. He could not be sure, but there were at least six or seven. He brought the rifle up and cocked the hammer. The horsemen abruptly reined up. All had their faces covered.

Rusty challenged them. "You-all are way off of the main road."

Someone exclaimed, "Who the hell—"

Someone else said, "It's Shannon. What business do you have here, Shannon?" The voice was filtered through a cloth sack covering the speaker's head.

"I'm visitin'. What about you-all?"

"We've come visitin' too. Where's that nigger?"

"I sent him away for safety." Rusty found it easy to lie in a worthy cause. "Looks like you've missed him."

"We'll see for ourselves."

Rusty raised the rifle to his shoulder.

The rider said, "You wouldn't shoot a white man."

"Maybe, and maybe not. But if you move any closer, you'll be sittin' on a dead horse."

A raspy voice spoke from behind the leader. "Rusty Shannon, you're a damned nigger-lovin' scallywag."

He would recognize Fowler Gaskin's voice if it spoke from the bottom of a well. Rusty said, "If you know me that well, Fowler, you know I'll do what I say I will. If you-all came here for mischief, you'd best turn around and go back. If you were just ridin' past, then you'd best circle around and give this place a wide roundance."

Gaskin argued, "He's by hisself. He can't get us all."

Rusty said, "No, but I could get one or two. Why don't you come up front, Fowler, where I can see you better?"

Gaskin did not budge from his position in the rear.

The leader said, "I still don't believe you'd shoot a white man."

From out in the moonlight Rusty saw two dark shapes rise up as if from the ground. He turned quickly, thinking someone had circled around him.

He heard the click of a hammer. A shotgun blasted, loud as a cannon in the night. The leader's horse jerked back and twisted around, tumbling its rider. The sack came off of the man's head. Rusty recognized the younger Brackett scrambling to get to his feet.

Gaskin shouted, "It's that crazy Indian kid. Look out, he'll kill somebody!"

Rusty realized that Andy had followed him but had remained hidden. The other figure had to be Len Tanner.

Tanner shouted, "I got me a rifle here too."

Farley Brackett turned angrily toward the men behind him. "Gaskin, this ain't like you said. Wasn't supposed to be nobody here but that nigger."

Gaskin argued, "How'd I know Shannon'd show up, him and them others? I ain't responsible for that."

Brackett said, "No use cryin' after the milk's been spilt. This'll keep for another day . . . or another night."

After one lie, the next came even easier for Rusty. "I know who most of you are. Anything happens here, I'll know where to go lookin'."

Brackett reined his horse around. "So will we, Shannon. If them Yankee soldiers hear about this, we'll know who to blame."

Rusty had no intention of getting mixed up with Yankee soldiers, but he chose not to say so. Let these yahoos worry about it, he thought.

The riders retreated, the sound of hoofbeats diminishing as they disappeared into darkness. The dog trailed after them, barking them on their way, as self-important as if he had routed them single-handedly.

Rusty turned as Andy walked up to him. His voice was sharp. "Boy, you could've got yourself killed."

"Not by them. They're cowards."

"That's the most dangerous kind there is. Cowards take every advantage they can. What possessed you to trail after me?"

"You acted like you were afraid for Shanty. I figured I could help."

Rusty glared at Tanner. "Thought I told you to keep him at home."

"Andy's got too much Indian in him. When he makes up his mind to somethin', all hell can't prize him loose. Wasn't nothin' I could do but come along and try to keep him from gettin' hurt."

Shanty came walking up. He had put on trousers, but he was barefoot. He held a shotgun.

Surprised, Rusty asked, "What were you goin' to do with that thing?" He had never seen or heard of Shanty picking up a firearm except to kill something for the cooking pot.

"I was afraid they might hurt you, Mr. Rusty."

"Thanks," Rusty replied, "but the only thing hurt was some feelin's. You know they had a notion to give you a whippin'. They'll do it yet if you stay here."

Shanty stared off in the direction the visitors had taken. Rusty sensed that he was assessing the danger not only to himself but to his friends. Shanty said, "Even if I was to go with you, they'd still know where I was at."

"But you won't be by yourself."

Reluctantly Shanty accepted the inevitable. "I'll gather up my needfuls first thing in the mornin'." He looked toward the dog, which had returned from seeing the riders off. "I don't know how Ol' Rough will take to movin'."

"Ol' Rough doesn't have the Ku Klux on his tail."

*　*　*

Riding toward Tom Blessing's cabin, Rusty heard hammering and reined Alamo toward a shed that served as a blacksmith shop, among other functions. Blessing stood before a glowing forge, beating a heated horseshoe against an anvil. He had removed his shirt. His long underwear was streaked with sweat and dirt. As Rusty dismounted, Blessing lifted the horseshoe with tongs and dipped it into a wooden tub half full of water. It sizzled. Blessing raised a big hand to shield his face from the steam.

He was a large man in advanced middle age, a contemporary of Daddy Mike and Preacher Webb. Tall, broadshouldered and all muscle, he looked at home beside a blacksmith's forge. He said, "Git down, Rusty. You come to get ol' Alamo shod? The coals are hot."

Blessing grasped Rusty's hand. He had a crushing grip that made Rusty's bones ache. "Me and Len Tanner took care of that already."

Blessing seated himself on a bench in the shade and rubbed an underwear sleeve across his grimy face. He said, "I heard a little rumor over in town."

"What kind of yarn are they tellin'?"

"I didn't get this from anybody who was there. At least they didn't own up to it. But the story was that your boy Andy threatened some citizens and fired off a shotgun."

"Not *at* anybody. He fired it into the air to get their attention."

"He got it, all right. Nobody's admitted to bein' there. I don't imagine they want to explain what they were doin' at the time." He frowned. "What *were* they doin'?"

"A bunch of them figured on whippin' Shanty, or maybe worse." He explained his own role in the incident, then Andy's and Tanner's. "The boy puts a lot of store in him."

"Most folks around here respect Shanty, but there's always a few . . . You know who they were?"

"I told them I recognized them, but I didn't. Nobody except Fowler Gaskin and his nephew." He purposely neglected to mention Farley Brackett, for the man's father had a generally favorable reputation around the community even if he was extreme in his feelings toward the Union.

Blessing considered. "I'm not the sheriff anymore, not since the carpetbaggers took over. There's not much I can do. Not officially, anyway."

The Unionist state government had fired Blessing and appointed a new sheriff from among its own ranks. That gentleman had disappointed his sponsors by leaving between two days, taking with him several thousand dollars in Federal specie. They had appointed another who did not steal but seldom ventured beyond the town limits for fear of tangling with someone who did not appreciate the majesty of the law. To talk to him about Shanty's situation would be a waste of time.

Blessing said, "Let's mosey up to the house. My wife's gone to see some of the grandkids, but me and you ought to be able to brew us a pot of coffee."

Blessing's cabin was of a standard double type. An open dog run separated the two main sections, a common roof tying them together. A loft above the dog run had been sleeping quarters for the Blessing boys until they came of age. They had to remain hunkered down to keep from bumping their heads against the low ceiling. As they grew up to their father's height, that became a considerable problem. One by one, they had left home.

A longtime neighbor to the Shannons, Blessing had been with Daddy Mike and Preacher Webb as part of the Texan force that struck a huge Comanche raiding party at Plum Creek in 1840. They found there a small white boy, barely old enough to talk and unable to tell them anything more than that his name was Davy. His red hair had soon earned him the nickname Rusty. As far back as he could remember, Blessing had been an important part of his life.

Blessing said, "After I heard the rumor, I rode by Shanty's cabin to make sure he's all right. Didn't see hide nor hair of him."

"He's over at my place. I thought it was best if he stayed with us 'til this foolishness is done with."

Blessing's wrinkles deepened. "That could be a long

time. The way things are goin', with the Unionists and the Freedmen's Bureau on one side and a lot of hardheaded rebels on the other, I wouldn't be surprised none if the war busted out again."

"Sure makes me wish we had the rangers back."

Blessing said, "That's one reason Austin set up the new state police force. They're supposed to take the rangers' place, only with a different name and with Union people headin' them up."

"Most Texans ain't takin' kindly to a Unionist police force."

"At least the state police don't wear them damned blue uniforms of the Yankee army." Blessing's sympathies still lay with the rebels, though he seldom expressed them beyond his circle of closest friends.

Rusty said, "The question is whether the police will enforce the law or just keep chastisin' folks for the war."

"If they could get the right kind of men . . ." Blessing studied Rusty intently. "People like you, for instance. You spent a long time with the rangers. You could help put the state police on the gospel path."

"I doubt it. Lately both sides have come around to take my measure. Neither one seems to like me."

"There's some good men in the state police. They're not all bad."

"It wouldn't be the same as the rangers. The Unionists lean too far in one direction. As for the other side . . . some of them want to run Shanty off of his land. You know he won't fight back. He doesn't want to cause trouble."

"He causes trouble just by bein' there. He can't wash his skin white."

Rusty said, "He's a harmless old man. All he wants is to be left alone."

"It's liable to take some funerals before that can happen. But I've still got a little influence. I'll ride around and offer a few folks a Preacher Webb sermon . . . with a little smell of hellfire and brimstone."

"You'd best watch your back, Tom. There's some folks

that might not dare to face you, but they'd be willin' to shoot you when you're not lookin'."

"It's been tried. Hasn't worked yet."

Rusty finished his coffee and shook hands, then started for the door. Blessing said, "Wait." The look of regret in his eyes told Rusty that he was about to say something he disliked.

"Rusty, that Indian boy of yours—"

"Why does everybody keep callin' him an Indian?"

"He acts like one in so many ways, like the scraps he keeps gettin' into."

"He hasn't had many fights lately."

"That's because he's already whipped just about everybody who might challenge him. People are talkin' about him, Rusty. They wish you'd send him away."

"What if Daddy Mike and Mother Dora had sent *me* away?"

"With you it was different. You hadn't been with the Indians long enough to pick up their ways. That Andy, though . . . folks are wonderin' when he's goin' to pull out a scalpin' knife and start takin' hair."

"I'll talk to him."

"I wish you would. There's a few people who might take it in their heads to do somethin' regrettable. I'd hate to see him put in the ground."

Len Tanner stepped out of the lamp-lighted cabin and spread his blanket in the dog run. Straightening up, he shouted, "Rusty, you better come look."

Excitement in Tanner's voice brought Rusty to his feet and out into the open space between the two sections of his cabin. Against the night sky, just at the horizon line, he saw a red glow.

Tanner said, "I don't think *that* is any eclipse."

Rusty muttered an oath. "It's the right direction to be Shanty's place." He slammed the flat of his hand against the log wall. "They're burnin' him out."

"Good thing we brought him home with us."

Shanty heard the voices and ventured from his sleeping place in the shed. Andy had taken to sleeping there too. Shanty looked at the glow, then hurried barefoot to Rusty's side. "Lordy, Mr. Rusty, they're burnin' down my place."

"I'm afraid that's what it looks like."

Andy came up, shoving his shirttail into his trousers. He wore buckskin moccasins. "If we hurry, maybe we can put the fire out."

Rusty shook his head. "By the time we got there, the cabin'd be burned to the ground. And whoever's done it, they might be waitin' to ambush Shanty or anybody else who rides in there."

Andy argued, "We can't just stand here and do nothin'."

Rusty stared at the glow, deploring his helplessness. "Best we wait 'til daylight so we can see what we're gettin' into."

Andy seemed more agitated even than Shanty. "One thing we *can* do. The people that done this, they've got houses too."

Rusty knew what Andy was driving at. "A house for a house?"

"Seems fair to me."

"The law doesn't work that way."

"Don't look to me like the law works at all."

Shanty's shoulders slumped. Always thin and spare, he seemed to shrink even smaller. "I ain't never done nothin' against nobody."

Rusty said, "You're a free man. Nobody owns you, and some folks can't accept that."

"I ain't free if people won't let me alone. I wish Mr. Isaac was still livin'. They wouldn't burn the place if it was still Mr. Isaac's."

Rusty started to say Isaac York was white. But he knew Shanty was well aware of the reason for the hostility.

Shanty said, "They wouldn't do nothin' like this if you was to say *you* own me."

"The war settled that question. Nobody owns anybody anymore. That's the law."

"I wisht there hadn't been no war. I wisht things could go back to what they used to be. Them wasn't really bad times."

"You didn't have freedom then."

"Don't seem like I got much freedom now."

Rusty bade Andy and Shanty to stay back while he and Tanner circled around the blackened ruins of the cabin and made certain no one had set up an ambush. Tanner said,

"Looks safe to me. They done their dirty work, then cleared out."

The chimney stood like a tall tombstone above the charred remnants. By contrast, the shed was only moderately damaged. Though it had been set afire, the flames had flickered out. Chickens pecked in the dirt, oblivious of the carnage about them. The shed had been their roosting place.

Len pointed. "Yonder lays Shanty's plow mule."

He gave vent to his anger as he rode up to the dead animal. It had been shot and left to die slowly, for the ground was torn up where it had lain and kicked in agony while its blood drained away. "Any man who would do this ought to be gut shot and left to fight off the buzzards."

Rusty nodded solemnly. "They didn't find Shanty. They had to take it out on somethin'."

He shivered, picturing Shanty lying here instead of the mule. On reflection, he figured they would more likely have shot Shanty at the cabin and burned him with it.

He signaled for Shanty and Andy to come in. Shanty stopped to study the cabin ruins, then came out and looked down at the dead mule. "Poor ol' Solomon. *He* wasn't black like me, he was brown."

Rusty said, "But he belonged to you."

"I ought to've been here. They wouldn't have done this to him."

"They'd have done it to *you*."

Andy clenched his fists, his face reddened. "Ought to be somethin' we can do about this."

Shanty said, "The Lord keeps a tally. Come Judgment Day, He'll call on trangressors to settle their due."

Tanner added, "He'll send them to hell."

Andy demanded, "Why wait on the Lord? Why don't we give Him some help and do it ourselves?"

Despite lectures on the subject from Preacher Webb, Andy had never quite grasped the white man's concept of a fiery hell. The vision of eternal damnation was not part of Comanche tradition. The Comanche preferred immediate punishment, duly witnessed. He said, "I've heard of the

Kiowas tyin' a man to a wagon wheel and burnin' him alive. I can believe in that kind of hell."

Shanty dismounted and stood in anguish where the cabin door had been. "Me and Mr. Isaac, we built this with our own two hands." He raised his palms and looked at them. "Wasn't nobody else, just us. He'd be mighty grieved to see this."

Rusty thought Shanty was too old to be raising a cabin anymore, at least by himself. "We'll help you build it back, but we'd best wait awhile. They'd just burn it again."

Tanner said, "What this country needs is for Preacher Webb to do the honors at a few good funerals."

Rusty demurred. "There's been too many funerals already. The wrong folks got buried." He rode out to the dead mule and drew the loop of a rawhide reata tight around the animal's hind feet. He dragged the mule off a couple of hundred yards, out of sight from the burned cabin. There he found Shanty's milk cow, killed as the mule had been.

Shanty's dog Rough would probably have been shot too, had Shanty not tied him to a post at Rusty's place. The dog had kept trying to run off back to the home it knew.

The raiders had flung a few torches over into Shanty's garden, but the plants had been too green to burn.

Rusty rode back to where the others waited. He said, "You-all go on home. I've got to make a visit."

Tanner said, "You fixin' to call on Fowler Gaskin? This has got his earmarks all over it."

"Fowler can wait. There's somebody else who might listen to reason. I'll give him a try."

Like most farms in the Colorado River country, Jeremiah Brackett's had suffered hard times. Some of the old rail fencing that enclosed his main field had been replaced, but long stretches threatened to collapse, supported by temporary bracing that was makeshift at best. Recovery from the war had been slow and painful and was far from complete.

Rusty's acquaintanceship with the man was limited.

Brackett apparently had brought some money with him when he settled on this land several years before the war. He had built a home larger than most in the area and had plowed a lot of grassland into fields. Fortune's warm smile had turned cold during the war, however. Becoming an officer himself, he had urged his sons to join the Confederate service. His wife had bitterly blamed him after two of them died in battle. The third son, Farley, had been so badly warped by the war that he rebelled against all authority. Toward the end he had deserted the army and taken up with fugitive brush men hiding beyond the western settlements. Now he rode precariously along the hazy-edged line that divided law and outlaw.

Brackett had paid heavily for his allegiance to the Confederacy. Rusty could respect that; the same had happened to many of his friends. But some, like the Monahans, had paid an even heavier price for their opposition.

Passing a field, he noticed a young black man guiding a moldboard plow drawn by a pair of mules. Rusty lifted one hand in a modest show of friendliness, receiving a nod and a white-toothed smile in return.

Evidently Brackett did not hate all blacks. Or, if he did, his hatred did not prevent his using them.

The house, of rough-hewn lumber, had gone for years without fresh paint. Remnants of white still clung, emphasizing patterns of grain in the exposed and darkened wood. Like much else he saw, it bespoke a long, slow fall from prosperity.

In front of the house stood a wooden carving of a boy in a jockey's uniform, holding a brass ring for tying a horse. Like the house, the carving had lost most of its original paint. Rusty dismounted and tied Alamo's reins to the ring after first checking to be sure the hitching post had not rotted off at ground level. One of the plank steps yielded under his weight. It was cracked and needed replacement.

Beyond the front door a woman stood in semi-darkness just inside a hallway. He tipped his hat. "Miz Brackett?"

The woman moved closer, into brighter light. "I am *Miss*

Brackett. Is there something we can do for you?"

"I'm lookin' for Jeremiah Brackett."

He could see now that the woman was actually a girl of perhaps fifteen or sixteen years, too young to be Brackett's wife.

She said, "My father is somewhere out in the fields. He'll be home directly for dinner. You'd be welcome to stay and eat with us."

Rusty was hungry, but he felt his mission was too awkward for him to break bread with these people. "I'm much obliged for the hospitality, ma'am. I'm afraid I can't stay."

She said, "You'd be Mr. Shannon, wouldn't you? I've seen you over in town."

Rusty could not remember that he had ever seen the girl before, though he probably had. She was in that period of rapid change that comes just before womanhood. He found her face pleasant, her faint smile reinforced by friendly brown eyes.

He said, "I don't recollect hearin' that Mr. Brackett had a daughter." Unmarried ladies were scarce, even ones this young. They were outnumbered by unattached bachelors persistently striving to alter their marital status. Unless a woman was homely enough to frighten hogs and had a disposition to match, she stood scant risk of becoming a spinster.

"My name is Bethel," she said. "It comes from the Bible."

"Mine is Rusty. I don't expect you'll find it in the Book." He turned to look toward the fields. "I'll go hunt for your father."

She raised her arm to point, and he noticed that her sleeve had been mended, its cuffs fraying, the fabric faded. She said, "I think you'll find him over yonderway, in that field past the oak trees."

Turning away, he thought there ought to be at least enough money to buy that girl a decent dress. But he knew the reality was otherwise. Six years after the war, much of rural Texas was still flat on its back. Or, at best, up on one elbow.

He had made a modest amount of money gathering unclaimed cattle and throwing them into herds that James Monahan trekked north to the railroad, but it had been extremely difficult to hold on to much of it. He bought little, but what he did buy was high in price. Taxes had risen to near impossible levels. He was convinced that reconstruction officials were deliberately taxing old settlers off their land so they or their friends could have it. The stronger the tie to the Confederacy had been, the higher the taxes were set.

Jeremiah Brackett stood in the edge of the field, watching a black man follow a plow and team of mules. He became aware of Rusty's approach. For a moment his gaze went to a rifle leaning against the rail fence, but it was some distance away. He gave Rusty a second look and evidently saw no imminent threat. He picked his way through rows of corn, careful not to crush any growing plants.

"Howdy, Shannon. You've come to see me?"

That seemed obvious to Rusty, but he guessed it was a strained way of being polite. He dismounted. "I have. Wanted to ask you where you went last night."

The question seemed to surprise Brackett. "Nowhere. I was at home. I am at home just about every night. Where would you have me be?"

"Thought you might've gone over to pay Shanty another visit."

"I rarely visit my white neighbors, much less one of so dark a hue." Brackett peered intently as if trying to read what was back of Rusty's eyes. "I suspect you are about to tell me that something has happened."

"Somebody burned down his cabin."

Brackett blinked as if the news was unexpected. "Was he in it?"

"No, I'd taken him home with me. But I figured you knew that."

"I had no reason to know."

"Figured your son Farley would've told you."

"Farley hasn't been there since the night your Indian boy fired a shotgun and got him thrown from his horse."

"Andy didn't shoot *at* him. He just wanted to be sure he had everybody's attention."

"He had it, and that is a fact. The boy is a menace."

"Some folks must figure Shanty to be some kind of a menace too, the way they keep tryin' to run him off."

"We don't need his kind in this country."

Rusty nodded toward the black man with the plow. "I've seen three of them in your fields."

"That's different. They're working for me. They have no claim on any of the land."

"Where do they live?"

"In a cabin out by my barn."

"Then they're livin' a whole lot closer to you than Shanty is. How come he puts such a burr under your blanket?"

Brackett's face twisted. "If you were any kind of a white man you wouldn't have to ask. Working for somebody is one thing. For a darkey to own land is something else. It is like saying he is equal to the rest of us. That, I cannot accept. Those people were brought here to serve. Let one become too independent and the others start thinking they should be too. Worst thing Lincoln ever did was to free those people. Everybody was a lot happier before that."

"Except maybe the slaves."

"They had plenty to eat and a place to sleep, probably far better than in Africa. Now there are hundreds of them adrift without work, without a place to sleep or anything to eat unless they steal it. Do you think freedom has made *them* better off?" Brackett waved a hand toward the man with the plow. "Do you know why I'm out here watching him? Because if I don't, he'll stop at the end of the row and lie down in the shade. Left on their own, they'd not work enough for their own subsistence."

"Shanty has done all right on his own."

"But it was given to him."

"Whatever that little place amounts to, Shanty made it so with his own muscle and sweat. His master was drunk more than he was sober."

Brackett shrugged away further argument. "I see I am not going to sway your opinion, and certainly you are not going to sway mine. I know nothing about the burning of that darkey's cabin. You'll have to take my word on that."

Rusty did not want to believe him, but something in Brackett's eyes told him he spoke the truth. He asked, "What about your son Farley?"

"I regret to say that Farley was in jail last night. Some altercation with a state policeman."

"You wouldn't have any idea who did burn Shanty out?"

"Ideas do not stand up in court. You have to show proof."

"Not always, not in a Yankee court." Rusty decided upon a flanking approach. "It has the look of somethin' Fowler Gaskin might do, him and his dim-witted nephew." He watched in vain for anything in Brackett's expression that might reinforce his suspicion. He decided the farmer must be a good poker player.

Brackett said, "Fowler Gaskin is a lazy, ignorant lout, and no confidant of mine."

Rusty nodded. "At least there's *somethin'* we can agree on. It's a mystery to me why good men die young while reprobates like Fowler Gaskin live on and on."

"Perhaps it is because the Lord wants no part of him, and hell is already filled up with Unionists."

Rusty said, "Those who fought for the Union side were honest in their opinions."

"They were wrong. And if you sympathized with them— which seems to be the case—then you were wrong."

"Looks like we've about used up our conversation." Rusty put his foot into the stirrup.

"Wait a minute." Brackett raised a hand. "It's about dinnertime, and you're miles from home. You're welcome to stay and eat with us."

That caught Rusty by surprise. "You're invitin' *me*?"

"I have never turned a hungry man away from my door, be he white, black or somewhere between."

"I'd figured myself lucky if I got away from here without bein' shot at."

"I even fed the tax collector, though he made me sell off more than half of my farm so I could keep the rest."

"That's a second thing we can agree on. I don't like the governor's tax men either."

A bell clanged at the house. Rusty saw the black man stop the mules in the middle of a row and begin to unhitch them. Brackett said, "That's Bethel, letting us know that dinner is about ready."

Brackett had evidently walked to the field. Rusty saw no horse for him to ride. The plowman rode one of the mules and led the other, but Brackett made no move toward the second mule. Either he did not like to ride mules or he would rather walk than ride beside the black.

To keep from outdoing the host, Rusty also walked, leading Alamo. Brackett showed an interest in the animal.

Rusty admitted, "He's gettin' up in years, and I wouldn't take him out anymore if I was called on to chase Indians. But he's still the best horse I ever had just for ridin' the country and workin' stock."

Brackett gave Alamo a look of approval. "You can tell a lot about a man by the horse he rides."

Rusty, by the same token, had always been able to overlook at least some faults in a man who took good care of his horses.

Brackett's daughter stood on the porch, one hand shading her eyes as she watched for her father's coming. Brackett stamped his boots against the bottom step, dislodging a little field dirt. He said, "I brought company for dinner."

"I figured you would. I set an extra plate." She motioned toward the open door. "You-all go on ahead. There's a fresh bucket of water and some soap on the back porch."

Brackett led the way. Rusty saw a black woman and a white one in the kitchen. He surmised the white woman was Mrs. Brackett, but she did not turn to greet him. He heard Bethel say, "They're here, Mama." He heard no acknowledgment. Perhaps Mrs. Brackett did not care for company. Or, from what he had heard, she no longer cared for Mr. Brackett.

Bethel was pleasant through the meal, passing food around the table, asking Rusty if he needed anything else. Mrs. Brackett took her place at one end, but Rusty soon realized she had not once looked toward her husband. She had probably been a handsome woman in a younger, happier time, but her face had frozen into a bitter, pinched expression. She kept her attention focused on her plate and the food immediately in front of her.

He caught Brackett glancing at his wife, pain in his eyes.

Bethel made polite small talk, seemingly oblivious of the wall of silence that stood between her parents. But the forced quality in her voice told Rusty she was achingly aware of it.

The war had cost this family dearly, but it had cost others just as much. He pondered the wide contrast—and the parallels—between the Bracketts and the Monahans.

Mrs. Brackett arose from the table before the others had finished. She picked up her plate and utensils and disappeared into the kitchen. Brackett stared after her, saying nothing.

Uncomfortable, Rusty pushed back his chair. "I'm much obliged for the good dinner, but I'd best be headed home." He started to pick up his plate, but Bethel signaled him to leave it.

She said, "I'll take care of it, Mr. Shannon. You needn't bother."

He sensed that she was sparing him another meeting with her mother. Or perhaps it was her mother she was sparing.

Brackett said, "Come back any time, Shannon. You're welcome here so long as you don't bring up politics."

Bethel followed Rusty out onto the porch. In a quiet voice she said, "I hope you'll pardon my mother's behavior. She hasn't been the same since my brothers died. She blames Papa for that." She looked intently into his face.

"It's odd, but you look a little like them, especially John, the oldest. I think my mother saw that."

He twisted his hat in his hands. "I'm sorry about your brothers."

"We still have Farley." She looked away as if mention of the name brought sorrow. "He follows after calls that the rest of us can't hear."

Riding away, he felt sympathy for the Brackett family . . . Mrs. Brackett, driven inward, still unable to reconcile herself to the loss of two sons. Bethel, trying to bring even false cheer into a house that had no cheer at all. And Jeremiah Brackett . . . Rusty felt that he could bring himself to like the man, even granted that he had some unreasoning attitudes.

His thoughts turned to Bethel's comment about her brothers, and the fact that Rusty resembled them a little. Could it be . . . no, surely not. No one had ever been able to determine who Rusty's real parents had been. It was taken for granted that they had fallen victim to the great Comanche raid. It was probable he had blood kin somewhere, kin who did not know he existed.

But the Bracketts? No, the chance was too slender to contemplate. He probably resembled a lot of people. For most of thirty years he had lived without knowing who he was. He thought it unlikely that he would ever know.

He wished he could. Occasionally he awoke from a dream in which he could almost see the faces of his real mother and father, could faintly hear his mother's voice singing to him. At such a time he felt adrift, alone in a world of strangers.

A ndy Pickard sat on his moccasined heels in the shadow of his horse, his attention focused on an open spot where the grass was thin and short. Chopping weeds in the garden, Shanty had eyed him awhile. Finally, laying down his hoe, he moved through the open gate and walked out to join Andy.

He asked, "Where'd you leave Mr. Len?"

"Me and him found that lost milk cow of Tom Blessing's. She'd had a new calf. Len took her home. I don't expect he'll come back tonight."

"And Mr. Rusty?"

"Out lookin' for a couple of strayed horses."

Shanty bent to see what was holding Andy's attention. "What you studyin' so hard, boy?"

"Ants."

Puzzled, Shanty asked, "What's to look at with an ant? One looks the same as another. I don't pay them no mind long as they ain't crawlin' up my britches leg."

"These are fightin' a hell of a war."

Shanty frowned at the word *hell*, but Andy had taken to using it so casually that there seemed little chance of breaking the habit.

"It's passin' strange," Shanty said, "how easy it is for a young feller to learn words he ain't supposed to say, and how hard for him to learn the gospel."

Andy pointed. "They're killin' one another by the hundreds."

Shanty's interest quickened as he braced his hands against his thin knees and leaned down. "I see what you been lookin' at. Dead ants layin' all over. They're just like people. This whole country to share, and they fight over one little bitty piece of ground."

"I remember a medicine man tellin' about watchin' a big ant war one time. Said it went on from daylight 'til the sun went down. Said he saw more dead ants than there was stars in the sky."

"That's a lot of ants."

"He said it was a sign from the spirits. The winnin' ants was Comanche, he said. The losin' ants was the Texans. Said pretty soon the Comanche nation was goin' to rise up and take back everything the white men stole, clear to the edge of the big water. Then everything would be like it was in the old days when the Comanches drove the Apaches out."

"I don't reckon he said when that was goin' to happen, seein' as it ain't yet?"

Andy sensed that Shanty was not taking the prediction seriously. "It's bad luck to make fun of a medicine man. They say some can turn a man into a crow or a bullfrog, even a snake."

"You ever seen it done?"

"No, but I've heard tell."

"I don't reckon you know a medicine man who can turn a black skin white? If I was white, maybe I could live over at my own place and not have to burden nobody."

Andy brushed away two ants that started to crawl up on his moccasins. "No tellin'. Medicine men have a lot of power. They know how to reach spirits nobody else can talk to."

Shanty frowned. "Listen at you, talkin' about spirits and

such. Preacher Webb'd be mighty disappointed. He's taught you all about the Good Book and tried to help you put away them heathen notions."

"Who's to say they're all wrong? I expect Preacher Webb is closer to the Lord than anybody I know, but when I was with The People I saw things he nor no other white man could explain. Not everybody talks to the Lord the same way. I'll bet before your folks was brought to this country they talked to Him different than what you do."

Shanty mused. "When I was a shirttail young'un, before I was sold off, I remember my granddaddy tellin' about a far-off place way across the water. Said *his* daddy was a king before the slave catchers come. Said he fought the chains and took many a bad whippin', but he never did give up the notion of bein' a king. Died claimin' he still was."

"Then by blood rights you'd ought to be a king yourself."

"King of what? A little old dirt farm that I dassn't even go to unless I got somebody with me?" Shanty pointed to the ground. "If I was an ant—if my people was ants—they'd be the ones gettin' whipped yonder, the ones with their heads bit off. And I'm afraid your medicine man was wrong about which ones was Comanche and which was white. It's the Comanches that's losin'. Or fixin' to."

Andy noticed his horse beginning to paw the ground and realized ants were climbing up its legs. He brushed them off and led the horse out of harm's way. "We ought to be smarter than ants. Looks like we could figure out some way to divvy up the land and not fight over it."

"That's been tried. Never did seem to work. There's too much difference in the way white folks and Indians look at things. I remember once the government started a reservation up on the Brazos River. Folks blamed a lot of the Indian raids on tribes from there. Maybe they was right and maybe not, but it didn't make no difference. The Indians was forced off of the reserve and pushed up north of the Red River. Even the peaceable ones."

Andy said with a touch of pride, "The Comanches I was with never let the white men put them on a reservation in the first place. They still run free."

Shanty's brow furrowed. "I hope you ain't thinkin' you'd like to go back and run with them."

"The notion strikes me sometimes. I've got no kin here that wants me. I ain't forgot the time my uncle came and looked me over. Said even though I was a Pickard, like him, I was too savage to live with his family. He went off and left me."

"Folks here have treated you good . . . Mr. Rusty and Mr. Len, Tom Blessing and them."

"That makes it hard, in a way. Every time I take a notion I'd rather be Comanche, Rusty or somebody does me some special kindness. Then I don't know whichaway to turn."

"Don't forget that it was Indians who killed your real mama and daddy."

"I was too little to remember much about that. Mostly I just remember that the Comanches gave me a good life." He grimaced. "I guess it's easier bein' an ant. They always know which tribe they belong to."

Shanty straightened his back and groaned at the pain the move brought him. "Everybody wants to live to get old, but it sure don't come cheap." He turned his head and stared off down the wagon road. "We got company comin'. He's runnin' like he had Indians chasin' him."

Andy did not recognize the rider at first. "Looks like he's pushed his horse about as far as it can go."

Shanty nodded. "A man don't abuse an animal that way without he's got reason."

The bay labored for breath, sweat lathering its hide. Andy thought the horse might go to its knees when its rider brought it to a stop. The man slipped from the saddle and almost went down from fatigue. Andy judged him to be about Rusty's age, though his eyes were hard in a way that Rusty's never were. A scar cut through the whiskers on one side of his face, all the way up to the corner of an eye.

Andy guessed he had probably earned it in a fight. It was a scar a Comanche warrior would envy.

The visitor paid no attention to Shanty. He acted as if the black man were invisible. Laboring for breath, he said, "This is Shannon's place, ain't it?"

Andy said, "Yep, but he ain't here."

Looking closer, he realized he had seen this man the night the riders had come to challenge Shanty. He remembered the scar. Rusty had said his name was Farley Brackett. Andy immediately felt a rising antagonism.

Brackett said, "I don't need Shannon noway. I just need one of his horses." He looked at Andy's. "That one will do."

Andy took a tight grip on the reins. "Not this one. I can see how you've treated yours."

"Couldn't help it. I've got Federal soldiers comin' behind me. And the state police."

"Anyway, I been ridin' mine, and he's tired. He wouldn't carry you far."

Shanty lifted his hat to arm's length, shading his eyes. "I don't see nobody back there."

The fugitive seemed irritated that Shanty made so bold as to speak to him. "They're comin', and they're hell-bent to stretch my neck."

Though Andy had seen little of the state police, they had been the topic of much conversation. Most people seemed to regard them more as an oppressive arm of the Federal military than as an independent law-enforcement body like the old-time rangers had been.

Shanty said, "Even if you was to have a fresh horse, you look mighty tuckered yourself. Best you lay low and let them go on by."

The man acted as if he had not heard. He was probably not used to listening to black people's opinions. Andy didn't like the man, but he figured anyone who had aroused the state police and the Federal troops must have redeeming qualities.

He pondered the advisability of the question, then asked, "You kill somebody?"

"Best you-all don't know what I done. Just give me a fresh horse."

Shanty said, "I seen a blue roan down on the river a while ago. Ought to be easy caught."

Brackett looked to Andy for confirmation, not trusting Shanty. Andy said, "I don't know what Rusty would say."

Brackett declared, "It don't matter what he says. I need me a horse." He looked back for evidence of pursuit. "Them Yankees will ask if you've seen me."

Andy said, "If we don't watch you leave, we can't tell them whichaway you went."

The man looked suspiciously at Shanty. "You won't let this nigger tell them?"

"Shanty and me'll both be too busy to see where you go."

Brackett remounted and soon disappeared amid the trees and low brush that screened the river from view.

Andy said, "Maybe you shouldn't have mentioned that roan. Looks to me like Rusty's lost a horse."

Shanty smiled wickedly. "You know that roan ain't much account. He may not even outrun them Yankees. Mr. Rusty's been talkin' about swappin' him off."

Andy shaded his eyes. "I see the soldiers now, just like he said. I don't know if I can lie to them." Beyond a little creative boasting of their exploits in battle, Comanches had taken pride in veracity.

"Ain't hard to tell a lie if you set your mind to it. From the time I was a young'un I learned how to bow my head and make a big grin and tell folks what they wanted to hear. Had to, else somebody was apt to take a quirt to me."

Andy saw a fleeting resentment in Shanty's eyes, reflecting a lifetime of suppressed reaction to neglect and mistreatment. It troubled him to realize that despite his concern for the Comanche viewpoint he had never fully considered Shanty's.

Shanty said, "If you don't want to lie, ain't no reason

you have to for Farley Brackett. Whatever trouble he's in, he got in it by hisself. You don't owe him nothin'."

Andy wrestled with his conscience. "I don't owe the soldiers nothin' either."

It occurred to him that if he and Shanty remained where they were some sharp-eyed trooper might notice the fugitive's tracks leading toward the river. He said, "Let's walk over to the corral and wait."

As he expected, the soldiers veered toward the corral, missing the garden and whatever trail the scar-faced Brackett might have left.

Blue-coated troopers had always made Andy uneasy. He remembered warrior accounts of fights with them before the conflict between North and South. Since returning to Texas after the war the soldiers seemed not to bother much about Indians, even when the Indians came raiding. They appeared more interested in complicating life for those Texans who had supported the South.

Though Rusty had never borne arms against the Union, the soldiers and Federal officials treated him as if he had. That added to Andy's mistrust.

Shanty spoke softly and with confidence. "Stand easy. They ain't apt to do nothin' to a boy of your age, nor to a gentleman of color."

"I ain't afraid of them. Me and half a dozen Comanche warriors could whip the whole damned bunch."

"The rebs thought thataway too."

The troopers were black, their officer white. Andy recognized from his insignia that he was a lieutenant. Two other white men were in civilian clothes. Andy assumed they were state policemen. He was almost certain he had seen them somewhere. One had a pinned-up sleeve.

The officer raised his hand, signaling the soldiers to stop. He gave Shanty a quick, dismissive glance, shifting his attention to Andy. He demanded, "Whose farm is this?"

The superior attitude tempted Andy to tell the officer to go to hell. He deferred to better judgment. "It belongs to Rusty Shannon."

The civilians showed surprise at the name. One leaned forward in the saddle. "Shannon, you say? Him that used to be a ranger?"

"He was. But not anymore."

The man smiled. "Well, I'll be damned. I had no idee what part of the country he was in." The smile was cold.

Andy suddenly remembered when he and Rusty had made a fast departure from the Monahan farm to avoid a potentially violent showdown with two men named Oldham. This was Clyde Oldham. The man with one arm was the brother everybody called Buddy-Boy. Andy's skin prickled.

The lieutenant stared hard at Andy, first at his braided hair, then his moccasins. "What kind of a Hottentot do you call yourself?"

"My name's Andy Pickard. I ain't no Hottentot, whatever that is."

"One might think at first glance that you had escaped from the reservation."

A black sergeant pushed forward. "I've heard talk in town, sir. This young man was raised by the Comanches."

The officer sniffed. "He does not appear to have left them far behind. Where is this Rusty Shannon?"

Andy's face warmed. He felt no inclination to answer.

Shanty broke the silence. "He's out huntin' for horses, sir. I expect he'll be comin' along directly."

The lieutenant gave Shanty a closer study than before. "I take it that you work here, boy."

"Can't get a lot of work out of an old man like me, but I live here."

"Does Shannon pay you?"

"Well, no sir, but you see—"

"Boy, don't you know slavery is forbidden anymore? You need not work for anyone unless you are paid for it."

Andy could not hold his anger. "Night riders burned Shanty out of his own place, and there wasn't none of you yellow-legs anywhere in sight."

"Young man, you are addressing an officer of the United States Army."

Shanty whispered, "Careful. Soldiers been known to carry people away, and some never was heard from again."

"I ain't afraid of no soldiers." He dismissed any thought of telling the truth about Farley Brackett.

The officer frowned darkly. "I can see that you are too young to have served in the rebel army, but that kind of attitude got your elders into a war they could only lose."

Andy clenched his fists. "Not my *Comanche* elders. They whipped you bluecoats every time they met you."

The officer turned to the sergeant. "You say you've heard about this lad. I take it Shannon is not his father."

"Way I heard it, the boy's folks got killed by Indians. I don't 'spect him and Shannon is blood kin."

The lieutenant nodded as he looked back at Andy. "So Shannon uses you for free labor, just like this poor darkey. We'll look into that. But right now we have more pressing business. We are on the trail of a fugitive. If you'd seen him, I don't suppose you'd tell us?"

Angry, Andy wanted to say he had not, but the reply seemed to swell in his throat. It would not come out.

Shanty feigned innocence. "What sort of a man you talkin' about?"

The civilian spoke up. "His name is Farley Brackett. He shot a state policeman."

Because the fugitive was a son of Jeremiah Brackett and had once tried to do Shanty harm, Shanty had no real cause to lie for him. But he said, "A feller come by a while ago, ridin' like there was Indians after him."

"Heading west?"

Shanty hesitated. Andy quickly said, "He was when we seen him." That was a half truth. Brackett had been traveling west when he first appeared.

The officer accepted the statement. "Then we'll be on our way. Don't forget to tell Shannon we'll be back to have some words with him."

Clyde Oldham leaned forward in the saddle. "Tell Shannon that the Oldham brothers have got some words for him too. He'll remember us."

The lieutenant said, "Shannon can wait. Right now we have to try to catch Brackett."

Oldham turned in the saddle as the others started away. "Me and Buddy'll be back. That is a promise."

Andy watched the soldiers and the Oldhams move off.

Trouble in his eyes, Shanty asked, "Who are these Oldhams? What they got to do with Mr. Rusty?"

"Seems like they had bad trouble a long time ago. Now they know where Rusty lives."

Shanty worried, "Maybe we made the trouble worse, lettin' them soldiers go in the wrong direction."

"Maybe so. I've got no reason to like Farley Brackett, and you have every right to hate his guts."

"Hate just burns a hole in your belly. Like that Farley. Folks say the war turned him ornerier than a badger in a trap. He was probably cocked and primed to shoot that state policeman."

"I kind of wish now I'd told the soldiers the truth. Lyin' don't set well on my stomach."

"You didn't lie, exactly. You just didn't tell them all of it. Other people's quarrels are best left alone. Most of us got troubles enough of our own."

Once the soldiers were well gone, Brackett emerged from the timber by the river. He was riding the blue roan. As before, he spoke to Andy and paid no attention to Shanty. "I'm obliged to you for sendin' the soldiers on their way. And I'm obliged for the horse trade." The scar-edged eye twitched.

Andy said, "Don't thank us 'til you've rode that roan awhile." He frowned. "Just curiosity, but how come you to shoot a state policeman?"

"It needed doin', and I didn't see nobody else fixin' to."

"You'd best not tarry long. The soldiers'll figure out pretty soon that they're draggin' an empty sack."

Brackett said, "If you happen to see my old daddy, tell

him that snotty policeman ain't goin' to be messin' with him no more."

The soldiers and the Oldhams had ridden westward. Brackett rode southward, quickly disappearing. That puzzled Andy a little. "I figured he'd go north. There wouldn't be as many people up that way to tell the soldiers where he went."

Shanty said, "Don't matter. People south of here ain't tellin' the soldiers nothin' neither. Especially since it was a state policeman he shot. Them old rebels lost the war, but they didn't lose none of their will."

Andy had just finished milking when Rusty came in about sundown, leading a bay horse on a rawhide rope. It was the horse Farley Brackett had been riding. Andy and Shanty met him at the corral.

Rusty seemed puzzled. "Found him down by the river. You-all know anything about him?"

Andy saw that Shanty was waiting for him to give the answer. He said, "Farley Brackett came by a while ago in a hurry to make a swap. He took that blue roan. Looks to me like you got the best end of the trade."

"Not hardly." Rusty turned the horse around. "Look at the brand on his hip."

It was a US. Andy slumped. "Army horse. I didn't notice that." He glanced at Shanty, who shook his head. Shanty could not read, so the brand might have meant nothing to him even if he had seen it.

Rusty asked, "What was Farley doin' with an army horse?"

Reluctantly Andy explained about the shooting of a state policeman.

Rusty said, "And you lied to the soldiers?"

"Not exactly. Just sort of."

Shanty offered, "I'll lead that horse back down to the river and hide him to where them soldiers won't see him."

Rusty looked westward. "Good idea, but it's too late. They're already comin'."

Andy could see the horsemen approaching. He said, "One more thing you better know before they get here. The Oldham brothers are with them."

Rusty's face fell. He said something under his breath, then, "Bad luck. I was hopin' they'd never find out where I live."

"What's more, they're state policemen."

Rusty expelled a long, painful breath. "That gives them authority to do just about anything they want to."

Horses and men looked whipped down and subdued. Questions were unnecessary. Andy wondered how far west they had ridden before they accepted the fact that Brackett had given them the slip. He understood why Federal soldiers had managed so little success in trailing Indians. Anyone with watchful eyes could have seen the fugitive's tracks leading down toward the river, then turning about and heading south.

The army sometimes employed friendly Indians such as the Tonkawas to do its trailing, but there had been no Indian with the lieutenant's detail.

Rusty raised one hand in a civil but less than enthusiastic greeting. The lieutenant's gaze fastened immediately upon the bay horse.

Rusty said, "I found him down on the river. Looks like the man you were after left him and took one of mine."

The lieutenant cast a suspicious eye in Andy's direction. "How could he do that without somebody seeing him?"

Rusty said, "By swappin' in the timber, out of sight from up here."

The lieutenant was suspicious to the point of belligerency. He pointed a finger at Andy. "You and that darkey claimed the fugitive rode by here and went west."

Andy fumbled for words. "That ain't exactly what we

said. He was ridin' west when we first seen him. We didn't say whichaway he went after that."

"We didn't find any tracks to the west."

Rusty said, "Like as not your man doubled back. Even a coyote is smart enough to do that."

Clyde Oldham fixed a hard gaze on Rusty. His brother beside him, he pushed up abreast of the officer. "Sounds thin to me, Lieutenant. Remember, Shannon was a ranger under the rebels. I'm bettin' he helped Brackett get away and put that boy and that nigger up to lyin' for him."

Shanty declared, "Mr. Rusty didn't do no such thing. He wasn't even here."

The lieutenant showed no inclination toward believing. He jerked his head at the black sergeant. "Ride down toward the river and see if you find any tracks."

Andy watched nervously as the soldier walked his horse along, looking at the ground. If the sergeant had good eyes, Andy thought, he was likely to pick up Brackett's trail. Surely enough, the trooper paused a minute, riding back and forth, then proceeded to the river. In a little while he returned and saluted the lieutenant. "Tracks are clear as day, sir. They go from here straight down to the river. By the looks of it, he changed horses and rode back up this way. Never went west at all."

Clyde Oldham declared, "This is the horse that Brackett stole off of the street after he shot the policeman." He turned a wicked gaze on Rusty. "What do you say now, Shannon?"

"Looks like I've lost a horse."

The younger Oldham had a malevolent grin. "You're fixin' to lose a lot more than a damned horse."

Clyde Oldham's eyes were cold as he looked at the lieutenant. "We've found Shannon in possession of a stolen horse, an army horse at that. Looks clear to me that he aided and abetted an escapin' criminal."

The lieutenant addressed Rusty. "I had intended to come back and talk to you about other matters, such as not paying that darkey for his labor, or this young man either. But now we have a more serious violation to consider." He glanced at Oldham. "Inasmuch as this affair began with the shooting of one of your fellow policemen, the army defers to the state. You may make the arrest."

Clyde's eyes seemed even colder. He drew a pistol and pointed it in Rusty's face. "Much obliged. Rusty Shannon, I arrest you as an accessory after the fact."

Rusty argued, "Lieutenant, this man and his brother have an old grudge against me."

Clyde said, "Damned right we do. He's the Confederate ranger that crippled Buddy." He waved the pistol. "Get your hands up, Shannon."

Rusty said, "I don't have a gun on me."

"Just the same, raise them hands. High."

Andy felt the blood rise in his face. He tried again to intercede. "Rusty wasn't even here when that feller came by."

The lieutenant pushed his horse in front of Andy. "Young man, if you interfere any farther your youth will not be taken into account. I can have you sent away to a correctional institution where they will work the wild Indian out of you . . . or beat it out."

Shanty said, "The boy's right. Wasn't none of Mr. Rusty's doin'."

The black sergeant was the only one who even looked at Shanty. The white men did not acknowledge his presence. Shanty protested directly to the sergeant, who studiously looked away, his jaw firmly set, and pretended not to hear.

The lieutenant finally acknowledged Shanty by giving him an order. "Boy, put Shannon's saddle on that bay horse. Mr. Oldham and his brother will take him to town while the rest of us pursue our fugitive."

Shanty gave Rusty a plaintive look. Rusty nodded for him to do as the officer ordered. Shanty soon brought the bay horse. Clyde motioned with the pistol's barrel. "Mount up, Shannon. We got a ways to ride."

Rusty shrugged in futility and swung into the saddle.

"Andy, you and Shanty take care of things while I'm gone."

Buddy Oldham motioned for Rusty to start moving. "You're liable to be gone a long time. You may *never* come back."

The tone of his voice sent a chill down Andy's spine.

The lieutenant led his soldiers out toward the place where the sergeant had found the tracks leading southward. It would soon be dark, so they would not be able to follow the trail long.

Shanty worried, "Ain't nothin' to keep them Oldhams from shootin' Mr. Rusty in the back. They can claim he tried to get away in the dark."

Andy's belly went tight. He felt that it would be his fault if something happened to Rusty. "Let's catch up and go along. Maybe they won't do him no harm if we're there to witness."

Darkness fell by the time they saddled their horses and started. They set off in the direction the Oldhams had taken. They had not gone far before two pistol shots echoed through the trees.

Andy swallowed hard. "They've already done it." He put the animal into a hard run. He could hear Shanty behind him, trying futilely to catch up.

He heard Clyde Oldham's voice somewhere ahead. "Shannon! Where the hell did you go?"

Buddy Oldham called, "Shannon! Goddamn you!"

The two turned at the sound of Andy's and Shanty's horses. Clyde declared, "We had to do it, Lieutenant. Shannon was fixin' to get away." His voice changed abruptly as he realized these were not the soldiers. He aimed his pistol at them. "You stop where you're at or I'll shoot you both."

Andy drew rein. His voice almost broke from rage. "What did you do to Rusty?"

Clyde regained his composure. "I don't have to explain nothin' to a mouthy kid nor a nigger." He lowered the pistol when he saw that Andy and Shanty were not armed.

Buddy said excitedly, "He ran off, but I know I hit him. Like as not he's layin' dead out yonder somewhere."

Andy seethed. "If he is, you'll have a lot to answer for."

"I got a duty to shoot an escapin' prisoner. Anyhow, he shot me one time."

Andy said, "Folks around here think a lot of Rusty Shannon. If you've killed him they'll hunt you down like a sheep-killin' cur."

"I got the law on my side."

"Carpetbag law."

"Law just the same."

Clyde Oldham holstered his pistol. "You don't need to explain nothin' to the likes of them. We'll go and fetch help. Come mornin' we'll find Rusty Shannon no matter where he's at." He pointed a finger at Andy and Shanty. "You two better go home and stay there if you know what's good for you."

The brothers rode off into darkness. Shanty said, "Them Oldhams ain't goin' to let him live. We got to find him first."

The moon had not yet risen. Andy could barely see past Shanty. Anxiety made him shake. "He may be wounded and down."

They rode in a walk, calling Rusty's name. Andy worried, "We could go right past him and not know it."

"We can't wait for the moon to rise. He could bleed to death by then."

Andy felt cold all the way to his boots. "If he dies I swear I'll nail the Oldhams' scalps to the courthouse door."

"This ain't no time to be talkin' like a Comanche. Better you talk a little to the Lord."

A horse nickered. Andy turned toward the sound. "Rusty! Rusty, can you hear me?"

He came upon the horse. In the darkness he could not see the color, but he knew he had found the government bay.

Shanty pointed. "There, Andy."

Andy saw a dark shape on the ground. He dismounted quickly, but Shanty reached Rusty first. "Still breathin'," he said. "Mr. Rusty, it's me and Andy."

Rusty was on his stomach. He groaned. Andy dropped to his knees and reached to touch him. He drew his hand away, sticky with warm blood. "Took a bullet in his shoulder. From the back, I'd guess."

He jerked his neckerchief loose and pressed it against the seeping wound.

Shanty said, "Let's turn him over real easy. See if the bullet came out the front."

It had. At least the slug was not lodged in Rusty's body.

Andy felt like crying but managed to choke it off. He forced the words. "Rusty, we have to move you away from here. Think you can ride?"

The only answer was a groan.

Shanty said, "We got to get him to the house."

"They'll look there in the mornin'."

"Where else can we go?"

Andy thought a minute. "Tom Blessing's. He'll know what to do." Andy touched Rusty's arm. "Rusty, can you hear me?"

The voice was weak. "I hear."

"We'll take you home and get the wagon. Then we'll haul you to Tom Blessing's. Think you can ride if we hold on to you?"

Rusty murmured, "Try."

Shanty brought the bay horse and helped Andy lift Rusty to his feet. Andy had to place Rusty's foot in the stirrup. The two managed to boost him into the saddle. Shanty held him in place while Andy mounted his own horse, then Andy took over.

Andy said, "Grit your teeth, Rusty. It won't be long."

Rusty drifted in and out of consciousness. Andy held on to him but came near losing him once. "Grab on, Shanty. He's about to fall."

The cabin was a welcome sight as the moon emerged. They eased Rusty down and carried him inside. Andy worked to stop the bleeding and bind the wounds while

Shanty went out to fetch the wagon and team.

Andy felt compelled to keep talking whether Rusty heard him or not. Otherwise he would break down and cry. "Damn it all, Rusty, it's my fault. I ought to've let them have Farley Brackett. Better him than you."

Rusty made a small cough. Throat aching, Andy said, "Hang on. Hang on tight. Don't you be goin' off and leavin' with me owin' you so much." He rubbed a sleeve across his eyes.

Rusty did not respond. Andy decided it was better that he remain unconscious. Perhaps the trip would not hurt him so badly.

Andy and Shanty carried Rusty outside and placed him on blankets spread in the bed of the wagon.

Shanty fretted, "A wagon won't be no trouble for the Oldhams to follow."

"We'll use the town road as far as we can. I doubt they can tell one wagon track from another."

Tying two horses on behind, they started toward the road that led to the settlement.

Rusty lay quiet and still, reacting only when the wagon hit a bump that jarred him. Andy remained on the road awhile, then turned onto a lesser-used trail that led to Tom Blessing's place. He stopped for a minute and made an effort to brush out the tracks.

Past midnight, he saw the cabin ahead.

He said, "We're there, Rusty. We've made it." He did not know if Rusty heard him.

A dog barked. A man emerged from beneath a shed. Andy recognized the lanky form of Len Tanner. "Len," he shouted, "come a-runnin'."

Barefoot and in his long underwear, Tanner came in a trot. "What's the trouble?"

"Rusty's been shot. Go rouse Tom Blessing, would you?"

Tanner demanded, "Who done this to him?"

"Clyde and Buddy Oldham. Go, would you?"

"Oldham?" Tanner spat the name. He hurried away, cursing the Oldhams, all their antecedents and any progeny they might ever have.

Rusty regained consciousness enough to ask where they were. Blessing came out of the bedroom side of the double cabin, buttoning his britches, bringing his suspenders up over his shoulders. He was barefoot and without a shirt. Tanner trotted alongside him, looking thin enough for a strong wind to blow him away.

Blessing peered into the bed of the wagon. "How bad is it?"

Rusty had become completely aware. He managed a raspy answer. "I ain't dead yet."

Blessing slid strong arms beneath him. He shouted at his wife to bring a light to the door, then set some water on to boil in the fireplace. He carried Rusty inside the bedroom. To Andy, Blessing seemed an old man, yet he had the strength of a bull. Mrs. Blessing held a lantern, setting it down on a table as her husband gently placed Rusty on the warm bed the couple had just vacated. She hurried to the cabin's other side to stir the coals in the fireplace and set a kettle of water on.

Blessing cautiously unwrapped the binding and examined the wounds.

Andy told him, "The bullet went plumb through. He lost a right smart of blood before we could stop it."

Shanty said, "It was God's mercy that he didn't bleed to death."

Andy explained about the fugitive Brackett, about the soldiers and the Oldhams.

Tanner swore. "Me and Rusty ought to've shot them damned Oldhams years ago when we had the chance."

Blessing grunted. "Now they're state policemen. They can get away with just about anything."

Andy said, "You've been the sheriff. You know the law. What can we do?"

"Not much. The state police and the military just barely tolerate us old rebels."

"But Rusty never was a rebel, and he had no part in

Brackett gettin' away. I don't see how they'd have a case against him."

"The law is whatever the carpetbag courts say it is. As long as men of the Oldhams' caliber wear a badge, Rusty has a sword hangin' over his head."

Andy clenched a fist. "I wish I could bring the Comanches down here."

Blessing pointed out, "They'd hit a lot of the rest of us too. No, we've got trouble enough as it is."

Mrs. Blessing washed the wounds with water as hot as her hands could stand it. Her husband poured whiskey into the bullet hole, front and rear. Rusty arched his back and sucked air between his teeth.

Blessing said, "I wish Preacher Webb was here. He can heal the body as well as the soul."

Mrs. Blessing replied, "If he *was* here, he'd wonder how come we keep whiskey in the house."

Shanty had watched gravely but said little. "I doubt the Lord minds folks takin' a little nip, long as it's in a healin' way."

The rough handling had brought Rusty to full consciousness. Blessing asked him, "How'd this happen?"

Rusty struggled with his answer. "I had a notion what they were goin' to do. When I heard the hammer click I set the horse to runnin'. I reckon the first flash blinded them. They couldn't see where I went."

Andy worried, "When they can't find you, they'll start figurin' all the places we might've took you. How long before they come here?"

Blessing finished wrapping the wounds with clean cloth. "Not long. Some damned fool is bound to tell them me and Rusty have been friends since the battle of Plum Creek."

"Where can we take him?"

Rusty said, "The Monahan place."

Tanner nodded vigorously. "Back when we was rangers, Rusty caught a Comanche arrow in his leg. The Monahans took care of him 'til he was on his feet. They'd do it again."

Blessing cautioned, "The Oldhams might guess where he went."

Tanner's face twisted ominously. "It'd be their own fault if they did. Was Clyde and Buddy-Boy to go up there, they might not come back. Them Monahans get real serious when they're provoked."

Blessing said, "Rusty would have the benefit of Preacher Webb's doctorin'."

Andy remembered, "It's a long ways. It'll take several days in a wagon."

Rusty said in a weak voice, "I can make it."

Tanner declared, "Sure you can. Damned if we'll let the likes of Clyde and Buddy-Boy do you in."

Rusty reached up to touch Andy's arm. "Len knows the way. He can take me. I wish you and Shanty would stay and watch out for the place."

Andy felt a rush of disappointment at not going. "Whatever you want."

"Fowler Gaskin will carry off everything but the dirt if somebody's not there."

Andy's disappointment was quickly overcome by the realization that he was being trusted with heavy responsibility. "We'll take care of things, me and Shanty." He looked to Shanty for support.

Tanner asked, "You sure Andy's man enough?"

Rusty grunted. "He's almost grown."

Andy thought if he were still with the Comanches he would be taking scalps by now. He would start with the Oldhams'. He decided not to say so because it might be taken for immature blustering.

Mrs. Blessing said, "I'll be fixin' us some breakfast. Andy, there's ham in the smokehouse. Fetch a shoulder in here for Rusty and Len, would you? I'll put some salt and flour and coffee together."

Like most settlers along the river, Tom Blessing let hogs range free. Butchering was done on cold winter days and the meat slow-smoked in a small log structure behind the cabin. It took a minute for Andy's eyes to adjust to the darkness. He found the mixed smells of pork and charred wood pungent but not unpleasant. He chose a cloth-wrapped shoulder and lifted it from its hook.

Returning to the cabin, he found Rusty on his feet but supported by both Tanner and Blessing. Rusty said, "I believe I can sit up if you'll put me on the wagon seat."

Tanner said, "And go to bleedin' again? You'll lay down on them blankets and not give us no argument. I don't aim to dig a grave for you all by myself."

After a hasty breakfast the two men got Rusty safely situated in the wagon bed. Rusty looked with concern at Andy and Shanty. "The Oldhams may talk pretty rough. Shanty, you'll see that Andy keeps a cork on his temper, won't you?"

Shanty said, "We'll do just fine, Mr. Rusty. Don't you worry yourself about us."

Andy said, "I'm sorry, Rusty. I'd give anything not to've brought this trouble on you."

"Don't you be feelin' guilty. With the Oldhams, if it hadn't been this it would've been somethin' else. You just step careful and don't fall into any trouble."

Andy watched the wagon move away in the first pale light of morning, Len's horse tied on behind. He did not want anybody to see him choke up, so he took a broom from the dog run and began to brush out the tracks.

Blessing watched him quizzically. "You aim to sweep all the way to the Monahans'?"

Andy recognized the futility of what he was doing. "I can brush out the trail for a little ways, at least. I don't want anything to be easy for the Oldhams."

Blessing pointed to clouds building in the east. They would hide the sunrise. Andy saw a few faint flashes of lightning, so far away that he did not hear the thunder. Blessing said, "Looks like we may get some rain after a while. If we do, it should take care of the tracks. You-all like a little more coffee before you start home?"

Shanty shook his head. "We need to hurry and get there

before the Oldhams do. Me and Andy got to figure out a lie to tell them."

Andy said ruefully, "It was a lie that started all this."

They had not been home long before Clyde and Buddy Oldham appeared with several men on horseback. Andy recognized none of them except Fowler Gaskin and his nephew, Euclid Summerville. Fowler had long and loudly proclaimed his allegiance to the Confederacy, though he had been quick to take the oath of loyalty to the Union once it was clear the rebel cause was lost and there might be advantages to reconciliation. Now he rode beside the state police, symbol of the occupation. It stood to reason that he would join the search for Rusty, given the long enmity between them.

Only the Oldhams wore badges, but the others all bore a gravely officious look that told Andy they had a high regard for their authority.

Clyde leaned forward in the saddle, his face as stormy as the clouds that rose behind him. "All right, where's he at?"

Andy and Shanty glanced at one another. "Who?"

"You know damned well who I mean. Rusty Shannon."

Andy said, "Couldn't you find him with all this bunch to help you?"

"Buddy hit him last night. He couldn't have got far without help."

"We ain't seen him." Andy found that the lie spilled out easily. In the Comanche culture the coyote was regarded as a trickster, always trying to lead humans astray. The People looked upon it with a mixture of dismay and admiration. Playing the role of the coyote gave Andy a wicked satisfaction.

Clyde said, "I figure you're hidin' him. We're goin' to look around."

Andy shifted his gaze to Gaskin. "Just don't carry away anything that don't belong to you."

Clyde gestured. "Search the place, men. Don't overlook nothin'."

Some went into the cabin. Andy was glad he had thought to burn the bloody pieces of cloth that would have been a giveaway. Others went to the barn and shed. Gaskin and Summerville headed straight to the smokehouse. Gaskin came out carrying a ham.

Andy said, "Just because you're runnin' with the scalawag state police don't mean you got a right to steal."

Buddy Oldham said, "Keep it, Gaskin. When we get through with Shannon, he ain't goin' to care about one little old ham. He ain't goin' to care about *nothin'*."

Emboldened, Summerville went into the smokehouse and fetched another.

Shortly the men gathered in front of the cabin, empty-handed except for Gaskin's hams. Clyde's temper had not cooled. "Seems to me like I saw a wagon under that shed yesterday. I don't see it there now."

"You don't?" Trying to appear innocent, Andy looked again at Fowler Gaskin. "There's thieves everywhere."

One of the riders pointed out, "I see fresh wagon tracks leadin' off yonderway."

Buddy's voice crackled. "I wounded him. He couldn't have rode far on his horse. One of you—maybe both of you—hauled him someplace. Tell us where you took him."

Neither Andy nor Shanty spoke. Buddy lifted a quirt from his saddlehorn. He rode forward, lashing Shanty first. Andy saw the next strike was coming at him and tried to shield his face. The quirt stung like fire across his cheek and down his shoulder. He looked up, burning with anger but determined to take the next strike like a warrior, without flinching.

Summerfield shouted, "Hit him again. And that nigger too."

One of the policemen rebuked Buddy. "Headquarters ain't goin' to take it kindly, you quirtin' a darkey. You'll have the Freedmen's Bureau down on us."

"Mind your own business. I'm tryin' to make them talk."

"They ain't goin' to. Look at the fire in that kid's eyes. Right now he's pure-dee Comanche. He'd cut your gizzard out and feed it to you."

Clyde Oldham said reluctantly, "Back off, Buddy."

The policeman said, "Oldham, looks to me like we ought to be huntin' Farley Brackett instead of wastin' so much time on Shannon. The worst he did was let Brackett have a horse to get away on."

Andy declared, "He didn't even do that, and Oldham knows it. He's tryin' to get even for somethin' that happened back in the war."

Buddy raised the quirt as if to strike Andy again.

The policeman caught Buddy's arm. "Been enough whippin' done. We're fixin' to get caught in a frog-stranglin' rain. I'm for goin' back to town."

The others seemed to agree. Clyde trembled with rage. "You-all quittin' on us? Then me and Buddy'll keep lookin' by ourselves."

"If you keep on lookin', it'll *be* by yourselves."

Clyde cursed them to no avail. All turned and started riding away except Fowler Gaskin and his nephew. Gaskin advised Clyde, "Between Rusty Shannon and the Comanches, they've plumb ruined that boy. You ought to take that quirt and make a Christian out of him."

Andy said sarcastically, "You're a great one for usin' a whip on people. And burnin' cabins, too."

Gaskin said, "We ought to burn this one. Teach them all a lesson."

Summerfield offered, "I'll do it, Uncle Fowler."

Clyde said, "Forget it. I got plans for this place. I'll need that house."

The four were so intent on Andy that they did not notice Shanty ease into the cabin. He came out with a rifle and a look of determination. "You-all are about done here, ain't you?"

Gaskin's voice went shrill. "Aim that thing somewheres else. Damned fool nigger, you're liable to touch it off and kill somebody."

Shanty agreed. "Sure might."

Gaskin began backing his horse away. Shanty swung the muzzle toward Clyde and Buddy.

Fear leaped into Clyde's eyes before he could check it. He said, "We ain't goin' to get nothin' out of these two. Let's see if we can follow them wagon tracks."

Shortly after they turned away, the rain began. It started with large drops, widely scattered, then became a drenching downpour. Andy and Shanty stood in the dog run, beneath the roof. Wind carried a cool spray into their faces. It eased the burning where Buddy's quirt had stung Andy's cheek.

Shanty looked closely at Andy's face. "That quirt marked you pretty good."

"It'll pass."

Shanty said, "With this rain, they ain't goin' to follow no tracks for long."

"Maybe they'll all drown."

Rusty and Tanner were probably caught in the same heavy rain, Andy thought. At least they had slickers and a tarp. The Oldhams, Gaskin and Summerville didn't. Maybe they *would* drown.

He grinned. His cheek no longer burned so badly.

But Shanty spoiled his good feeling. He said, "It ain't done yet. Looks like them Oldhams ain't goin' to rest 'til they ruin Mr. Rusty, or kill him."

Andy was chopping a seasoned live-oak limb for firewood while Shanty took the shade on the dog run after a day's work in the field. Andy said, "That feller hidin' down by the river is gettin' careless. I've seen him twice."

Someone had been camped in the timber for the last three days, watching the cabin. Andy knew it was probably an Oldham or some other state policeman assigned to the duty. He said, "Maybe I ought to go and invite him up for supper."

Shanty smiled but dismissed the idea. "That'd just make the Oldhams madder than they already are. They don't think we know anybody's down there."

"They're liable to take root and grow if they're waitin' for Rusty to show up."

Andy returned to his wood cutting. It struck him that in a Comanche camp, gathering wood was woman's work. But there was no woman here, and he had seen little sign that Rusty was looking for one. He remembered that the Monahan daughter named Josie had taken a shine to him. Maybe she would have time and opportunity to work on him now while he was hurt and helpless.

He had not gotten a good look at Jeremiah Brackett the night a group of riders visited Shanty's place, so he did not recognize him when the man came riding up on a long-legged sorrel horse. A wagon followed. Andy was intrigued to see that a girl was driving it.

At least they were not state police. He walked out to meet them, the dog Rough trotting ahead of him, barking. Shanty remained beneath the dog run, mending harness.

"Howdy," Andy said to the rider. "Light and hitch." It was a greeting he had often heard Rusty address to visitors.

He judged the horseman to be well into his late fifties, maybe even his sixties, roughly the same as Tom Blessing. Except for a stiff military bearing he had the look of a hardworking farmer, not a man from town.

The visitor said, "I'm Jeremiah Brackett." He gave Andy's braids a moment's quiet attention. "You'd be the young man my son told me about."

"Andy Pickard. I suppose your son is Farley Brackett."

"He is. It seems the Brackett family owes you-all a horse. We always pay our debts. I brought this one in exchange for the one Farley took from you."

Andy walked around the sorrel, giving it a close inspection. "He's a sight better-lookin' than the roan your son took. You're gettin' the short end of the trade."

"Farley said that horse almost got him caught by the state police. He would have shot him, but that would have left him afoot."

The wagon stopped. Brackett unsaddled the sorrel and threw his saddle behind the seat. He said, "This young lady is my daughter Bethel."

Andy stared at the girl, trying to remember the rules of behavior Rusty and Shanty had lectured him about. He removed his hat. He struggled for the proper words. "Damned pleased to meet you, ma'am." His face warmed. He knew he had made a mess of it.

He had not seen a lot of girls to compare her by. He thought she might be the prettiest he had ever looked upon, though his notion of what constituted *pretty* tended to change with each new one he saw. He tried to remember if he might have encountered her in town. It seemed to him that if he had, he wouldn't have forgotten.

She said, "Your name would be Andy, I suppose. I've heard about you."

He wondered what she had heard. Probably not good if she had heard it in town. He said, "Don't believe them. There's an awful lot of liars in this country."

"It wasn't *all* bad. We appreciate what you did for my brother."

Shanty came out from the dog run. Andy nodded in his direction. "It was Shanty's doin' as much as mine."

Brackett grunted. "I'll pay him for it. I don't want to stay beholden to a darkey." He reached in his pocket and withdrew a silver coin. He handed it to Shanty. "Here. This is yours."

Bethel gave her father a quick look of disapproval, then turned away.

Shanty fingered the coin, his eyes confused. "What's this for?"

"For your part in helping my son escape. It should buy you a pint of whiskey."

"I ain't a whiskey drinker, sir."

"Well then, some tobacco or whatever you like. It's Yankee. Anybody in town will accept it."

Shanty tried to give back the coin, but Brackett waved him away. "Keep it. We're even now."

Andy felt he should extend the hospitality of the house, such as it was. "We've got some coffee inside. Or some fresh buttermilk I just churned last night."

He immediately wished he had not admitted that. Churning was something else that would have been woman's work in a Comanche camp except that the Comanches did not have milk and butter.

Brackett climbed into the wagon. His daughter moved over on the seat and handed him the reins. He said, "Thank you, but we should be getting back. There is always more work to do than time to do it."

The girl gave Andy a thin smile as her father turned the team around. "Come and see us."

"I'd like to." Watching them leave, he thought, First time there's a reason. Maybe if he studied on it he could *find* a reason.

Shanty was still rubbing the coin between his thumb and forefinger. "I didn't see him give *you* nothin'."

Andy shook his head. "He didn't."

"Then how come him to pay *me*?"

Andy knew. Brackett would feel compromised if he owed a debt to a black man. Unable to think of any painless way to explain it, Andy decided to let Shanty figure it out for himself.

He did, and quickly. Shanty drew back and sailed the coin as far as he could throw it.

The Oldhams' state police gave up any pretense of secrecy in their watching post by the river, but they did not give up the stakeout. By the time Brackett and his daughter pulled away from the cabin, a rider was already trotting his horse up to overtake them. He circled the cabin and stopped the pair. After questioning them a few minutes he let them proceed and came back to where Andy and Shanty stood watching.

This was a deputy, not an Oldham. He looked disappointed. "Thought that might be Shannon."

Andy said, "You'll have to get up mighty early in the mornin' to catch Rusty. But keep on tryin'." He had wanted to needle the deputies and, if possible, the Oldhams, but Shanty had advised against it.

The deputy said, "Just followin' orders. Clyde says do it, and we do it. Tell you the truth, I'm gettin' almighty tired of campin' down there by the river."

"Come on up here, why don't you, where you can watch us a lot closer? Spread your blankets in the dog run. Even eat with us if you'll bring the grub."

"Clyde and Buddy would raise hell. Can't get friendly with the enemy, they'd say."

Andy said, "Don't it hurt your conscience, workin' for the state police, takin' orders from people like the Old-hams?"

"It's a livin'. All our officers ain't like them. Most of them are honest men just tryin' to do a dirty job the cleanest way they can."

"Like houndin' Rusty when you know he didn't do anything wrong?"

"That's Clyde's doin'. He's got the authority, and he's friends with a judge who goes along with whatever he wants to do. They've squeezed the old rebels around here for all they could get out of them. Stole some farms and stuck most of the money in their pockets, except for what they sent to Austin to keep the higher authorities happy."

"You could quit."

"I've got a family to feed. I grit my teeth and look the other way."

"This reconstruction government won't last forever. What'll you do when it's gone?"

"Been thinkin' about California. Maybe there's still some gold left out there. Ain't none in Texas. But 'til I can save enough to make the trip, I'll bide my time, do what Clyde tells me and hope I don't have to help him starve any wid-ders and orphans."

He started to ride away but stopped and turned back. He seemed to have a hard time getting the words out. "I oughtn't to be tellin' you-all this, but I think you deserve to know. Clyde's fixin' to steal this place from Shannon the same way he's stole them others."

The statement hit Andy in the stomach. "How could he do that?"

"Rig the tax books, say that Shannon ain't paid all his assessments. It's worked for him before, him and his judge. You-all had just as well pack up whatever you'll want to take with you. There ain't no stoppin' him."

In a moment of anger Andy thought there was one way.

He considered whether he should shoot Oldham in the head, in the chest or in the belly. Any of the three would do the job. But he knew it was a futile notion.

Preacher Webb had often spoken about the wages of sin. Watching the deputy ride back toward the river, Andy said, "Yonder goes a man who hates the sin, but he's willin' enough to take its wages."

Shanty replied, "I'm glad I won't be wearin' his shoes when he walks up to the Golden Gates."

"He's wearin' better shoes than me and you."

"I'd rather be barefooted."

Andy was almost finished with his chores when he recognized the blue roan horse approaching from the direction of the Brackett farm. It was too far to identify the rider. "Company comin'," he called. His first thought was that the elder Brackett was bringing back the roan.

"Damn! I'll bet he wants to take Long Red." That was the name Andy and Shanty had given to the sorrel.

Shanty arose from his wooden chair and entered the kitchen. He was back in a moment with the rifle. "Hope it ain't Clyde Oldham, comin' around to hound us again."

"He wouldn't be ridin' that roan. Anyway, I saw him down on the river a while ago, watchin' this place." He squinted. "That's not Old Man Brackett after all. It's his son Farley. They look a right smart alike."

"Him that caused us all this trouble?" Shanty made no secret of his disliking for the man. He handed Andy the rifle. "Mighty reckless, showin' hisself when the police are huntin' all over for him."

"Maybe he's come to thank us for that roan horse."

"He never looked like a man spillin' over with thankfulness."

Brackett reined up a little short of the cabin and studied the rifle with misgivings. The eye at the upper end of his facial scar was squinted almost shut. "Ain't no need for that."

Andy said, "I hope not, but I'd use it if you was to give me cause."

Brackett raised a hand, signaling peaceful intentions. "You and that nigger played a mean trick on me, puttin' me onto this roan. He ain't worth six bits in Yankee silver."

Andy shook his head. "You didn't do us no favor either, leavin' us with a horse that had a US brand on it. That's caused us no end of hell."

"So I've heard. I'm sorry for what happened to Shannon."

"Bein' sorry don't take Clyde Oldham off of his back, or ours."

"Ain't nothin' I can do about it."

"You could surrender to the state police. You could tell them how it really was. Then Rusty could come home."

"I'd just as well put a gun in my ear and pull the trigger as to give myself up to that bunch."

"Then what did you come here for?"

"Just wanted to say I appreciate you puttin' the soldiers off of my trail."

Andy said, "I'm wishin' now we hadn't done it."

Brackett leaned down to look closer at Andy. "That's quite a mark on your face."

"Quirt. Buddy Oldham did it."

"I'd like to take a bullwhip and write my name across his back with it. Him and all the others."

Andy said, "You've got trouble enough, shootin' a state policeman."

"He lived. Guess I'll have to try again."

Andy felt relieved. At least Rusty could not be charged as an accessory to murder. "After you do, run some other direction, would you? Don't come by here."

A smile flickered and was quickly gone. "If there's anything you need, go talk to my old daddy. If he's got it, you can have it."

Andy said, "He brought us a horse. We don't need nothin' else from him. But you might need a little advice from *us*."

"What's that?"

"Don't go down by the river. Clyde Oldham and one of his deputies are there watchin' to see if Rusty comes back."

"The hell you say!" Brackett looked toward the river. "I don't see anybody."

"We're not supposed to either, but they get careless now and again."

"You want me to go down there and shoot them?"

"Looks like you'd get tired of shootin' policemen."

"I ain't yet, but I guess this time I'll be movin' on." Brackett set the roan into a trot and disappeared around the cabin.

Relieved at his departure, Andy drew a deep breath. Shanty wiped a sleeve across his face.

Andy's relief quickly faded as he saw Clyde Oldham and a deputy riding up from the river. He growled, "Preacher Webb says trouble likes to travel in pairs." He cradled the rifle in his arms.

Oldham spat a stream of tobacco juice and gave Andy a fierce scowl as he approached. "That wasn't Rusty Shannon, was it?"

Andy said, "The shape you left Rusty in, he couldn't ride like that."

"Then who was it?"

"He didn't mention his name."

Oldham clenched a fist. "If it's somebody carryin' messages to Shannon . . . "

Andy tried not to betray his surprise as he saw Farley Brackett ride out from behind the cabin and move up behind Oldham. Oldham heard and turned quickly, then froze, gaze fixed on a pistol in Brackett's hand.

Brackett said, "No, I ain't Shannon."

Andy swallowed hard.

Oldham stammered, fear rising in his eyes. He raised his hands. "Brackett. Where . . . how . . . " His voice choked off.

Brackett reached forward and took Oldham's pistol from its holster, then the deputy's. "Don't worry, I ain't made plans to kill anybody today unless I'm provoked. For what it's worth, the time I stopped by this place and took a fresh horse, Shannon wasn't even here. Besides, what I did wasn't much."

"You shot a state policeman."

"He oughtn't to've messed with me and my folks. But I didn't kill him."

"You tried."

"Yes, I did. Some days I can't shoot worth a damn. Anyway, you've got nothin' to blame Shannon for. I stole his horse, same as I'm fixin' to steal yours." He nodded at the deputy. "You heard what I just said? You can bear witness to it."

The deputy looked uneasily at Oldham. "I heard."

"Don't forget it, or I'm liable to come lookin' for *you* on one of the days when my shootin' eye is sharp." He nodded toward the roan. "Now, Deputy, I wish you'd take the saddle off of this horse and put it on Oldham's."

Oldham sputtered. "You'd leave me afoot?"

"You'll have the roan. I warn you, though, he ain't much of a horse."

The deputy switched saddles. Brackett looked Oldham's brown horse over and nodded approval. "Too good for a state policeman. The roan is more your caliber."

Oldham fumed. "I'll get you someday."

"Be damned careful that I don't get *you*." Brackett mounted and rode away in a stiff trot.

Left without a weapon, Oldham could only stare, his eyes smoldering.

With a touch of malice, Andy said, "You want to stay for supper? We'll be servin' crow."

Shanty frowned at him.

Oldham said, "It don't make any difference what Farley Brackett says, I'm still goin' to get Shannon."

Andy protested, "But you heard him say Rusty wasn't here to give him that roan horse. He just took it."

Oldham acted as if he did not hear.

*   *   *

Four weeks had passed without word from or about Rusty. Andy was uneasy, but he knew it would not do for Rusty or the Monahans to write a letter. Any mail would almost certainly be opened and read by the Oldhams or the Federally appointed postmaster.

He found that in a perverse way he enjoyed the present situation except for being concerned about Rusty's condition and a continuing guilty feeling that he was responsible for it. He felt a sense of being on his own and given a high level of responsibility. With the Comanches the equivalent would be if he were allowed to participate in running of the buffalo or raiding into Texas settlements and Mexico. The Comanches did not count birthdays quite as white men did. A boy became a man when he proved he could carry his weight. For some, that could be as little as fifteen or sixteen summers. For others, it took longer.

Shanty came into the cabin's kitchen, carrying a slab of bacon from the smokehouse. His eyes were troubled. "Andy, did you hear my dog barkin' last night?"

"No. At least, he didn't wake me up."

"Me neither. I slept real good. But there's some hog meat missin' from the smokehouse."

Andy's first thought was that whoever stood guard at the river might have run out of meat and decided to replenish his supply. That idea gave way to a more likely answer. "Fowler Gaskin or his nephew Euclid. Clyde let them take those hams from us the day they came lookin' for Rusty. They probably figure they've got the law's blessin' to do it again."

Shanty said, "Can't always trust that fool dog to raise a ruckus. Maybe I better take to sleepin' out by the smokehouse."

A delicious thought came to Andy. "I wonder if anybody's got a wolf trap we could borrow."

"There's some over at my place, in the old shed. Me and Mr. Isaac used to do a bit of winter trappin'. Mostly for coons and ringtails and such, but now and then we caught us a wolf."

"I'm thinkin' more about catchin' us a hog. Your field probably needs weedin' again. We'll go over there tomorrow."

They had been working at Shanty's farm every few days, taking care of the field and garden. Because the cabin had been burned, they had been going early in the morning, then returning to Rusty's place late in the day to do the chores, fix supper and sleep. Before they started home Andy sorted through several steel traps hanging in Shanty's shed, picking two of the largest. He set one of them, then tripped it. The jaws snapped hard enough to break a dry stick he used to trigger the mechanism.

"Not strong enough to bust an ankle," he judged, "but he's liable to hop around on one foot for a few days."

"Kind of mean, don't you think?" Shanty tried to sound dubious, but Andy could see mischief in his eyes.

"Not half mean enough for the likes of Gaskin."

Though he doubted that Fowler or Summerville would show up so soon, he set a trap that evening just inside the smokehouse door. Entering in darkness, the thief was not likely to see it until he put his foot in it.

Andy checked on the trap the next morning. It was just as he had left it. For safety he tripped it. He set it again the second night, and again no one came.

The third night Andy awakened to a loud cry of surprise and pain. He stepped out onto the dog run in time to see a spider-legged figure dancing furiously in the dim light of the moon, a chain clanking as it dragged behind him.

The voice was Fowler Gaskin's. A second voice quavered. "What's the matter, Uncle Fowler?"

Gaskin launched a formidable string of profanity. "Fetch my horse, you damned idiot!" Howling, he dropped to the ground and labored to free his foot. He cast the trap as far as he could throw it and limped to the horse Summerville led up.

"You sons of bitches!" he shouted toward the cabin. His

voice was shrill. "You dirty sons of bitches!" He fired a parting shot toward the cabin. Andy heard the slug smack into a log.

He grinned. "Fowler Gaskin, that'll teach you to stop suckin' eggs."

He had not seen Rusty's black horse Alamo in a couple of days and set out after breakfast to search for it. Toward noon he found it with a couple of the neighbors' plow horses grazing in a draw, tributary to the river. "Come on, boy," he said, dropping a rawhide loop over Alamo's neck, "you better stay closer to home or somebody like Fowler Gaskin is liable to hook you to a plow."

He expected to see Shanty working in the field or the garden, but instead he was at the cabin, loading something into one of two wagons that stood nearby. Two men were leading harnessed teams up from the river, where they had evidently been taken to drink.

One of the men was tall Tom Blessing. The other, who looked much like him but was younger, Andy recognized as a son. Blessing saw Andy coming but continued leading his team to the front wagon.

Andy dismounted and extended his hand. "Howdy, Tom." He nodded at the younger Blessing. "What brings you-all over here?"

Tom Blessing's face was grim. "Bad news. Clyde and Buddy Oldham are fixin' to take over this farm and everything on it."

Andy felt as if his stomach were turning over. He remembered what the deputy had told him. He had not really believed it could happen. "How can they do that?"

"I heard about it in town. Clyde claims the records show that Rusty is way behind on his taxes."

"Rusty's paid all the taxes they asked for. It took just about everything he got for sendin' cattle north."

"Tax records are easy to alter if you've got the keys to the courthouse. My son and I hoped we'd beat the Oldhams out here and haul off everything Rusty might want to keep."

Shanty came out with an armful of blankets. Blessing's son had Rusty's plow in his wagon, along with all the harness and tools from the shed.

Tom Blessing said, "Pity we can't take cabin and all."

Blood hot in his face, Andy demanded, "What about the field? The crops are half grown already."

Blessing replied, "Pity, but I reckon the Oldhams'll get the benefit of all that. You want to help me empty the smokehouse? No need in leavin' the meat to them."

Andy trembled with outrage. "And I thought Fowler Gaskin was a thief. Ain't there somethin' we can do?"

"I don't know what. Clyde has got the scalawag government on his side."

"We could shoot him," Andy said.

Shanty shook his gray head sadly. "That's the Comanche in you talkin'. Killin' ain't the way the Lord meant for folks to doctor what ails them."

"Once it's done, it's damned sure permanent."

"So is a hangin' rope, and that's what you'd get. Them Oldham brothers are like a pair of hungry wolves."

"No, they're just coyotes."

"Anyway, it ain't for me and you to decide. Best let Mr. Rusty know what's happened and see what he wants."

They soon had the two wagons loaded with about everything not too heavy to lift or too bulky to carry. Andy said, "It's up to me to go tell Rusty about this. He ain't goin' to take it kindly."

Blessing nodded. "Kindly or not, he'll have to take it for now. Maybe someday when things change he'll find a way to get the farm back. At least there's this much the Oldhams won't get."

Andy gazed in the direction of the plot where Rusty's Daddy Mike and Mother Dora lay. "He won't even own the ground where his folks are buried."

Blessing's expression was grave. "I can imagine what old Mike would say. He was a fire-eater, that one. But it finally got him killed." He climbed onto the wagon.

Shanty asked, "What about me? Where will I go?"

Blessing replied, "With me, Shanty. You can stay at my place 'til things straighten out."

Shanty hesitated. "Andy, you goin' to go tell Mr. Rusty?"

"He's got to know."

"Like as not them Oldhams'll figure on that. They'll follow you. They won't be satisfied 'til they've killed him dead."

"I'll wait 'til night, and I'll ride in the edge of the river a ways so they'll have hell findin' my tracks." He reached up to shake Shanty's hand, then Blessing's. "I don't know when I'll be comin' back. A lot'll depend on what Rusty wants to do."

Blessing said, "Tell him we'll be back and gather up all of his livestock that we can find. We'll drift them west to some empty country I know of. I doubt the Oldhams will find them any time soon."

Andy stood hunched in sadness, watching the wagons roll away. For six years this place had been home to him, at least the only home he had. He felt the same emptiness as when he had turned his back on Comanchería. There were times when he wondered if dark spirits dogged his steps and did not mean for him to have a home.

The cabin appeared almost empty, bereft of most of its handmade furniture except for the beds, too cumbersome for the wagons. The cooking ware, the cups and plates, were gone. The smokehouse was empty except for a large slab of bacon Andy had saved for his trip north. He had kept back salt, coffee and a small sack of flour so he could make bread on the trail. These he carried out to the corral and placed in a wooden trough near his saddle. He planned to ride the Brackett sorrel, Long Red, and use Alamo as a packhorse. For no amount of money would he leave Rusty's favorite mount to be taken by the Oldhams or perhaps Fowler Gaskin, whichever showed up first.

Clyde and Buddy Oldham arrived a while before sundown, accompanied by a sour-faced deputy. Clyde

dismounted and waved some folded papers in Andy's face.
"I got eviction papers for Rusty Shannon. Since I know he
ain't here, I'm servin' them on you. These papers tell you
to vacate."

Andy feigned ignorance. "What do you mean, vacate?"

Buddy spoke up sharply. "He means get the hell off, and
the quicker the better." Buddy lifted the quirt from the horn
of his saddle and raised it.

Clyde blocked the blow with his arm. "He's still got a
mark from when you done that before, and it didn't do no
good. He may be half Indian, but I expect he understands
English when it's spoke good and plain. Put your stuff together, boy. You're leavin' here."

"Where do you expect me to go?"

"Back to the Comanches, for all we care. That's probably
where you belong."

Andy knew argument was futile, but he did not want to
give in to them without raising a little dust first. "You've
got no right to this place. It's Rusty's, and it belonged to
his folks before that. What if I don't want to leave?"

"Then I'll turn Buddy loose with that quirt. He's only
got one arm, but you know it's a strong one."

While the deputy waited with Andy, Clyde and his
brother walked up to the cabin. They paused a moment at
the dog run to look at the empty iron hooks on which fresh
meat often hung, wrapped in canvas. They then went into
the kitchen. Clyde was out again in a moment, crossing
quickly over to the bedroom side. He stayed there but little
longer before striding down from the dog run and marching
angrily toward Andy.

"What the hell has happened here? Where's everything
gone?"

Andy continued to feign ignorance. "I been away most
of the day. Maybe Fowler Gaskin paid us a visit. He never
leaves without takin' somethin'."

"Gaskin hell! Everything on this place belongs to me.
These papers say so."

"You just now served them. 'Til you did that, I reckon

everything still belonged to Rusty." Andy knew little about legalities, but that seemed logical enough.

The deputy put in, "I told you I seen a couple of wagons earlier in the day. They left here loaded."

Buddy declared, "Somebody tipped this Indian off. Whoever it was needs a good stompin'."

Clyde said, "We'll save the stompin' for Rusty Shannon, when we find him."

Buddy said eagerly, "Stomp on him awhile, then shoot him."

Clyde looked toward the field. "What was in the house wasn't worth much anyhow. They couldn't carry off that plowed ground out yonder. It's ours."

He turned again to Andy. "We'll be back first thing in the mornin'. You better not be here. Come on, Buddy, we're headed to town."

Andy watched them so long as they were in sight. Though they left by the town road, he had a strong hunch they would circle back and keep a lookout on him. Clyde was surely shrewd enough to guess that Andy would go immediately to notify Rusty what had happened. All he and his brother had to do was follow.

He raked banked coals in the fireplace and coaxed the flames with dry shavings, then built up a blaze with larger pieces of wood. He broiled bacon on a stick and waited for night.

In the dark of the moon he packed blankets and food on Alamo and saddled Long Red. He had built up a big fire, hoping the watchers would think he was still in the cabin. For a while he had entertained the notion of burning the cabin so the Oldhams could not have it. He gave that up as a bad idea. The cabin was Rusty's main tie to the memory of Mike and Dora Shannon. He would not want it destroyed, even to keep it from the hands of his enemies.

Besides, Andy held out hope that Rusty would eventually find a way to get the farm back. He would appreciate having the cabin remain intact.

He swung into the saddle and tugged on the lead rope. "Come on, Red, Alamo. We're goin' north."

There was no clearly marked trail at first, but Andy did not need one. He had confidence in his sense of direction and his memory for landmarks. As he had told Shanty, he rode a couple of miles in the edge of the river, then found a gravelly bank on which he could quit the water without leaving obvious tracks. He traveled until he figured it was past midnight, then halted for a dry camp. He had eaten his supper in the cabin.

He hoped the Oldhams had not noted his departure. Even if they guessed his direction and started at daylight, he should be several hours ahead of them.

Awakening at daybreak, he glanced around to be certain where he was. He had a good memory for places. More than once during the years he had lived with Rusty, he had become helplessly homesick for the plains and had slipped away alone, returning to Comanche land. There he had lived off the land and watched The People's camps from afar, wishing but not daring to enter. He had been like an estranged family member who still felt the kinship but knew the path to reconciliation was too treacherous to try.

He prepared a hasty breakfast of bacon and bread wrapped around a stick and broiled over a low flame. The bread tasted flat, so he salted it a little and made it more palatable. Shanty had taught him how to bake corn dodgers on the flat side of a hoe, but here he had neither hoe nor cornmeal. Looking behind him he saw no sign of pursuit, but he was uneasy. He felt instinctively that the Oldhams were back there somewhere. They might be greedy, they might be vicious, but they were not altogether stupid. Sooner or later they were bound to cut his trail.

Andy followed a route he had ridden with Rusty. He remembered he had also ridden this way, though southbound, following his Comanche brother Steals the Ponies and several other young warriors intent upon a horse-stealing raid. Because they considered him too young they had not let him ride with them, but he had followed at a distance. He had not allowed himself to be discovered until they were too deep in the Texan country to send him back. Misfortune had dogged him, however. In a running fight his horse fell on him, breaking his leg. That was when Rusty Shannon found him and carried him home.

Andy had relived that event a thousand times in his mind. He toyed with the fantasy that it had never happened, that he had never reentered the white man's world and traveled the white man's road. He often wondered where he would be now and what he would be doing. By this time he fancied that The People would have accepted him as a warrior and a skilled hunter of buffalo. He would ride with pride through camp after each exploit, knowing The People were watching him and telling stories of his deeds.

He had been called Badger Boy, but surely by now he would have earned a nobler name reflecting his status as a man. He would not be just that Indian-looking young'un Andy Pickard, getting into fights at the settlement, a kid whose blood kin had rejected him and who lived as a ward of Rusty Shannon. Among the Comanches, he would be a man worth noticing.

At least now he was on a mission worthy of him, to warn Rusty of danger and perhaps to help protect him from his enemies. The responsibility was heavy, a little daunting, yet exhilarating.

Late on the first full day of travel he came upon a creek. He had known it would be there, yet he had not allowed himself to give it much thought beforehand. Now, suddenly, the sight of it took him back six years. He remembered what Rusty had shown him then, and he shuddered. This was a bad place.

His instincts pressed him to cross the creek hurriedly and ride on, but something within would not allow him that avoidance. It was if other hands took hold of the reins and guided the sorrel horse against his will.

He watched for a landmark tree. He almost rode past, for it had fallen since his last visit. It lay dry and broken on the ground. A scattering of chips indicated that travelers had chopped up much of it for campfire wood. He rode a small circle and found the mound of stones just as he remembered them.

Stomach cold, Andy made himself dismount and tie Alamo's lead rope to the horn of his saddle. He hitched Long Red to a sapling at the top of the creek bank. He stood at the grave, skin prickling, his throat swelling to a rush of confused feelings.

This was where his white mother had died.

Rusty had told him how he and Daddy Mike and others had ridden this way, following the trail of a war party. The Comanches had taken many horses and carried with them two prisoners, a small boy and his mother. Here the pursuing Texans had found the woman cruelly butchered. Lacking digging tools, Rusty and Preacher Webb had covered her with stones the best they could.

They had not overtaken the warriors, and they had given the captive boy up for dead.

That boy had been Andy.

Rusty had shown him the place, hoping it would revive memories of his life before the Indians had taken him. Here Andy had imagined he felt the spirit of his mother, and images suppressed during his years with the Comanches had come rushing, overwhelming him. He had relived the horror of her death. He had tried ever since to rebury that memory, but the specter rose up now and then in the dark of night, chilling him, destroying any chance of rest.

Logic told him he should hate the Comanches for what they had done, but he could not. They had killed his original family—his mother and father—then in compensation had given him a new family, making him one of their own.

As he looked down at the grave now, a grief long denied came welling up. He tried to remember his mother as she was before her capture and not as she had been in the last terrifying moments of life. He could not quite see her face, but in his mind he could hear her voice. He remembered that she used to sing a lot. He tried to remember the songs. It was like trying to grasp a fluttering butterfly that remained teasingly out of his reach. As with the details of her face, the old melodies eluded him.

He said, "Mother." The word seemed strange on his tongue. He said it again, knowing he must have spoken it to her often when he was small. He had had an Indian mother, too, but he had addressed her as *Nerbeahr*, in the Comanche tongue.

"Mother," he said, feeling choked, "I wish I could remember more. It's just not there. I wish . . ." But there was nothing more to say.

A faint smell of smoke drew him back to the reality of the present. For a panicked moment he wondered if the Oldhams had outthought him, if they had already been here. Perhaps Clyde had guessed where Andy was headed and had cut around him. He found a disturbed spot on the ground beneath the creek bank, near the edge of the water. Campfire coals still smoldered beneath a cover of sand, which appeared to have been kicked over it to snuff it out.

The sorrel horse nickered, its alert ears pointed forward. Taking a quick breath, Andy saw a dozen riders spill over the top of the bank where it made a bend fifty yards away.

One glance told him they were Comanche. It was not Clyde and Buddy Oldham who had camped here.

Heart pounding, he ran for the horses, jerked the reins loose and swung into the saddle. He had to tug on the lead rope to get Alamo moving. The warriors shouted eagerly, yelping like coyotes. Andy set the sorrel into a run but quickly realized he had no chance. Though he turned Alamo loose, he saw that the Indians would overtake him in a minute.

Mouth dry, blood racing, he turned to face the threat. Trying to remember one of Preacher Webb's prayers, he made a show of dropping his rifle. He raised his hand as a sign of peace, or at least of resignation.

In the Comanche tongue he shouted, "Brothers. I am Comanche. I do not fight you."

They quickly circled around him. Several held bows with arrows fitted and ready to fly, but they hesitated.

One ventured nearer than the others, eyes narrowed with suspicion. "You are white. How is it you call us brothers? How is it you know our words?"

Andy swallowed hard. They could drive a dozen arrows into him before his heart could beat twice. He hoped they would give him time to speak. He hoped also he could remember the words, for he had not used them in a long time. He said, "I was raised to be Comanche." For emphasis he took off his hat and lifted one of his braids. "My heart is still Comanche."

The one he assumed to be the leader said, "We do not know you."

"I do not know you either." Andy struggled with the language. "But it may be that you know my brother. He is called Steals the Ponies."

Someone spoke from the edge of the circle. "I know such a man. Was not his father known for finding buffalo when others could not?"

"That is right." Steals the Ponies's father had been known as Buffalo Caller, but one avoided speaking the name of the dead lest it disturb the sleeping spirit. Andy said, "The one who was his father was a great hunter. So is Steals the Ponies a great hunter, and a brave warrior."

The leader was not quite satisfied. "How is it that you are white and you wear the clothes of a white man if you were raised Comanche?"

Andy's heartbeat began to ease. That they even listened to him was a favorable omen. He drew a deep breath and explained briefly the circumstances of his capture as a small boy. "It was here at this place," he said, "that those who took us killed my white mother. Then the one who was Steals the Ponies's father carried me away. I became Comanche." He told how years later he had foolishly followed his brother's raiding party, had broken his leg and had been found by friendly Texans.

He said, "They have tried to make me white again." He touched his hand to his heart. "But I do not forget that I am also Comanche."

The leader's face twisted as he pondered such an unfamiliar concept. "I do not understand how two men can live in one body. What medicine makes this possible?"

"It is not easy," Andy admitted. "For a long time I have had to follow the white man's road. But I still know the Comanche ways."

"Why have you not left the Texans and come back to The People?"

Andy was slow to reply, unsure how his answer might be received. He said only, "There was trouble. I cannot return." He did not want to tell it all, that he could not return because he had killed a fellow Comanche.

The leader speculated, "You were too young to have stolen another man's wife. Perhaps the trouble was over horses."

Andy sensed that this would be accepted. Technically he did not confirm that horses had been the cause, but he did not challenge the suggestion. He made a grunt which could be taken in any way the warriors chose.

The leader laughed. "At least it was over something of importance. A good horse is worth fighting for." The laugh faded. "Why are you here? Where do you go?"

Andy knew he could not explain the complex political

struggle between the reconstruction government and the former rebels, for he did not fully understand it himself. He simply related that he was on his way to warn a friend and benefactor that men of bad spirit were after him.

The leader asked, "Can your friend not fight for himself?"

"He has been wounded. He will need help."

"Perhaps *we* can stop these bad spirits. We have taken horses on this trip, but we have not yet taken scalps."

Andy felt a surge of enthusiasm. The Indian side of him thought how perfect it would be if the Oldhams were brought down by Comanches. No one could blame Rusty or Andy for that. But a white man's doubts intruded. Not even Clyde and Buddy deserved to die the kind of death the Comanches could administer when their blood was up. "They may not come this way."

"But they might. We had started to make camp. You will stay with us. We want you to tell us how it is to live in the white man's country."

Andy felt trapped. He had no assurance that the Oldhams were trying to follow him. Though there had been enough travel along this way to beat out a faint wagon trail, they might not be using it. They might have realized where he was going. If so, they could miss this place by miles, circling and hurrying on ahead of him. But he could see that the Comanches had no intention of letting him proceed. Not yet. Perhaps when they were all asleep he could steal away in the dark. He would have to control his impatience, difficult as that might be.

The Indians stirred the fire they had hastily smothered and kindled the coals back into life. They took Andy's slab of bacon, though if divided equally it would not be large enough to provide much for each man. Most yielded their shares to the leader and a couple of the men who seemed closest to him. The rest ate typical Comanche traveling rations, dried meat pounded almost to a powder and combined with fat, berries and nuts, whatever had been available at the time it was prepared. They shared this with Andy.

It reminded him of earlier times, and for a change it was pleasant. But it was not nearly so tasteful as what Shanty cooked up back home, or even Rusty.

Len Tanner, by contrast, could not boil water without giving it a scorched flavor.

Andy tried to feel at ease, but it was difficult so long as one warrior kept glaring at him and sharpening his knife.

He learned that the leader was known as Horse Runner, a name probably earned either snaring wild horses or stealing tame ones. Horse Runner and several others pressed him with questions. They exhibited much curiosity about the white man's world and the puzzling things they had seen on their forays through the settlements. Why did the white man tolerate the weak taste of his beef cattle when buffalo meat was available, so much stronger and more flavorful? How could he not be sickened by the stench of his pigs? How could the white man bear to live in a wooden tepee that could not be moved when the campsite became fouled with waste and when his horses had eaten off all the grass?

Most of all, why did each white man lay personal claim to one piece of land when the Great Spirit had provided so much to roam over and to share?

Andy felt that each question was a personal challenge, that he was called upon to defend the white man's ways. That meant these raiders did not entirely accept him as Comanche, just as many people around the settlements did not fully accept him as white.

He explained, "In the white man's eyes, to own land is a thing of honor. It means he is free and does not have to do as another bids him."

"But *we* are free," Horse Runner argued. "We do not have to do as any man tells us unless it is our wish. Yet we do not each claim one piece of land." He made a long sweep with his hand. "Together, we own it all."

You own it until the white man decides to take it, and

he will, Andy thought. "All people do not have the same ways," he said.

Horse Runner grunted. "The whites are not true human beings. I do not understand how you can live among them."

"There are some bad ones," Andy conceded. "But there are many more who have good hearts."

"If their hearts are good, why do they take away what is ours? We won this land. Our grandfathers fought many battles to take it from the Apaches. The white man has no right."

Andy could see the inconsistency in Horse Runner's viewpoint. Rusty would say the Comanche had won the land by conquest from weaker people and now was losing it the same way to a stronger people. But nevertheless Andy's sympathy lay heavily with the Comanche.

He was relieved of the necessity for further argument when a young warrior hurried down the creek bank, motioning excitedly. "Three horsemen come. They are *teibo*."

White men. Andy moved up the bank far enough to see over the edge. The riders were three hundred yards away. They could not see the danger that awaited them, for the warriors had camped beneath the creek bank, out of sight. He wondered that they did not detect the smell of wood smoke, for the breeze was moving in their direction. They were blissfully complacent. Carelessness was a white-man trait that had brought many to a sudden death.

The warriors quickly caught and mounted their horses. Andy sensed the electricity of their excitement, though they remained quiet so they would not alarm their quarry too soon.

Horse Runner said, "Get on your horse and ride with us. Three good scalps are there for the taking."

"They may not be the right ones."

"It does not matter. They are Texans."

Andy wished he could be somewhere else, anywhere else. He had killed once and regretted it ever since. Though he occasionally made bold talk, he had no real wish to bloody his hands again, especially on strangers who had done him no wrong.

He squinted, trying to see more clearly. His breath stopped for a moment. One of the horsemen was Clyde Oldham. Andy had learned to identify him at almost any distance by the way he sat a little off-center in the saddle, comfortable for him perhaps but tiring to his mount. Another rider had but one arm. This must be Buddy Oldham. The third was probably the deputy who had been with them before.

Horse Runner grabbed the back of Andy's shirt and almost lifted him onto the sorrel horse. "Come on," he shouted. "You may take one of the scalps." Given no choice, Andy mounted as Horse Runner and the other warriors scrambled up the creek bank.

Around him, the men began whooping and yelping, eager for the kill.

The three riders instantly saw their peril and jerked their mounts around, whipping them furiously. Hooves pounded the earth and sent clods of dirt flying behind them.

Andy soon realized that the race was uneven. The Oldhams and the deputy rode grain-fed horses, whereas the warriors' mounts subsisted on grass. Andy found himself ahead of the Comanches, for the sorrel was stronger than their horses. But his incentive for catching the Oldhams was less compelling than the Oldhams' for getting away.

The chase stretched for more than a mile before it became obvious that the white men would escape. Andy began drawing on the reins. Most of the Indians pulled up on either side of him. A few were still determined to continue the contest though it was clearly lost.

Horse Runner eased to a stop, patting his mount on the neck in recognition of a good though unsuccessful run. He said, "At least we gave them a scare. They will tell their grandchildren about it."

Except they will probably claim to have killed half the Indians, Andy thought. "They will keep running until dark."

"Were they the bad spirits you spoke of?"

"They were."

"It is unfortunate we did not catch them."

"It is," Andy said, though he felt more relieved than disappointed. He would have had no stomach for watching the warriors murder the Oldhams and the deputy. That would rekindle old and bitter memories of the brutal way his mother had been butchered near here.

He could not be sure Clyde and Buddy would give up and go home. Once they recovered from the scare they might well continue their quest for Rusty, though they would probably circle far around this place.

At least this incident had given Andy time.

The Indians straggled back toward the creek. The last holdouts gave up the chase and trailed behind. Horse Runner said, "Would you like to go with us?"

"To the reservation?"

Horse Runner snorted. "The reservation? We still live free, as our fathers lived free." He motioned toward the north. These warriors came from the open plains where few whites so far had penetrated much beyond the outer fringes. To Texans it was still an unknown land. The only outsiders who entered with little trepidation were Mexicans from mountains and valleys to the west. They came in great groaning two-wheel carts, carrying trade goods to exchange for buffalo hides and dried meat, as well as horses and mules and cattle taken from the Texans' settlements.

Occasionally these Comancheros had ransomed white captives. Andy remembered a time when one had tried to bargain for him, but Steals the Ponies had refused even to consider giving him up.

He said, "I cannot go with you. I still must go to my friend. Those who hunt for him will probably keep trying to do him harm."

"Look for us if you ever want to return to The People. You will be welcome, Badger Boy."

He waited until the Comanches had gone to sleep. It was a weakness of theirs as warriors that they often did not bother to post a guard at night. Andy managed to get his horses and slip away. He did not stop to rest until he had put many miles between him and the Indians.

He decided not to mention this encounter. Even Rusty might not understand how Andy could join hostile Comanches in pursuit of white men. Too, if he reported this horse-stealing party, Texans were almost certain to organize a pursuit. He might be responsible for casualties on both sides.

No, he would keep his mouth shut.

◆ 11 ◆

Rusty kept rubbing his shoulder, trying to convince himself it had healed, but the wound was still inflamed around the edges and sore to the touch. He remembered it had taken a long time for his leg to recover from his arrow wound years ago. Even when the pain was gone, the shoulder would not soon regain full strength.

Damned poor farmer I am going to be, he thought.

He had been concerned about the farm, about how Andy and Shanty were getting along down there by themselves. He had wanted to send Len Tanner back to see about them, but Tanner had thrown himself into the routine here on the Monahan place and seemed in no hurry to go south again. Besides, he had taken down with a bad case of infatuation for the youngest Monahan daughter, Alice. She had blossomed into a pretty young lady with sparkling eyes and a laugh like music.

Tanner had expressed concern about several young men of the area who went out of their way to visit the Monahan farm more often than any legitimate business would seem to call for. "Somebody's got to keep an eye on Alice," he told Rusty. "She's too innocent to know what them young heathens have got on their minds."

"And you figure you're the one to keep her innocent?"

"Somebody has got to."

Maybe he *was* the one, Rusty thought. In some ways Tanner was about as innocent as any grown man he had ever known. As loyal a friend as anyone could hope for, Tanner had pulled Rusty out of tight spots more than once. But he was inclined to talk more than he listened and to jump into deep water before he considered whether or not he could swim. That had made him a good ranger when there was a necessity for fighting, but it also got him into some fights that need not have happened.

James Monahan had returned after being gone a couple of weeks, searching for cattle he might buy and put on the trail to Kansas. In the first years after the war he had been able to gather unclaimed cattle that had run wild, unattended during the conflict, but those had become scarce. Other men had observed James's success in converting them into cash and had followed his example. Now it was rare that an animal as much as a year old turned up without someone's brand already burned on its hide. James and brother-in-law Evan Gifford had turned more of their time and attention to breaking out additional land, expanding the farm's cultivated acreage.

The family's costly pro-Union stance during the war had finally turned to their benefit. The reconstruction government, often punitive in its relations with former rebels, treated the Monahans with respect in view of the heavy price they had paid for loyalty. It did not burden them with the high property appraisals and ruinous taxes often levied against others.

Rusty fretted over not being able to help with the physical labor. He spent his days finding small tasks he *could* manage such as mending harness and sharpening tools. He could not swing an ax, but he could fetch light armloads of firewood into the house after someone else cut it, usually despite protests from Josie Monahan. Clemmie Monahan's second daughter had appointed herself his nurse, his overseer, his guardian.

Josie took half the wood from his arms to lighten the load before he could dump it into a woodbox beside the cast-iron stove. She scolded, "Rusty Shannon, you'll never get well if you don't give yourself time."

"I don't like idlin' around. I want to earn my way."

"You earned your way with this family a long time ago. Now you go sit down in yonder and get some rest."

Rusty seated himself in a rocker in the front room. He could hear Clemmie in the kitchen, telling her daughter, "You treat him like you were already married. There'll be time enough to give him orders after you've stood together in front of Preacher Webb."

"I don't remember Papa ever takin' orders from you. For that matter, I don't see Preacher Webb doin' it, either."

"Your father did, and so does Warren Webb. I've just tried to give my orders in a way to where they think it was their own idea."

Rusty smiled. He was aware that Josie had set her cap for him years earlier, even when he was involved with her older sister Geneva, now Evan Gifford's wife. From things said and not said, Rusty knew several young men had tried to court Josie, but she had offered them no encouragement. At least a couple of these had transferred their attentions to the youngest sister, causing Len Tanner considerable loss of sleep.

Rusty would admit to himself, but to no one else, that he enjoyed Josie's attentions. Perhaps it would be easier if she did not remind him so much of Geneva, for he would know his feelings were for Josie herself. Yet, if she did not, he might have no such feelings. It was hard to be sure of his own mind.

Tiring of the rocker, he walked out onto the dog run. The log house was still relatively new, built after the war to replace an older one burned one night by Confederate zealots in a show of spite against the Monahans. A porch had recently been added to extend the dog run's shade.

A boy of six rode a pony into the yard. He swung a rawhide rope over his head and cast it at one of Clemmie's hens, missing by a foot but setting the hen into a squawking fit. This was Geneva and Evan's son Billy, named after the Monahan son killed years ago with his father for the family's Union leanings. The Giffords had a second child, a girl about two years old. Rusty suspected Billy had been sent outside to play so he would not awaken his sister.

The boy had been riding horseback as long as he had been walking. He was most often somewhere close to his great-grandfather, Vince Purdy, riding with him or walking alongside him when the old man worked in the field. The patient Purdy walked slowly to let the boy keep up with him, though Billy's short legs forced him to take a lot more steps. Sometimes Purdy pulled out a pocket watch James had brought him from a cattle trip to Kansas. He held it to the boy's ear and let Billy grin over a little tune it played.

Watching them together reinforced Rusty's acute sense of the value of family, and his own lack of one.

Vince is going to make a cowboy out of that kid, he thought. It was by no means the worst thing that could happen to him. Right now Texas was pulling itself up by its bootstraps from war's economic depression. It was doing so mainly with cattle and cotton. This was a little far west for cotton because of the cost of transporting it by wagon to distant railroads. If rails were one day laid across this part of the country, the arable lands would turn white with ripe bolls, he thought.

He watched Billy make a run at a cat. The loop went around it, but the cat was gone before the boy could jerk the slack.

Purdy walked up and patted his great-grandson on the leg. "You're doin' fine, Billy. Only what were you goin' to do with that cat when you caught him? He would've clawed you somethin' fierce. Come, let's see if you can rope the goat."

"If I do, will you let me hear the watch?"

"Sure. We'll find out if it plays Dixie." It wouldn't, of course. James had bought it in Kansas for his grandfather. That was Yankee country.

Billy laughed and rode off after Purdy, hunting for another target. The boy's got no fear, Rusty thought. The Monahan blood ran strong in him. He could imagine the pride crusty Lon Monahan would have felt in his grandson had he lived to know him.

A troubling thought came unbidden. Billy could have been his own. Rusty would have married Geneva Monahan had frontier duty not called him away too soon and kept him too long.

From almost as far back as he could remember, he had been acutely conscious of having no real identity. No one had ever been able to discover who his parents had been or if he had other kin. Mike and Dora Shannon had been like family, but theirs was not a blood tie. He had felt a strong attachment to the Monahans, yet they were not of his own blood either.

Andy Pickard was an orphan too, but at least he knew who he was. He had blood kin. In spite of the fact that they had rejected him, it must be a comfort of sorts to know they existed. Rusty would always have to wonder about his own.

Preacher Webb came in from the field, shirt darkened with sweat. He stopped at the cistern and drew up a bucket of water. After drinking liberally from a dipper, he joined Rusty on the porch and said, "The Lord has sent us another beautiful day."

Rusty agreed. "But sometimes I think he sends us too many. We could stand a little more rain."

"This has always been a one-more-rain country. It always will be. But most of the time He provides just enough. How's your shoulder?"

"Better every day. I feel like I'll be able to start back home most any time now."

"Are you sure you should? The trouble you got away from will still be there waitin'."

"I've been afraid it would come up here lookin' for me. I don't want it to spill over and hurt the Monahan family."

"You've helped them through their troubles in the past. They'd help you through yours now."

"It's better if they don't have to. After so much grief, the sun is finally shinin' on them. I'd hate to see them run afoul of the state police on my account."

Josie stepped out onto the porch for a quick look at Rusty. "Good. You're sittin' down. I was afraid you might've found yourself another job to do."

Webb smiled. "I'll keep an eye on him."

Webb watched her as she went back into the house. "I wonder if you know how much she thinks of you, Rusty."

"I think so. I just don't know what to do about it."

"She'd marry you in a minute if you asked her."

"What if somebody else was still on my mind? That wouldn't be fair to her, would it?"

He did not feel he had to be more specific. He was sure Webb understood the feelings he had long carried for Josie's older sister.

The minister said, "That's a question you might need to do some prayin' over."

"I've tried, but I've never heard the Lord say anything back."

"He speaks not to the ears but to the spirit. You'll hear Him when you're ready." Webb stood up. "I'd best return to the field. That plow won't move by itself."

"I wish I could do it for you. I feel like a broken wheel on a wagon."

"We all have an appointed place in the Lord's plan. It isn't always given to us to know just what it is. Yours will be revealed to you when it needs to be."

Concern about the Oldham brothers had everybody on the place watchful. Vince Purdy limped into the front room where Rusty was seated in the rocker, trying to read a romance novel Josie had handed him but making little headway. He did not relate to the genteel ballroom adventures of English society.

"Rusty, somebody's comin'. One man, leadin' a horse."

"Just one man? I doubt it's an Oldham. They generally ride together." Travelers had passed by the Monahan farm almost every day he had been here. Nevertheless he rose, trying to ignore the pain in his shoulder. He reached for his pistol, hanging in its holster from a wooden peg.

He found Len Tanner standing protectively at the edge of the porch, rifle in his hand.

Rusty said, "I doubt you'll need that."

"Rather have it and not need it than need it and not have it. You never know when you'll see a son of a bitch that needs shootin'."

Preacher Webb approached from the direction of the field. "You won't neither of you need a gun. That's Andy Pickard comin' yonder."

"Andy?" Rusty squinted, trying to see better. It seemed to him that his vision was not completely recovered from several days' fever caused by the wound. "What do you suppose—"

Tanner said, "It won't be good news. Nobody travels this far to tell you somethin' you want to hear."

Rusty walked out to meet Andy as he neared the barn. Webb, Purdy and Tanner followed him. Andy was riding an unfamiliar sorrel and leading Alamo. The black horse had never been used as a pack animal before. It was probably a wound to his pride, Rusty thought.

Andy drew rein but seemed reluctant to dismount. His dark expression indicated that Tanner had been right. Rusty asked, "What's wrong back home? Somebody killed?"

Andy said, "Not yet, but somebody ought to be." He swung a moccasined foot over the sorrel's back and dropped to the ground. He licked dry lips and looked toward the cistern at a corner of the house. "I sure need a drink of water. Used up my canteen a good ways back."

He drank two dippersful, then poured a third over his head. "Rusty, they've taken your farm away from you."

Rusty's first reaction was disbelief. "They can't do that."

But doubt set in. He felt as if Andy had struck him with the butt of a rifle. "How could they?"

"The Oldhams came out with some papers that said they could. Told me if I didn't want a good quirtin' I'd better hit the trail in a trot. So I trotted." He rubbed a hand across his face. "I already had a taste of Buddy's quirt."

"What became of Shanty?"

"He went with Tom Blessing. We cleaned out the cabin, and Tom hauled off everything that wasn't nailed down tight. Said him and his boys would gather all your stock they could find and try to get them out of the Oldhams' reach."

"Good old Tom. I never had a better friend." Rusty glanced at Webb and Tanner. "Except you-all."

Andy said, "Wasn't nothin' we could do about the land, though. We couldn't move that."

Rusty felt a weight growing heavy and cold in his stomach. He told Andy, "You did what you could. That's all anybody could ask. Maybe there's somethin' we can still do about the land." At the moment he had no idea what that might be.

Andy said, "I asked Tom. He didn't know of anything. The law goes along with whatever the Oldhams want to do."

Tanner declared, "There's one thing we *can* do. We can shoot us a couple of Oldhams and tell the law they bit one another like rattlesnakes."

Preacher Webb watched with misgivings, probably wondering if Rusty took Tanner seriously. Rusty said, "Don't worry, Preacher. I found out a long time ago that a shootin' doesn't settle anything. It just muddies up the water."

Andy grimaced. "One more thing I hate to tell you. The Oldhams were followin' me, at least at the beginnin'."

"You reckon they still are?"

"I saw them turn back, but they might not have stayed turned back. They wanted you awful bad."

Tanner said, "If they're still comin', we ought to go and

meet them. Nobody would ever have to know what went with them. Not many would even ask."

Webb pointed out, "That would not get Rusty's farm back. If the Oldhams disappeared it would revert to the government."

Tanner complained, "Every time I come up with a good idea, somebody shoots a hole in it."

Webb said, "You'd best go to the house, Andy. I expect you're hungry. We'll take care of your horses."

Rusty looked at the sorrel. It was unfamiliar to him. "Where'd you get him?"

Andy said, "Jeremiah Brackett brought him to pay for the roan his son took. He's a heap sight better horse than that roan was. You can be proud of him."

Rusty shook his head. "No, *you* be proud of him. He's yours."

Andy grinned, but the grin did not last long. "We'd better keep watchin' for them Oldhams."

Len Tanner came the next morning to warn of approaching strangers. Standing on the porch, eyes pinched, Rusty counted seven horsemen. "You don't reckon the Oldhams have fetched along a posse?"

Tanner grunted. "Might figure that's the only way they can drag you away from this place."

When the riders were close enough, Rusty determined that the Oldhams were not among them. A gray-bearded man of military bearing rode slightly ahead of the others. Something about him struck Rusty as familiar.

"Captain Burmeister!" he yelled.

The leader gave Rusty a moment's close scrutiny. "Private Shannon?" He shifted his gaze. "And Private Tanner, if my memory correct is."

There was no mistaking the voice and the accent, or the gray mustache turned up on the ends in the Prussian military style. Rusty and Tanner had served in a ranger company headed by Captain August Burmeister before the war began. After long service to Texas, Burmeister remained loyal to the Union and vocally opposed secession. He resigned at the outbreak of the conflict and rode north in hopes he could join a Federal army unit.

The old captain dismounted painfully, his legs stiff. He extended a gnarled hand, knuckles swollen with arthritis. "The time has been long, but no handsomer you are, either of you."

Rusty quickly surveyed the other six men. They had the grim and determined look he associated with those who enforced law. "Are you a state policeman now?" he asked.

Burmeister shook his head. "I am of a special ranging company set up by Governor Davis. Not rangers of the old kind, exactly, but also not state police. We are sent to the frontier to do what we can about the Indians."

James Monahan and Evan Gifford had walked out from the corral. Rusty introduced them to the captain, who remembered James from before. James said, "We hear about Indian trouble in other places, but there ain't been any around here lately."

Burmeister said, "Settlers have reported a raiding party not far from here. Comanches, they think. They have with them some stolen horses."

James pressed, "How close to here?"

"Reports say not far. A little south."

Andy had come out to listen. Rusty noticed that he seemed ill at ease. "Blood brothers of yours, Andy?"

With reluctance Andy said, "They could be. I ran across some Comanches on my way up here. They were the reason the Oldhams turned back."

Burmeister demanded, "You saw that? When, and how far from here?"

"Three days ago, two days' ride."

Rusty asked, "Why didn't you say anything?"

"I figured they were on their way out of the country anyhow."

James declared, "They could be anyplace. And if you saw one bunch, there could be others."

Evan looked around quickly. "The pony's gone. Where's Billy?"

Tanner said, "The wagon team didn't come for feed last night. Vince said him and Billy was goin' out to find them and bring them in."

James's eyes narrowed with concern. "We'd better go fetch them back. If there's Comanches prowlin' about, we don't want to have anybody out there."

Evan did not wait. He ran to the corral to throw his saddle on a horse. Rusty started to follow, but James stopped him. "You're not in shape to ride. You and Preacher stay and look out for the womenfolks."

Rusty knew James was right. He did not argue.

Andy said firmly, "I'm goin'."

Rusty watched as Andy saddled the sorrel horse. "I wish you'd told us about the Indians," he said.

"They treated me good. I was afraid if folks went chasin' after them somebody was apt to get killed, white and Comanche both."

"I still wish you'd told us."

"This colonel, is he a good man to follow?"

"As good as ever won a commission."

James finished saddling. He told Rusty, "With any luck we'll be back in a little while. No use sayin' anything to Mama and them. It'd just get them all roused up. We can tell them about it when we've got Billy and Granddad back home."

Rusty watched them ride out . . . James, Evan, Andy, Tanner and the cowboy named Macy, who had made himself a home here since soon after the end of the war.

Turning, he saw that Preacher Webb had his head down, whispering a prayer.

❖ 12 ❖

Andy hung back a little, stricken with remorse. Hindsight told him he should have mentioned running into the Comanche party, but at the time it had seemed prudent not to do so. Horse Runner and the others had said they were on their way home. Whatever damage they had caused was over and done with. It could not be undone. Andy had seen nothing to be gained by setting off a pursuit that might result in casualties for both sides.

One of Burmeister's men quickly picked up the trail left by Purdy and Billy. Burmeister told James, "When we see that your people are safe, we will go on and try the Indians to find."

James said, "That wagon team has always been inclined to stray off, but they don't generally go far."

Because Tanner had put in lengthy service with Burmeister before the war, he took advantage of the opportunity to renew an old acquaintanceship. Riding beside the captain, he talked of his experiences and Rusty's in the intervening years. Tanner's natural tendency was to go into considerable detail, repeating some parts for emphasis and adding modest embellishments from time to time in the interests of a better story.

Burmeister told Tanner that after leaving the ranger post near Fort Belknap he had ridden up into Kansas and offered his services to the Union Army. His long years as a ranger had given him solid experience in campaigning. He had put this to use in training troops.

Tanner said, "I hope you wasn't with none of them Yankee outfits that kept tryin' to invade Texas." A few had succeeded, mainly along the lower Rio Grande, but others had been beaten back after paying a heavy price for their effort.

"*Nein*. Texas was too long my home. I asked not to raise arms against it."

"How come now you're servin' Governor Davis's carpetbag government?"

"The word *carpetbag* I do not like. An outsider I am not. The word *reconstruction* is better. It means to build back, to fix what is broken."

"Some are breakin' more than they fix." Tanner told what he knew about the confiscation of Rusty's farm.

Burmeister listened with interest. He said, "Too often those who stand first at the trough are those who did not the work or the fighting."

The tracker, forty yards out in front, raised his hand as a signal for a halt. He turned back, his expression grave. "Captain, you better come."

Andy did not like the look in the tracker's face. Neither did James and Evan, for they spurred out ahead of Burmeister. Andy trailed with the rest of Burmeister's men. He heard James shout in dismay and jump to the ground, then kneel beside a body.

Evan cried out in anguish, "Where's Billy? For God's sake, somebody find Billy."

Andy knew whose body it would be, though James and Evan and Tanner blocked it from his view.

Burmeister raised a hand. "Everybody else stay back. We must study the tracks."

Evan called out, "Billy! Billy, where are you?"

James covered Vince Purdy's bloodied face with his

neckerchief, but not before Andy saw that the scalp had been taken. He felt stunned. His throat was blocked so that he could barely breathe. Misery settled over him like a suffocating blanket.

If only I had said something, he thought.

He had brought the Oldham trouble upon Rusty by something he had done. He had brought this trouble to the Monahans by something he had *not* done.

The tracker and Burmeister moved ahead of the others, searching the ground for a sign. Tanner joined them, for he had shown himself to be better than average at reading tracks. They conferred among themselves, then rode back to where James and Evan knelt beside Purdy's lifeless body.

Burmeister said, "I fear the boy is taken."

Tanner said, "There's his bootprints where he jumped down to see about Vince. And here you can see where they drug him a little ways. Then the prints stop. They must've put him back on his pony." Tanner looked at Andy. "They've taken him the same way they took you once, and like they took Rusty a long time ago."

Andy's eyes burned. For a while he wished he had let Tonkawa Killer finish him years ago.

Evan jumped to his feet, trembling. "We've got to catch them. We've got to get him back." He rubbed a hand across his eyes. "My God, how can I tell Geneva?"

James folded his grandfather's arms across the thin chest. "There ain't no easy way, but you've got it to do. Take Granddad home and tell her." He checked Purdy's pockets. "They even took his watch."

Evan said, "I can't go home now. I've got to find my boy."

James accepted his brother-in-law's decision. "All right, I'll go and help you." He turned to the cowboy Macy. "You take Granddad home. It'll be up to you to break the news to Mama and them. Andy, why don't you go with him?"

Andy had already made up his mind. He felt a heavy weight of guilt for what had happened. "You'll need me if there's parleyin' to be done. I can talk to them."

"I wish you'd parleyed with us about the Indians you saw."

Andy saw blame in James's eyes, or thought he did. He could understand that. James could not blame him half so much as he blamed himself.

Burmeister detailed one of his special rangers to go with Macy. "When you are done at the Monahans', you will go to the neighbors. Warn them. Tell them Indians prowl about."

The ranger made a poor excuse of a salute. "Yes sir, better to do it a little late than not do it at all." He looked straight at Andy. Andy looked at the ground.

Burmeister pointed his finger at the tracker, a gesture so small that Andy almost missed it. The tracker made a nod equally small and turned to pick up the tracks. Burmeister said, "Private Tanner, it comes back to me that you were better than fair at trailing."

"Yes sir, I was middlin' good."

"Then go forward and help Smith." He nodded toward the tracker. "Do not however get in his way. You are good, but he is better."

Tanner accepted with an ironic smile, taking no offense.

Burmeister waited until Smith and Tanner were fifty yards ahead, then put his horse into an easy trot. The rest followed his example without his having to give an order. Burmeister beckoned Andy with a quick jerk of his head. "Ride beside me. We will talk."

Andy complied, though he could not imagine that he and this old German frontiersman had much to talk about.

Burmeister asked, "Know you much of history?"

This seemed no time to talk of history, but Andy said, "I read about the American revolution in a book. All those people are dead now."

"The people are dead, but history is alive. What happened before will happen again. If we know what people have done before, we know what they may do again."

"You mean we'll have another revolution?"

"I was thinking of a time ... it is now thirty years past ... when a big battle we fought with the Comanches. We found at Plum Creek a small boy with red hair. Stolen, you see, by the Indians. Then many years after, when that boy was a man, he found another boy who had been taken by the Comanches. That was you. Now the Indians have a third boy. Perhaps you can help find him as Private Shannon found you and as the rangers found *him*."

"You're sayin' Rusty paid his debt, and now it's time for me to pay mine?"

"We all have debts to people of the past. We cannot go back to those people, so our debts we pay to people who live now. Somewhere ..." he pointed skyward, "... there is a bookkeeper."

Andy felt crushed by the heavy weight of his new debt. "I don't know how I can ever pay enough. Vince Purdy was killed and Billy stolen because I didn't tell anybody I had seen Indians. But if I had told, and a bunch had rode out to chase them, there might've been even more people killed. I wouldn't have wanted to be the cause of that either." He lowered his chin in frustration. "I wish somebody would tell me what I ought to've done."

"Always do what you think is right. Most times it will be so. The other times we leave to God."

"You sound like Preacher Webb," Andy said. He intended it as a compliment.

Though tracks indicated that the Comanches were driving as many as a dozen stolen horses in addition to the ones they rode, they had ways of making those tracks suddenly disappear. It would seem as if horses and men had simply evaporated. At such points much time would be lost while the two trackers circled farther and farther outward until they picked up sign again.

Evan seemed about to come apart. James remained close, trying to reassure him that they would find his son. To Andy they seemed more like blood brothers than brothers-in-law. Andy remembered what Rusty had told him about Evan's fighting for the Confederacy and almost dying of the wound that sent him home from battle. Yet this was almost certainly the most important fight of his life. Andy wanted to go to him and tell him how sorry he felt about Billy, but he could not bring himself to do it. Words were not enough.

By nightfall it was obvious that the pursuit would be difficult to sustain. Only the rangers had provisions. The others had ridden out from Monahan headquarters in hopes they would quickly find Purdy and Billy. They had not taken time to pick up food, canteens or blankets. Though the rangers would share the food they carried, it was clear that all would soon depend upon what they could obtain from the land itself.

Most maps were sketchy about details of the country beyond the settlements and military posts. Some had large areas virtually blank except for the word *Comanche*.

James hunched over a small campfire built in a shallow hole so the flames might not be seen from afar. He said, "We're comin' into country I don't know. Never came this far huntin' wild cattle. Len, did you ride over it in your ranger days?"

Tanner nodded. "That's too long ago. Hard to remember landmarks. And we was too busy trailin' Indians to stop and draw maps."

Both men turned toward Andy. Tanner said, "Maybe you know it from when you rode with the Comanches."

Andy was heartened by their acknowledgment that he might have some value on this quest. He would not have been surprised had they ordered him away. "Parts of it. We moved here and yonder, followin' the water and the buffalo."

Burmeister joined the conversation. "Most important is the water. They must have water for their horses. We must have water for *our* horses."

Their general direction was northwestward. The farther they traveled, the more critical water sources would be. A spring rich in flow on one trip might be reduced to a bare seep or even dried and caked mud on another. Creeks that ran bank-full after a good rain often went dry within a matter of weeks, or even days. One reason Texans had made slow headway in penetrating the plains homeland of the Comanches was that the Indians always knew where the water was. Texans rarely did.

By noon of the second day the horses were suffering. Andy remembered a spring where The People had camped a couple of times. But he did not know how to make the dried-up spring produce water.

"Rum luck," James complained, punching at the dry mud with the pointed end of a broken willow branch. All he raised was dust.

One of the rangers told Burmeister, "These horses are stretchin' their limit. We'll be walkin' home if we try to push them any further."

Evan protested, "We can't just give up. For all we know, Billy might not be more than a mile or two ahead of us."

Burmeister said, "He might not be ahead of us at all. You know the Indians have split. We do not follow as many today as yesterday. Those we follow now perhaps do not even have your boy."

Evan turned away from the others, fixing his eyes on the northwest. He trembled in silence. James placed a comforting hand on Evan's shoulder. "They're right. Besides, Billy ain't their boy. But he's *our* boy. Me and you will keep up the hunt."

Andy said, "And me."

Tanner said, "I'll stay with you."

Evan did not reply except with his eyes.

Burmeister was sympathetic, but he was a realist. "Think, gentlemen. How many times have Indians brought captives this far, and how many times has anyone been able a rescue to make?"

James argued, "But he's our own. We can't just back off and leave him in their hands."

"It will take much patience, but always there is a chance. We will alert all Indian agents to watch and listen. Sometimes they ransom captives if they can find them. And there are traders from New Mexico who go among the Indians. They are at heart decent people, most of them. We will find a way to let them know. It is not unknown that they buy captives and send them home."

Evan said bitterly, "That means you're givin' up."

"Not giving up. We go back to make a fresh start."

James said, "Time you show up here again they could carry that boy halfway to Canada."

"But they do not go to Canada. They will stay on the plains. And as long as they are on the plains there is a chance we find him. Have faith."

Four people glumly watched Burmeister turn back. The rangers left what provisions they had not already consumed as well as most of their ammunition.

Tanner said, "Don't get the notion old Captain is afraid. He ain't, and never was."

Evan retorted, "But he's left us."

"He gave you his reasons. Don't sell him short. One day when you think the world has slid within two feet of hell's rim, he'll come ridin' up with guns in both hands."

James turned to Andy. "You knew where this water hole was. There wasn't no way you could know it didn't have no water in it. Do you remember where the next one is at?"

Andy wished he could be more sure. "I think so."

"Point us the way."

He went by instinct as much as by memory, fearing all the way that they would find the place dry. These little pop-up seeps and springs depended heavily upon recent rainfall, and that could vary widely. He had seen rains cut a new gully in one place while dust continued to blow on the other side of the hill. That brought up one of the points that made it difficult for the Comanche side of him to understand the white man. The horseback Indians were always mobile. They could pack up and follow the rains. The white man tied himself to a specific piece of ground whether rain fell there or not.

No one had said anything in a while. Andy supposed the others were as dry-mouthed as he was, and as weary. His lips felt brittle and about to crack open. He could feel fatigue in the sorrel horse beneath him.

He felt a jolt of relief as he saw the tops of a few willows at some distance ahead. He had guided them right. At least the hole was there. There might or might not be water in it.

James seemed inclined to rush ahead and find out. Tanner quietly restrained him. "Might be some of Andy's cousins up there. They may be his kin, but not ours."

Evan said, "Billy could be there."

Tanner nodded. "There, or a hundred miles from there."

Andy said, "You-all wait. I will go." He peeled off his shirt, handing it and his hat to Tanner. "I won't look so much like a white man." He set Long Red into an easy walk. The horse had perked up. He probably sensed that water waited.

He caught the smell of wood smoke before he saw the camp. He slipped to the ground and tied his reins to a tall weed that would not hold the horse for even a moment if it should decide to travel. He saw nothing that would hold better.

Carefully he walked in the direction of the willows. He dropped to his belly and crawled to the top of each rise as he came to it, lifting his head slowly, surveying the ground ahead. Finally the water hole and the camp were in full view. There were no tepees. This was a temporary transit camp for whoever was down there. He counted two horses grazing among the willow trees. Beyond them several oxen had their heads down in the green grass. Two Mexican carts stood near the water. They appeared to be piled high with goods, though the cargo was covered with canvas.

Comancheros, Andy realized. These were the people who came out of villages in eastern New Mexico to trade among the Comanches, the Kiowas and whatever other tribes they might come across.

Andy retreated carefully to his horse, then returned to where the others waited. "There are people at the spring.

Mexican traders. I don't know if you want to go among them."

Evan spoke quickly. "The captain said Comancheros might be able to buy Billy back."

James said, "What would we pay them with? I didn't bring any money. Even if I had, it wouldn't be near enough."

"We can promise to pay them when they deliver Billy to us at the farm."

"More likely they'll deliver *us* to the Comanches. You've been around them, Andy. What do you think?"

Andy wished he had an easy answer. "It's a risk. The People have traded with them a long time. I don't know that they've ever completely trusted them. But the Mexicans don't completely trust The People, either. You never catch one far from his guns."

Tanner said, "We can parley with them, at least. If we don't like their looks, I reckon we can shoot them."

James gave Tanner a quizzical look. "You talk a lot about shootin' people, but how many have you ever really shot?"

"I don't keep count on such as that. Maybe a hundred, a little over or a little under."

A practical question came to Andy. "Any of you talk Mexican?"

Tanner claimed he did, but Andy knew his knowledge was limited to a scattering of individual words, most of them profane. Evan said, "My daddy fought in the Mexican war. He was always against any of us learnin' their language."

Andy pointed out, "These yonder may not talk English."

James said, "If they're tradin' with the Indians, at least one of them ought to talk a little Comanche. You can auger with him, Andy."

Andy felt uplifted by the responsibility. "I'd better go first. They'll likely take me for an Indian long enough for me to talk my way in. I'll signal you-all when it's time to follow."

Evan said anxiously, "Ask them if they've seen Billy."

Andy rode boldly into the camp, holding one hand high and shouting a Comanche greeting. Four Mexican men quickly materialized, all armed. They had evidently been napping on blankets in the shade of the willows.

One stepped a little ahead of the others, raising his hand in guarded response to the greeting. Peering from beneath the sagging brim of a frayed sombrero were suspicious eyes so dark as to be almost black. He did not appear to be an old man, though heavy black whiskers and a thick mustache covered most of his features. His clothing had been patched and patched again and matched the color of the earth. "*Quién es*?" he demanded.

Andy answered him in Comanche. "I am known among The People as Badger Boy. Who are you?"

The dark eyes blinked as the man weighed the likelihood of a gringo boy speaking Comanche. "I am Pablo Martínez. Your talk is Indian, but your eyes are blue."

"I was stolen and raised among the Comanches."

The Mexican appeared to weigh the account carefully before conditionally accepting it. "It is not uncommon. I have seen it."

Andy said, "Three friends of mine wait to come in. Would you share the water?"

"God has provided it for all."

Andy turned and signaled. He watched anxiously for the reaction when the Mexicans realized these were not Comanches.

"*Tejanos*," Martínez exclaimed. He raised his rifle but stopped short of the shoulder.

Andy said, "They mean you no ill. They come to harm no one. They search for a missing boy."

"There is none in this camp."

"But perhaps you have seen him?"

"One sees many children in an Indian camp."

The other three Mexicans gathered beside Martínez, ready either to shake hands or to start shooting, whatever he decided upon. Andy was aware that the people of eastern

New Mexico had no love for Texans in general. A Texas
Confederate army had invaded them early in the Civil War
and, though soon defeated, left bitterness in its wake.

Like Martínez, these three appeared to have been lifelong
strangers to prosperity.

A few moments of awkward silence passed; then Andy
introduced James, Evan and Tanner.

Martínez switched languages. "I speak some the English.
Better than I speak Comanche. What is this about a boy?"

Evan eagerly told him about his son. "If you've been
tradin' in Comanche camps you might've seen him."

"One sees many captives, some Mexican, some gringo.
Not all want to go home."

Andy understood that from his own experience, but it
would be different with Billy. "This one would want very
much to go home."

James told Martínez, "If you're in good with the Indians,
we'd like you to take us to them and ask about the boy."

"*Señor*, it would be most dangerous."

"We'd pay you if you'd find him for us."

"Pay?" Martínez's mood escalated from indifference to
interest. "How much? You have it now?"

James ran his hands into his pockets. "We brought no
money with us. But we would pay you when we get home
with Billy."

Martínez seemed to be giving the matter deep consideration. "Water your horses, and yourselves. Then we eat
together. You like buffalo?"

Andy did, though he had tasted little in his years apart
from the Indians. Tanner said, "Ate a many a pound of it
ridin' with the rangers. Ain't but few things tastier when
you been livin' on water and air." Any kind of food
sounded good to Tanner.

Evan had a more urgent priority. "Then we will talk?"

Martínez nodded. "Then we talk."

The Texans had used up the few provisions Burmeister
had given them, so all they had eaten since yesterday was
one prairie chicken divided between them. They wolfed

down the roasted buffalo. For drink the Mexicans offered strong coffee, boiled with sugar.

Andy remembered being present when his band had traded with such people at the foot of a great escarpment, its dark rock walls steep and forbidding. The stream that meandered past was known as the River of Tongues because many languages were spoken there by the various tribes that gathered to barter. An informal truce kept old enemies from battling. They might try to kill one another on the way there or the way back, but it was bad manners to attack even a lowly Apache while commerce was under way. Plains Indians were dedicated traders, and unnecessary violence got in the way of business.

A similar honor system protected the Mexican traders at the site, though it was hardly unknown for warriors to trail after them and rob them on their way home. With luck, goods taken from one set of Comancheros might be foisted upon a second set unaware of the robbery. Such doings were generally frowned upon, however, not so much on moral grounds as on the practical consideration that traders might be discouraged from coming again. One should gather the prairie hen's eggs without killing the hen.

Evan was the first to finish eating. He trembled in eagerness to talk about recovering his son. Martínez pointed out the many difficulties involved, not the least of which was finding the boy in the first place. The Comanches tended to scatter across the plains in many small bands. They had their pick of dozens of campsites, most known only to themselves.

Martínez said, "Then, if he is found, he may not be for sale. For money the Comanche has no use. He cannot eat it. He cannot go to town like you and I and spend it. You must offer him something he will want more than the boy. Usually that is horses. A Comanche can never get enough horses."

James said, "Then horses is what we'll give him. How many you reckon it'd take?"

Martínez shrugged. "Who can say? If he is a young warrior and has not many horses, he will be happy with a few more. If he is old and has many horses, a few will not interest him. He will require many more."

Andy could see obstacles no one else had brought up. For one, how would the horses be delivered? It was unlikely the Comanches would ride openly down to the Monahan place to receive them, risking not only treachery by the Monahans but attack by other whites who would know nothing of the trade and would simply consider them invaders. For the Monahans to attempt to drive the horses up into Comanche country for delivery would involve the same general risk.

As he saw it, both sides would have to trust the Comancheros to make the delivery. He wondered if either would have so much faith. But when Martínez suggested that path of action, James and Evan agreed without squandering much time on consideration. Tanner remained out of the conversation because he had lost no boy and had no horses to offer.

To Andy the best answer seemed simple: find him, steal him and get the hell away from there.

Martínez said, "We will travel among the bands, my friends and I. We ask questions—carefully. If we find him, we bargain. If a trade is made, I will come for the horses. Without doubt the Indians will want to see horses before they let the boy go. When I get the boy, I take him home to you."

Evan insisted, "Couldn't you bring him when you come for the horses? Tell the Indians we won't cheat them. Tell them we're honest people."

"How can I tell them when I do not myself know you until today? No, they will believe when they see horses, and then only."

Evan spoke to James. "We'll need first of all to know that Billy is all right. When we see that he is, you'll go home and bring the horses. I'll stay with the Indians so they'll know we don't mean to pull any tricks."

It would take only one disgruntled warrior to put a knife

or an arrow into Evan. Andy was impressed with his willingness to accept so much danger. He wondered if his own white father would have done as much. He wanted to believe he would, had similar circumstances arisen. In all probability he had had no chance.

Martínez raised both hands. "Wait, gentlemen. You talk as if you would go with me. That you will not. You will go home and wait."

James demanded, "Why can't we go with you?"

"Think. Many a warrior would rather have three *Tejano* scalps than a few horses. The first Comanches we find would surely kill you. They might kill me also for letting you ride with me."

Andy said, "He's right. It's better the Indians never see you. But it's different with me. I'm the one who ought to go with him."

James argued, "You're a Texan too."

"But The People will accept me as Comanche. Whoever has Billy, I can talk to them. I can make sure he's all right. And I think I can make them believe me when I promise they'll get their horses."

Evan said, "That's too much to ask of you." Though he protested with his words, Andy could see in his eyes that he was desperate for Andy to go.

Andy said, "I owe you. Billy wouldn't be where he is . . . none of us would be where we are . . . if I'd told about runnin' into that raidin' party."

Martínez looked from one to another, trying to understand. He had no reason to know how much Andy blamed himself, or why.

Tanner studied Andy with strong misgivings. "Rusty told me to look after you. How am I goin' to do that if you ride off and leave me behind?"

Andy tried to smile, but it did not work. "All this time I thought I was lookin' out for *you*."

• 13 •

The horses were hungry as well as tired. All afternoon they hardly raised their heads from the grass upon which they were staked. Andy took a careful look at Long Red, examining his legs, his hooves.

"No tellin' how far we'll have to travel," he told the horse. "I don't want you goin' lame on me." He rubbed a hand over the animal's back in search of possible saddle sores.

Tanner complained, "I've half a mind to stay with you. Rusty'll raise hell with me for lettin' a boy go on a man's job."

"I'm not a boy anymore, and you know why you can't go. You'd get yourself killed. Maybe the rest of us too. Tell Rusty the only way you could've stopped me was to shoot me."

"You don't hardly even know Billy."

"I know his folks. I know he belongs with them, and he'd be with them now if it wasn't for me. And I can remember enough to know what he's goin' through. They'll be whippin' on him to see if he shows fight."

"If he doesn't?"

"They may decide they can never make him into a warrior. Like as not they'll kill him."

"That might've already happened. What we've done, and what you're fixin' to do, could go for nothin'."

"I'm bettin' on him showin' enough fight that they'll want to keep him." Andy had seen the boy's pony take him under some low-lying limbs and knock him out of the saddle. Billy had immediately gotten up, used some language his mother would not have wanted to hear and gotten right back on. He had used his quirt a little heavier than necessary.

Tanner said, "If they decide he'll do to keep, they may want more horses than the Monahans can gather. It might take the whole Yankee army to pry him loose."

"We don't want soldiers gettin' into this. Billy would be the first person killed."

Tanner gave up with great reluctance. "Then I reckon it's up to you and that Martínez. Keep a sharp eye on him. I ain't trusted Mexicans since the fall of the Alamo."

"You wasn't even born then."

"I started distrustin' them *before* I was born."

Andy was not sure what James and Evan had promised Martinez as a reward for his part in finding and recovering Billy. Money, probably, or part of the horses. It didn't matter. In the dark of the night, wrapped in a thin blanket he had brought tied behind his saddle, he had time to think, to consider the probabilities. The more he examined them, the more problems he saw.

The odds were heavily against finding the boy in the first place, though Andy intended to press the hunt however far it led him. He stood a worrisome chance of falling among some of Tonkawa Killer's vengeful friends before he found Billy. They would probably murder him, leaving Rusty and the Monahans to forever ponder two mysteries: whatever became of Billy, and what happened to Andy Pickard?

He ate but little breakfast. The coffee seemed sour on a stomach already in turmoil from worry and lack of sleep.

Against their will, Tanner, James and Evan saddled their

horses and prepared to ride south. Evan squeezed Andy's hand so hard the bones felt as if they would break. Tears welled in Evan's eyes. His lips were pressed shut. He could not speak.

Andy's throat tightened. "If there's any way—"

James said, "We don't want you dyin' for a lost cause. Been too many people done that already."

Tanner almost crunched Andy's shoulder with a grip stronger than the former ranger probably realized. "You've been a damned good boy, Andy. Don't you do nothin' foolish and get yourself killed before you have a chance to become a damned good man. If things get too hot, peel off and run like hell. Won't nobody blame you."

Andy knew he would blame himself. "Tell Rusty . . ." What he really wanted to say would not come. Instead he said, "Tell him that when we get Billy back, we'll go home together and shoot Clyde Oldham."

"A deal." Tanner forced a smile. "And I'll shoot Buddy-Boy."

Watching the three ride away, Andy felt desperately alone despite the presence of the four Mexicans.

Pablo Martínez busied himself breaking camp and gave Andy time to recover from the stress of parting. Finally he said, "No Indians come here today. We must go to the Indians."

The cart men had the ox teams hitched. Andy said, "I'm ready." He led Alamo to the spring to let him drink. Martínez was not certain they would reach another watering place before night. They might be forced to a dry camp. Each cart carried a wooden barrel freshly filled so the animals would not suffer.

Andy had seen only a little of what was in the carts, but he assumed it would be the usual trading goods that Indians had come to regard as necessities: blankets, cooking utensils, knives and such. It would include luxuries to which Indians had become somewhat addicted: sugar, coffee, tobacco. Very possibly it might include rifles and ammunition.

He hoped it would not include whiskey, but he had to accept that possibility. When whiskey entered the picture, the unwritten rules against violence at the trading place had been known to go up in smoke.

Andy had never considered how much slower an ox team traveled than did horses or mules. They plodded along, straining in their heavy wooden yokes. He wondered if anything could excite them. A horse or mule team would occasionally take fright and bolt from something as innocent as a rabbit suddenly jumping up in front of them. The oxen looked half asleep.

For the likes of these, the white man would trade the buffalo. Andy grimaced at the thought.

He remembered that when he lived with the Indians on the plains, the wind rarely died down completely. It blew now out of the west, warm and dry. It was not unpleasant. The movement of air kept the sun from feeling quite so hot as it otherwise would.

He had time now, as he had last night, to assess the hazards and consider his possible moves. He saw little point in devising detailed plans. He could make only the wildest guess about the situation that might confront him when and if he and the Mexicans found Billy. In the beginning, at least, he would have to let Martínez take the lead. Andy saw few options for himself unless for some reason the whole business fell apart. Then he would play whatever hand luck presented to him.

Martínez gestured for Andy to ride beside him. Martínez was mounted on a long-legged fine-boned brown horse that Andy took to be a Thoroughbred. Martínez seemed proud of him, for he put on a show of turning the animal one direction and then another with almost no pressure on the reins. "I won him in a race at Taos," he said. "He is of the *sangre puro*, the pure blood. Where did you get that sorrel?"

"Got him in a trade. Don't have no idea about his blood. I expect it's red, same as any other horse."

"You ever been to New Mexico?"

The Comanches had traveled over wide areas, but they had little knowledge of or interest in boundary lines. "I suppose so. I don't know where it starts."

"We come from a place called Anton Chico. A valley between the mountains. We farm, we raise sheep, we trade. A very long time my people have lived in that valley. Maybe longer than the Comanche has been in this country, who can say?"

Andy had once assumed that the Comanches had been in Texas since the mountains were built and the rivers set to running, but Preacher Webb had told him it was not true. They had migrated south from somewhere far up in the big shining mountains in the very early 1700s. Somewhere, probably by stealing from the Spaniards, they had acquired the horse and soon were able to roam wherever and however far they wanted to go. They had become the most fearsome warriors on the plains.

Martínez said, "First we were Spanish. Then there was war between Mexico and Spain, and they told us we were Mexicans. Then there was war between Mexico and the *Estados Unidos*, and they told us we were Americans. Always, people from outside come and try to tell us who we are. We *know* who we are.

"Do you wonder that we do not trust people from the outside? They never come with good news. Always they come to take something, like the *Americanos* and the Texans."

"The Comanches do the same thing, don't they?"

"In the past. But the way to make an enemy not be your enemy is to trade with him. Get him things he cannot get from somebody else. Then your enemy is his enemy. Long time ago we had much trouble with the Apaches. Not much anymore. They are afraid the Comanches will come and help us."

"But you trade with the Apaches too, don't you?"

"Better to trade than to fight. The Indian thinks he is different, but he is like all other men. Get him to want things. Get him enough of these things to keep him wanting more and he will do as you bid him. You think these oxen want to stand and wait for the yoke each morning? They do it because they know they will be fed. Feed them and they will serve you. Stop feeding them, and soon they are gone."

"You ever quit bringin' goods to the Indians, they're apt to come after you with a scalpin' knife."

"A little danger is to life as salt is to the meat."

Andy could see a serious flaw in Martínez's reasoning. "When you trade with the Comanches and Kiowas for whatever they steal out of Texas, don't you know that makes them raid and steal even more?"

"It is for the Texans to take care of themselves. When they came into our valley in the last war they fancied themselves better than anyone else. *Damned greasers*, they called us. Took what they wanted, did as they pleased. What is it to us if the Indians make them fight a little?"

"My friends are Texans. How is it you agreed to try to rescue the boy for them?"

"I am a merchant. I sell what others want to buy. The boy is trade goods, like coffee and sugar."

Andy frowned. The Comanchero was being bluntly honest. Martínez had never met Billy. The boy meant nothing to him except in terms of market value. At least Andy knew where the man stood. In event of crisis he was not likely to stand hitched.

Martínez kept a close watch on the horizon as if he expected Indians to appear at any time. None did. Before night he approached what Andy remembered had been a weak seep in the side of a usually dry creek bed. Martínez rode ahead to look it over. He returned, the slump of his shoulders telling the story before he came close enough to speak. "No water. Too long no rain."

The water barrels would have to suffice.

Andy asked, "No Indians either?"

"No Indians."

Andy put down disappointment. Reality told him he should not expect to overtake Billy's captors so soon, but one could always hope for a stroke of good fortune.

After a meager supper of tortillas, beans and a bit of buffalo meat, he told Martínez, "I'm goin' off out yonder by myself awhile. Got to think."

Martínez made a faint smile. "You expect some Indian spirit to whisper in your ear?"

"Maybe. It don't hurt to be listenin'."

"I will tell my priest about you. He will pray for your heathen soul."

Preacher Webb probably would not approve either. Andy was not sure what he believed and what he didn't. He had heard so many conflicting opinions about gods and spirits, those of the white man as well as of the Indians, that he was hopelessly confused. He knew only that he had observed the wise men of the tribe wandering off to meditate and seek truth wherever they could find it. Sometimes they claimed it had found them.

He did not have time for a proper vision quest. He was old enough. If he were still with The People he would probably have undergone one or more such searches by now. The proper way would be with the aid of a dependable shaman, who would purify him and give him instructions. Then, in some isolated place where he would not be distracted by small things, he would fast and pray and go through the specified procedures for as long as four days and nights. If he were fortunate, at some point a benevolent spirit would visit, counseling him, perhaps revealing his future. Such an experience was regarded as a rite of passage to manhood.

He could not expect all this in a single night, but he could lose nothing by laying himself open to whatever spirits might be roaming about in the darkness. He could only hope they would be of a kindly nature and not malevolent. It was well known that malevolent spirits were always on watch for the unwary. Even Preacher Webb recognized their evil presence and preached for vigilance against their snares.

He had no tobacco, so he could not perform the smoke

ritual except with a small campfire. He tried to blow and push the smoke in each of the four cardinal directions, then down to the earth and up to the stars. He sat back and waited.

He was still waiting at daybreak. He awoke with a start, aware that the eastern sky was turning pink. No voice had spoken to him, no vision had appeared. He tried to remember if he had dreamed. Sometimes visions were elusive and came disguised as dreams. He remembered only loose and random fragments, none that made any sense.

He trudged back to camp, where the smell of coffee told him the Mexicans were making breakfast. Martínez gave him a questioning glance. "Any message from the Comanche spirits?"

Andy did not want to talk about it.

Martínez said, "You are probably too much white. It is better you look for your white-man spirits in church."

"I've tried. Maybe they don't like the Comanche in me any more than the Comanche spirits like me bein' white."

Martínez lifted a crucifix from beneath his shirt and fingered it. "No people of your own and no God. You wander like a soul lost in darkness. You are to be pitied, Badger Boy."

The use of his Comanche name, though in English translation, startled him a little. For a long time he had heard no name except Andy other than in his brief meeting with Horse Runner's party on his way to the Monahans'.

The oxen complained but stepped into their proper places as Martínez cracked his whip. They slung their heads in brief protest, then submitted to the yoke. Andy wondered if their necks might be perpetually sore from the burden. They had long since developed heavy muscles and a thick hide to compensate. The wooden cart wheels groaned under the weight of their load. They needed grease, but the cart men seemed oblivious of the racket.

If any Indians were about, Andy thought, they would hear the carts before they saw them.

Toward the middle of the afternoon two horsemen

showed themselves where the prairie rose up gently into a halfhearted semblance of a hill. Their silhouettes indicated they were Comanche. Andy felt a quickening of pulse, an uncertain mixture of anticipation and anxiety. Martínez made a show of leaving his rifle atop one of the carts. He rode slowly out in the Indians' direction, holding one hand high to indicate he meant no harm. When he reached the halfway point the Comanches wheeled their ponies about and disappeared.

Andy felt disappointed, but Martínez seemed unconcerned on his return. "They will be ready when they are ready."

The vegetation began showing more life, indicating that more rain had fallen than farther to the south. Andy hoped this meant the evening campsite would offer live water. The carts' barrels were down by more than half, which would mean tight rationing if the site proved dry. The oxen had to be considered first, before the men.

Late in the afternoon they passed over a small swell in the prairie, and he saw that they would not be alone at the night's camp. He rough-counted thirty or forty horses loose-herded on the curing grass. A breeze from the north brought the faint odor of burning wood.

He wanted to ride directly to the horse herd and see if Billy's pony might be there. Martínez stopped him with a quick jerk of his head. "Better you stay with the carts. Make not too bold until they have looked us over."

Andy curbed his eagerness and remained beside one of the carts as it approached the camp. Comanches began walking out or in several cases riding their ponies to give the carts a full inspection. They paid less attention to the Mexican cart men than to what they brought with them. At first Andy thought none were going to notice him, but soon he found himself the object of considerable curiosity. One of the warriors pushed so close that Andy was almost nose to nose with him. Andy realized with a start that he had seen the man before. He recognized several of the warriors.

Looking around quickly, he spotted Horse Runner,

though the raiding party leader did not notice Andy right away.

"You," a warrior said, poking his finger at Andy, "you are the white Comanche."

That caused Horse Runner to turn around. "Badger Boy!" He hesitated as if he could not believe, then he moved forward to embrace Andy. "You have come back to live among your true people?"

"No, I have come on a quest."

"Quest for what? When we saw you, you were going to give warning to a friend. Did you not find him?"

"I found him. Now there is other trouble. I have come to find a small boy who was taken, a Texan boy. He belongs to my friends." He watched Horse Runner's dark eyes for any sign that the raider had knowledge of Billy.

The eyes betrayed nothing. "I know of no boy."

"He was with an old man. The old man was killed and the boy stolen."

"Not by us." Horse Runner made a sweeping motion toward the other warriors. "We took horses. We did not have the fortune to take scalps." He hastened to add, "You may look among us. You will not find a boy."

Disappointed in not finding Billy, Andy was nevertheless pleased that Horse Runner's party was not responsible for killing Vince Purdy. He had a friendly feeling toward these warriors. He had been revulsed at the thought of their having another friend's blood on their hands.

Yet his basic problem remained. If this group did not have Billy, who did? Where were they?

"Do you know of other such parties that might have taken the boy?" he asked.

"We have not met any other parties except a few hunters. We saw a few Kiowas who fought the blue-coat reservation soldiers. They had no boy with them." Horse Runner seemed little concerned. "Your friends who lost the boy, they have other children?"

"Just a little girl."

"They should have another boy, then they can forget this

one. He is better off with The People. *You* would be better off to stay with The People and not go back to the Texans."

"It is not an easy thing, losing a child and a grandfather. Their hearts are on the ground."

"Many times have *our* hearts been on the ground because of the Texans. I do not find it here . . ." he touched his chest, ". . . to weep for them."

"It is my fault . . . my shame . . . that they lost him." He explained that he had made it a point not to mention to anyone that he had seen Horse Runner's raiders before he reached the Monahan farm. "I feared they would send out men to stop you, and there would be deaths on both sides."

Horse Runner did not grasp the point. "What does it matter that you did not tell them about us? We are not the ones who took the boy."

"But if I had told them there was danger the boy and his grandfather would not have gone out alone."

"The spirits were against them. There was nothing you could do against the spirits."

Andy saw that he could not explain his logic to Horse Runner.

Horse Runner said, "Forget the boy. Stay with us if you would like. Soon we will be in our own camp and celebrate our victories. There will be feasting and dancing and singing."

"It is a matter of honor. I must find him."

Honor was something Horse Runner understood. He said, "If you like, I will go with you. I know most of the camps."

Andy explained in general terms about the agreement with Martínez and the Comancheros. "If I find the boy, I have nothing to trade for him. I must stay with the Mexicans."

The raiding party had evidently ransacked at least a couple of homes, for they had picked up such miscellaneous treasures as some cooking pots, a clock and a couple of hand-sewn quilts of intricate design. These had more appeal to them than to the Comancheros, but Martínez was receptive to trading for as many of their stolen horses and mules as they chose to offer. Because horses were precious commodities to the Indians, they were willing to part with only a few. They were happy to trade the mules, which they considered inferior to the horses.

Martínez and the cart men spread out their trading goods for the Indians' inspection. As Andy expected, they were mostly knives, hatchets, beads, blankets and the like. Negotiations seemed to continue for hours, jovial at first but taking on a more and more serious air as the evening wore on. At a critical stage Martínez uncovered a jug and offered it as a gesture of goodwill.

Andy turned away, wishing it had not happened. He had observed the chaos whiskey could cause in a Comanche camp. But Martínez wisely restricted the gift to a single jug, enough to loosen the Indians' spirits, yet not enough to get them recklessly drunk. Each time the jug was passed around, Martínez made a show of drinking from it. Andy doubted much actually passed his lips, for the trader would want to keep his wits sharp. As the stack of dry wood beside the campfire gradually dwindled, the Indians traded off more of their horses than they intended and settled for fewer of the trade goods.

Andy decided Martínez could skin a prairie chicken without mussing its feathers.

At daylight Martínez took stock of the horses and mules he had acquired. "These I can sell for good money in Taos or Santa Fe. Not bad for an evening of work."

Andy pointed out, "All these are stolen stock. They belong to somebody."

"Yes, they do. To me."

Martínez considered it good policy to move on early while most of the Indians still slept, lest some begin to reconsider their transactions in full sunlight. The extra animals were tied together on long ropes and led rather than herded. Not until they had put a couple of hours behind them did he allow the cart men to stop and fix a simple breakfast.

Andy said, "I thought you had no fear of Indians."

"Not fear. Caution. Indians sometimes change their minds."

"If you didn't cheat them, you wouldn't have to worry."

"Who cheated them? All was done in the open, where everyone could see. I made no one to trade. It was of their own choice."

"With a little help from the whiskey."

Martínez frowned. "Do you want to go with us and find that boy, or not?"

"I've got no choice."

"Then keep eyes open, and ears, but mouth shut."

• 14 •

Andy was reminded how formidable distances could be across the high plains. Movement had always been slow when the pace was set by horses dragging travois loaded down with camp equipment and folded tepee skins. Plodding ox teams made it equally slow now. Much of the time he was hard put to see landmarks. The prairie had a gentle rolling character, the seasoned grass short and near golden in the sun. He sensed that Martínez knew where he was going despite the sameness of the landscape, mile after mile. Now and again Andy saw wheel ruts cut during some long-forgotten rainy spell, but these would quickly disappear. Even more rarely he would see a horseman or two at long distance. They vanished like wraiths.

Toward evening the little caravan reached a small stream. Andy tried in vain to remember if he had been there before. One small watercourse looked much the same as another. They made camp, and before long a half-dozen Kiowas appeared as suddenly as if they had risen up from the ground. Using sign language and a few Kiowa words he knew, Martínez welcomed them to camp.

They sat and smoked around the fire, using it for ceremony but remaining back far enough not to be made uncomfortable by its heat. Andy quickly discerned that the Kiowas had little to trade, but nevertheless Martínez passed out a few cheap gifts, mostly small mirrors and shiny metal figures. One of the Indians had an ancient rifle but explained through motions that the hammer was broken. Martínez spoke in Spanish to one of the cart men, who took the rifle and examined it. Soon he was filing a replacement part from a piece of steel.

Andy wondered at Martínez's show of generosity when he had nothing evident to gain. The Comanchero told him he had much to learn if he should ever decide to become a merchant. "Next time they may have something to trade. They will remember us."

The Kiowas stayed to supper. By then the cart man had the rifle ready. He fired it once to demonstrate that it was again serviceable, though it missed its target by at least a foot. Andy saw that the sight was bent.

"Are you goin' to get him to fix that?" he asked Martínez.

The trader shook his head. "If they shot at you, would you want it fixed? They are happy enough that it fires."

"When are you goin' to ask them if they've seen some Comanches with a boy captive?"

"In time. With Indians one does not rush, or have you forgotten?"

Andy decided he had forgotten much. He had become accustomed to Texans' lack of ceremony when taking care of business. Like them, he wanted to get to the red meat first and handle the amenities later.

The Kiowas provided what Andy thought was the perfect opening. They were curious about him, for he was clearly white though he possessed many Comanche characteristics. With sign language Martínez told them that Andy had been stolen as a boy.

Impatiently Andy said, "Now's the time to ask them about Billy."

But the Kiowas moved on to other interests, and the question went unasked. Andy sat chafing, trying to control his frustration. At length he attempted to break into the hand-signal conversation, but the Kiowas ignored him.

Martínez quietly shook his head. "They get suspicious when you push. In time I will give them a little whiskey. It loosens the tongue. Go now, water your horse or something."

Andy forced himself to pull away from the conversation and put his trust in Martínez. But he kept looking back, trying to read the sign language from a distance, picking up only fragments of it. He watched Martínez produce a jug from beneath the stack of goods in one of the carts and pass it among the Indians. From the high level to which they had to tilt it, he knew Martínez had been careful not to give them a full container.

It took only a short time for the Kiowas to fall into a celebratory state. Not long afterward, they began falling to sleep, one by one.

Martínez appeared cold sober. He had made a show of drinking with them, but Andy doubted that much whiskey had gone down his throat. He walked up to Andy, nodding in satisfaction. "They told me they came across some Comanches yesterday, with many horses and mules." He pointed northwestward. "A boy was with them. The Kiowas thought the boy was white. He seemed to be a prisoner."

Andy's spirits lifted. "That'd be Billy for sure."

"Not for sure. Could be some other boy."

Andy dismissed a fleeting uncertainty. "After we've come so far, it's got to be Billy. When are we gettin' started?"

"Daylight."

"We could go a long ways in the dark."

"And get lost. You are like the Texans, too much hurry. If we do find the Comanches, and the boy is with them, do not show much interest. They would ask more ransom."

"I don't care about the price. I just want to get Billy back."

"You must care. What if they ask more than your friends can pay? You do more harm than good."

"I have a knack for that."

"That I have seen for myself."

More than once, Martínez warned Andy not to set his expectations too high. Riding along ahead of the carts, he said, "We may find they have moved on."

"Then we'll follow 'til we catch up."

"Often they divide. We follow one group, we may find that the boy is with another. The Comanche are not *gente de razón*, men of reason. They are not like us, who find a place for ourselves and build our house and plant our fields. They are like the wild animals of the prairie, they travel where it is their pleasure, and when."

Andy realized Martínez was being realistic, trying to build his resistance against disappointment. But he preferred to remain positive.

"Old Preacher Webb often said that when you've got faith enough, your faith will usually be rewarded. So I've got faith, and I'm hangin' on to it whether I really believe it or not."

Martínez shook his head. "I wish I could take you to my priest. There is much he could teach you."

By the middle of the afternoon Andy began seeing horse tracks. A substantial number had been made by iron shoes. These, he reasoned, were from horses recently taken. The tracks left by Billy's pony would probably be smaller than the average. He found several sets of pony tracks but had no way of knowing which, if any, were Billy's.

Martínez warned, "If we do find the boy, show no interest. Make as if you do not know him."

"He'll know *me*. He'll figure I've come to rescue him."

"And you have. But do not let the Comanches know it."

Martínez had been over this ground before. Obviously he did not appraise Andy's intelligence too highly. Andy resented that, but he was in no position to do much about it. He was here at Martínez's sufferance.

He toyed briefly with the notion that he might do better

on his own. He recognized it as an idle thought, even a dangerous one. But everything about this mission was dangerous. He had climbed out to the far edge of a bluff that could break off at any time.

Martínez said, "It is not far now. Soon there is water and a good place for camp."

The cart men were not the first to reach it. They came across a horse herd tended by two young warriors. Andy rode close, trying to appear curious rather than seriously interested. One of the warriors, armed only with a bow and arrows so far as Andy could see, rode over to challenge him. Andy spoke a greeting in Comanche. Still suspicious, the young man answered in kind. Andy complimented him on having so many fine horses. The warrior answered with a degree of pride that most had been obtained by honest theft from the Texans.

"Why are you with those Mexicans?" he asked.

"We visit many camps, trading."

"Do you think he would trade for some of these horses, and the mules?"

"On the right terms. Trading is his work."

"He has with him whiskey?"

"You must ask him about that."

All the while he talked, Andy's gaze roamed over the horses. He did not see Billy's pony. Though disappointed, he was not without hope. The pony might be tied in camp. Most warriors kept one or more horses tied near the tepee in case of need. They did not walk when they could ride.

He pulled away to join Martínez and the carts. The encampment was not large, a dozen tepees lined along a small creek, their flap openings facing east so the morning sunrise would bring its light inside. Andy judged that most of the men had been away on a raid and had rejoined families at this prearranged meeting place within the last day or two. He smelled cooking meat and knew it was not buffalo. He had seen a couple of mule carcasses at the edge of camp, stripped of any meat worth eating as well as the hides. Mules were for trading or eating, not for riding.

A small group of Indians ventured out to watch the carts pass. Andy saw no friendliness in their faces.

Martínez moved upstream a little way from the Comanches. "We camp here," he said. "Let them come to us. We do not wish to seem in a hurry to trade. They will expect too much."

"They didn't look all that glad to see us."

"There is a bad mood in this camp. I can feel it."

Andy guessed that something had gone wrong for the Indians. Perhaps there had been argument over dividing the spoils, or worse, the raiders had lost a man or two in skirmishes along the way.

Riding past the tepees, Andy had given each a moment's careful scrutiny. "I did not see Billy anywhere. If he is here he must be tied up inside one of the tepees." He wished he could search every one of them.

Martínez seemed to sense his thoughts. "Patience. I said from the first, he may not be here."

"But if he isn't, he has been. I can sense it."

Martínez snorted. "Sense it? You think you can smell him, like a dog?"

"I've got a feelin', that's all."

"Some day you will have a feeling that you are about to be killed, and you will be right. Patience. With patience, all things can be known." Martínez looked back toward the Indian camp. His eyes revealed misgivings.

One of the cart men spoke to him in Spanish. Andy did not understand the words, but he knew the man was concerned about something. Martínez told Andy, "He says we should not stop here at all. But we will look the coward if we go on. You must never let the Comanche think you are coward."

They finished making camp. Martínez looked apprehensively toward the tepees. "Maybe they do not come to trade at all. That might be best."

"But if they don't, how will we find out anything about Billy?"

Martínez gave him no answer.

They had finished a meager supper when three warriors walked into camp. They walked silently around the two carts, peering inside without touching anything, then went to the dwindling campfire and seated themselves on the ground. They did not speak a word. In a short while others appeared, more or less repeating the motions of the first group. Several stared at Andy, evidently trying to figure out who or what he was, but they asked no questions and he offered no answers. The mood was sullen. Andy looked vainly to Martínez for guidance. Whatever the Mexican was thinking, he did not allow it to show in his face. He produced a pipe, stuffed the bowl with tobacco, lighted it and handed it to the man sitting on the end. Each man took a couple of puffs and passed it on to the next.

They looked no friendlier.

With a combination of Comanche words and sign language, Martínez welcomed the men to camp and asked them what was their pleasure. Andy listened intently. He feared at first that he might have forgotten too much, but he found that he understood the talk. The gist was that most of these men had taken part in a raid that penetrated the Texas settlements, accumulating many horses and mules as well as other booty. They had returned to this place where their families waited. Dissension had broken out regarding division of the spoils, and this group had been left feeling robbed. A larger band had gone on with more than their share. These Comanches wanted to trade the mules and some of the horses.

Martínez replied that trade was his reason for being here. "Bring what you want to sell."

"First," said the man who seemed to be the leader, "you have whiskey?"

Reluctantly Martínez said, "Only a little. Afterward, we drink in celebration of a good trade."

"We drink now." The leader was emphatic.

Andy could sense a wreck coming. Angry at their fellow raiders, these Comanches were willing to take out their frustrations on whoever was handy.

Martínez went to the nearest cart and dug beneath a pile of trade goods. He brought forth a jug, shaking it to judge how full it was. "There is enough here so each can have a drink," he said. "After the trading, another drink."

The jug was passed, but Andy saw that the first who received it were partaking liberally of its contents. It was empty before the last three men had their turn. Quarreling among themselves, they turned on Martínez with a demand for more. Martínez spoke to one of the cart men, who hurriedly brought another jug. Andy could see tension rising in Martínez's face.

He decided this was his chance to look through the camp while the men were engrossed in the whiskey and the negotiations. He slipped away carefully, looking back to see if his leaving had been noticed. He saw no indication that anyone was paying attention to him. Walking down into the camp, he saw only women and a few children, most of them outside.

As he passed each tepee he called softly. "Billy! Are you in there?"

He received no answer. By the time he had walked through the entire camp he was satisfied that the boy was not here. But a nagging feeling persisted: he *had* been.

He approached a middle-aged woman who was cutting thin strips of mule meat to dry. He decided he had nothing to lose by asking outright. "Grandmother, I am looking for my brother. He has about six summers. He stands this high." He indicated Billy's height. "He was taken from my family not long ago. I believe he has been here."

She stared at him as if he had two heads. "You talk like one of The People, but you have the look of a *teibo*."

"I am both," he admitted. "But what of my brother? You have seen him?"

"Such a one was here. Those who cheated us took him and went on." She pointed her chin to the northwest. "He is a Texan boy. He is claimed as a son by one called Fights with Bears."

Andy could remember no one wearing such a name. He

might be of a different band than Andy's, or he could have changed his name from something else. It was customary among The People to shed an old name if a new one seemed more appropriate.

"Thank you, Grandmother." He started back to the cart camp, for he had found out what he wanted to know.

He knew from the racket that something had gone badly wrong in his absence. The Indians had emptied the carts in their search for more whiskey. Goods lay scattered and trampled on the ground. Shouting, quarreling, warriors wrestled each other for possession of the several jugs they had found. Andy looked for Martínez and found that the cart men had carried him out past the edge of camp. He lay on a blanket. One of his helpers pressed a folded cloth against a wound in Martínez's shoulder. Blood streaked the side of his head.

One of the cart men spoke to Andy in Spanish, but Andy could not understand. Martínez groaned. "I knew we should have gone on."

Andy saw that Martínez had been knifed in the shoulder. He had another wound on the side of his head, probably administered by a club. "I could not stop them," Martínez wheezed. "They wanted the whiskey."

"I could've told you that. It was a mistake, bringin' it in the first place."

"I need no lectures, boy."

Andy said, "I found out about Billy. He was here. That other bunch took him with them. I believe I know where they went."

Martínez was incredulous. "You think we can go after them now?"

"We have to."

"Look. Look what they have done to the camp. The trade goods. They took two of the oxen for beef. And see what they have done to me. I have not the strength to go on."

"But you promised."

"A dead man cannot keep promises, and I am nearly

dead. If I live to get back to Anton Chico, I will never go among the Comanches again."

"You're quittin'?"

"What else is to be done? If this time is not the death of me, the next will be."

Andy saw that argument was futile. Clearly, Martínez was in no condition to continue the search. He would be fortunate to get away from here with one cart and perhaps most of the horses and mules for which he had traded earlier. He would be doubly fortunate if his small crew did not have to bury him in some unmarked grave between here and his valley home.

Andy said, "I'm sorry. I had hoped we could get Billy without things comin' to this kind of pass."

"You should give up and come with us, or go home. You see here what can happen."

"I kept my mouth shut when I should've talked, and Billy got taken because of it. I promised myself I'd bring him back or never go home at all."

"You are a fool."

"I don't doubt that. But I'm goin' on by myself."

Martínez gave him a look of despair. "You do not have to be by yourself." He spoke in Spanish. A cart man removed a crucifix and chain from Martínez's neck. Martínez handed it to Andy.

"It has been blessed by a priest in Santa Fe. Wear this and you will not be alone."

"Doesn't look like it helped you much."

"I am alive. I do not ask more of God."

At first light, Andy saddled Long Red and was on his way. The tracks were many and easy to follow.

·15·

Rusty Shannon stood on the bottom rung of the corral fence, studying three riders approaching from the north. He recognized James Monahan, Evan Gifford and Len Tanner. He could not see Andy. He blinked in an effort to sharpen his sight, but still he saw only the three. Dread built a knot in his stomach.

Josie Monahan climbed up beside him. "What you lookin' at?"

"Riders comin'. Your brother James, Evan and Len."

Her eyes brightened for only a moment, then trouble darkened them again. "What about Billy? And Andy?"

Rusty shook his head.

Josie leaned against him and choked off a small cry of disappointment. She glanced back toward her sister's house. Geneva sat in a rocking chair on the dog run, rocking the baby girl.

Josie said, "She's gone half crazy with worry and grief. At least Evan is comin' back. Maybe that'll help."

Rusty had watched Geneva waste away. He knew she had eaten but little, and he doubted that she had slept much. She clung to the baby as if the girl were the only family left to her. She had drained herself of tears. Now her eyes were dry and hollow and haunted.

Josie said, "I'd better go tell Geneva, and Mama."

She seemed reluctant to start. Rusty hugged her for whatever comfort that might give her, then watched her move away toward her sister. He opened the corral gate and waited. He felt no need for a lot of questions. Despair in the dusty, bearded faces told him almost all he needed to know. He asked only, "Andy?"

Tanner's expression was grim. "He wouldn't come back with us. He's still out there somewhere, lookin'."

Geneva hurried out from her cabin, carrying the baby, and ran to meet her husband. He folded both of them into his arms. Rusty heard her cry. Clemmie came from the larger family house with Preacher Webb. She shaded her eyes with her hand a moment, then rushed to embrace her son. Webb trailed, letting her have her moment with James.

Rusty asked Tanner, "Find any trace of the boy?"

"We saw Indian sign, but there was no way to tell if they still had Billy or not."

Rusty's voice turned critical. "I don't see how you could've let Andy stay up there by himself."

"He wasn't by himself." Tanner explained about the Comancheros and the deal James had offered to barter the boy's freedom with horses.

Rusty protested, "But Andy's just a boy himself."

"Maybe you ain't paid enough attention to him lately. He don't act like a boy when he's got his mind made up. Said he was goin' to find Billy however long it took."

"You still ought to've stopped him."

"Tell you the truth, I don't think we really wanted to. He feels like it's his fault Billy got taken. Another thing, he can go places the rest of us can't. If anybody's to find Billy, it'll be him."

Rusty's anxiety was not appeased, but he saw it was useless to belabor the point. "Did you see Captain Burmeister anywhere?"

"Not since he turned back."

"He went out again, soon as his men got a little rest, supplies and some fresh horses. God knows where he is."

"I'm surprised you didn't go with him."

"I don't have the strength to keep up on a hard ride. I'd be a millstone around everybody's neck. And somebody needed to be here besides Preacher Webb and Macy in case some Comanches or Kiowas decided to pay another visit."

Rusty watched Geneva and the baby return to their cabin. Evan had an arm around his wife's shoulder. Rusty ached for all of them. He could imagine the hell Evan had endured in the futile search for his son, the heartbreak he must have suffered in turning back.

Preacher Webb moved up beside Rusty and Tanner. "We prayed mighty hard. Sometimes it takes a while, but you generally get an answer if you don't give up hope."

From someone else Rusty might have taken that as an empty platitude, but he knew Webb believed with all his soul.

Webb walked back to the family house with Clemmie and James. Rusty watched in silence. Clemmie had taken her father's death hard, but she had never let her back bend. She stood straight and determined.

Knowing it was futile, Rusty climbed onto the fence again and looked northward. Josie reached up and gripped his arm. "I can see in your face what you're thinkin'. Don't. You'd never find Andy. One boy alone, out in hundreds of miles of open prairie."

"A boy who considers himself a man."

Tanner declared, "He *is* a man, I tell you. He's given himself a job that few men would have the guts to try."

"I ought to be up there with him."

"You'd never make it past the first Comanche camp. But he will. He's got enough Indian in him."

Captain Burmeister returned in a couple of days with his little group of frontier guards. He was painfully frustrated, men and horses weary, dried out and hungry. "It is hopeless," he told Rusty. "Of water there is not enough. It will never be a country for white men, not while we live."

"There is water," Rusty argued. "Otherwise, the Indians couldn't stay."

"But only the Indian knows where it is."

"Tanner was tellin' me about runnin' across some ox-cart traders out of New Mexico. Looks like they know how to find water. Someday somebody will start markin' the water holes and the trails. Once it's done, that country won't be a mystery anymore. There won't be anyplace safe for Comanches to hide."

"Someday," Burmeister said. "But it is for now that we must worry. We know so little, and we are so few."

Rusty had been chewing on an idea for several days. "Captain, could you use another man?"

Burmeister's gray mustache lifted in a smile. "As in times past, before the fools on both sides carried us into war?"

"Like then. I realize it's not quite the same as the old-time rangers, and I know I'll be a while gettin' my full strength back. But I feel like there's things I can do to make myself useful."

"But you have your own home, far from here."

"Not anymore. I've been carpetbagged out of it. I need to stay up in this part of the country for now, but I don't want to keep bein' a burden to the Monahans."

Tanner's mouth sagged open. Rusty had not mentioned the idea to him.

Burmeister turned. "And you, Private Tanner? What of you?"

Tanner grinned. "Why the hell not? When I was a ranger I went hungry half the time, and I never got paid what they promised me. They was the best years of my life."

"I cannot guarantee you will be paid this time. In Austin promises are many, but the well is often dry."

Rusty had one reservation. "Somethin' you ought to know, Captain, before you swear me in. There's a charge against me down home. It's a false charge, but it's on the books just the same."

"Not murder, I hope."

"Nothin' like that. I'm charged with aidin' and abettin' the escape of a criminal. But I never did it. He took one of my horses without me knowin' it. They claim I gave it to him."

"They?"

"Two brothers by the name of Oldham. Durin' the war they hid out in the brush. I had some trouble with them."

"They did not serve in the Confederate Army?"

"Nor the Union Army either. But now they're state police."

Burmeister scowled. "Do not worry about the state police. There are some good men but also some rotten apples. They have no authority over my company."

Rusty's announcement took Josie by surprise. She was dismayed. "Rusty, you can't. You mustn't."

"I can't stay here just doin' nothin'."

"You have a home here as long as you want it."

"It's your home, not mine."

"But it could be your home. You could be one of us."

He took her hands. "The Monahans have been the nearest thing to family that I've had since Daddy Mike and Mother Dora. There's not a family anywhere that I'd rather be a part of."

"I've always hoped that you and me—"

"I know. If I was in a shape for marryin', you're the one I'd ask. But I'd have nothin' to offer you now, not so much as a roof over your head or a plot of ground for a garden. And there's Billy out yonder somewhere, and Andy. I can't be thinkin' of makin' a home 'til that's all settled."

"What do you think you can do?"

"Ride. Watch. Listen. Maybe somewhere out there I'll find somethin' or hear somethin'. I don't know what, and I won't know 'til it happens."

She pressed his hand against her lips. "When the job is done, you know where I'll be."

Burmeister had set up his base camp several miles from the Monahan place. On the way there Rusty was aware that Burmeister watched him with a critical eye. When they reached the camp, the captain asked him, "You are tired?"

Rusty was, but he chose not to acknowledge it. "I'm doin' better than I thought I might."

"We will not push you too hard, not at first."

"I'll tote my share of the load."

"You always did. Always you were a good man on patrol. There was not much you did not see."

"You're wantin' me to go on scout?"

"Tomorrow, and only as far as you feel strong. Take Private Tanner with you. Look for sign of Indians. But do not engage. Come back and report."

"Yes sir." It would feel good to be doing something useful again and not be considered an invalid. "There's nobody I'd rather have with me than Tanner. Even if he does sometimes talk 'til my ears hurt."

The camp reminded him of earlier times, before and during the war when he had served with the rangers in the Fort Belknap country. Burmeister maintained a loose form of military discipline and routine that lent at least some structure to each day. Rusty studied the men, quietly trying to assess their potential. He found that most had escaped Confederate service, a couple of them by going to Mexico, a couple more by serving in the Union Army. One or two he suspected of having been brush men, hiding out from conscription officers. That did not necessarily brand them in his view. James Monahan had done it. On the other hand, so had the Oldham brothers.

Rusty guessed that his first day's ride with Tanner covered about twenty miles, about as much as he could expect while watching the ground for tracks. The last few miles set his shoulder to throbbing and aggravated an old leg pain from his long-ago arrow wound.

Tanner commented, "You're lookin' a little peaked."

"It's your eyes. I'm doin' just fine."

"Well, I'm tired if you're not. I say it's time to make camp. Got to think of the horses."

The ride had not been long enough to tax the horses unduly. Rusty appreciated that Tanner was watching out for his welfare without making an issue of it.

They stopped at a small seep he remembered from scouting trips long ago. The seep fed a narrow creek, its water trailing for a couple of hundred yards before disappearing into the sand. Along the creek's short course a thin band of green grass offered grazing for the horses. Rusty and Tanner staked their mounts with long rawhide reatas that gave the animals considerable freedom to move around.

Tanner watched them. "Just like old times. The horses are gettin' fed better than we are. I can imagine the good supper Clemmie Monahan is servin' tonight."

Rusty chewed hard on a salty strip of dried jerky. "Andy may not have even this much to eat."

"He can get by on lizards and rattlesnakes if he has to. He's that much Comanche."

Rusty shuddered at the thought. "If I had any notion where he's at, any notion at all—"

"You'd go there and lose that red hair before it has a chance to start gettin' gray."

The only horse tracks he and Tanner had seen all day had been remnants of old ones, headed north. They found no sign of recent Indian incursion. Years ago, under the old loose frontier ranger organization, the men had scouted along established north-south lines a little beyond the settlements, riding until they met scouts coming from counterpart camps. At that point they turned back and re-rode the same line. The system had worked well so long as the frontier companies had manpower enough. Some Indian raids were broken up before they were well started. The system had become less and less effective as the war drew men away from the frontier and the ranger companies.

Rusty knew Captain Burmeister lacked men enough to make the routine work as well as it once had. Intercepting Indians would be as much a matter of luck—of being at the right place at the right time—as of organization.

Tanner said, "This ought to be the job of the United States Army, but them generals don't see Indians as a serious problem."

"They're mostly stayin' back in the settled parts of the state where Indians *aren't* a problem. They spend most of their time lookin' for Confederate conspiracies."

"Well, I've learned one thing for damned sure."

"What's that?"

"Don't ever lose a war. It don't pay."

They were within sight of the camp when one of the scouts rode out to intercept them. His expression indicated that he was not the bearer of good news. He said, "Captain Burmeister wanted me to let you know you've got company waitin' for you."

Rusty asked, "Who is it?"

"Couple of brothers. I don't recall the name. The younger one has just got one arm."

Rusty frowned at Tanner. "The Oldhams. I've wondered how long it would take them to figure out where I'm at." He looked back at the messenger. "Did the captain say what he wants me to do?"

"No, just said he didn't want you ridin' in unawares."

Tanner said, "You take Clyde. I'll take Buddy-Boy. We can put an end to them once and for all."

Rusty realized Tanner was serious. "I don't want us to kill anybody. Remember, they're state police."

"Damned poor recommendation."

The scout said, "There's a third man with them. Deputy of some kind, I think."

The Oldham brothers and the deputy waited outside Burmeister's tent, their stance stiff and expectant. Burmeister and two of his men stood nearby, watching them. Tanner's rifle lay across the pommel of his saddle, ready.

Rusty dismounted, keeping his horse between himself and the Oldhams. He said, "I expected you a lot sooner, Clyde."

"It ain't that we didn't try. You're a hard man to locate."

"Now that you've found me, what do you figure on doin'?"

"We've come to arrest you."

Rusty said, "If you plan on shootin' me in the back again, you've come a long ways on a fool's errand. I'm not goin' with you."

Clyde started to reach into his pocket but stopped abruptly when Tanner swung his rifle around. He swallowed hard. "I'm just goin' after my warrant."

Tanner said, "See that that's all you go after."

Buddy Oldham dropped his hand to the butt of a pistol on his hip but made no effort to draw the weapon. He stared into the muzzle of Tanner's rifle.

Tanner said, "Better raise that hand, Buddy, or this time you're liable to lose more than your arm."

Buddy lifted his hand clear, his eyes flashing anger.

Clyde demanded, "Where's that Indian kid of yours, Shannon?"

None of your damned business, Rusty thought. But he said, "He's not here."

"Probably runnin' with his Comanche friends." Clyde scowled. "When he left down yonder, we followed him. Second or third day out, a bunch of Comanches come swarmin' down on us. I'd swear on a stack of Bibles that boy was with them. He was after our scalps."

Rusty wondered. Andy hadn't told him about that, if it was true.

Tanner said, "Damned shame he didn't get them."

Captain Burmeister reached out for the warrant. "I will read that, if you please."

Clyde hesitated. "I come to serve it on Shannon."

"I am commanding officer here. I will read it first."

Grudgingly Clyde handed it over. Burmeister glanced at the paper. "This judge, his name is not known to me. How am I to know this document is real?"

"It's got the court seal on it."

"Perhaps it is real. Perhaps it is not. You will tell me about the charges against Private Shannon."

Clyde's eyes widened. "*Private* Shannon?"

"He is a member of my company. Therefore he is an officer of the state, as you claim to be. My authority as captain is superior to yours. He will go or not go, as I choose."

Buddy Oldham's face colored. "Authority! You sound like some kind of a Dutchman. Me and my brother don't have to take orders from no immigrant."

Burmeister's mustache twitched in growing anger. "I fought for this country already before you were born. Private Shannon tells me you spent the last war hiding in the brush. You fought for nobody."

Clyde said, "It wasn't our war. We had no stake in either side."

"But now you wear a badge that is too big for you and swear out charges against those from whom you would steal."

"We ain't stole nothin'—"

"You have taken Private Shannon's land, have you not?"

"He owed back taxes. I paid them fair and legal."

Rusty held his tongue. He wanted to refute what Oldham said, but the captain seemed to be doing a good job of it without his interference.

Burmeister said, "Once before you have arrested him, and you shot him in the back."

"He tried to escape."

"So you claim. It is an excuse as old as Pharaoh."

Tanner put in, "If you let them take Rusty, he'll never get halfway home. They'll kill him."

Burmeister nodded. "So we will put the boot on another foot. Mr. Oldham, if it is your will to take him I do not prevent you. But I will send Private Tanner and some of my other men as escort. If you make any move to kill him, any move whatever . . ." He did not finish. He did not have to.

Buddy Oldham's face went crimson. "Don't let them scare you, Clyde."

Clyde looked at Tanner with dread. He said, "They do scare me. It's *us* who wouldn't live to get back. They'd kill us sure as hell."

Burmeister agreed. "Possibly so. But is that not what you planned for Private Shannon?"

Clyde Oldham had the trapped look of an animal hemmed into a corner.

Buddy was too outraged to understand his brother's fear. "Ain't we goin' to take him?" He raised the stump of an arm. "Look what he done. He left me half a man. You swore to me, Clyde. You swore we'd kill him for that."

"Shut up, Buddy. You don't see what we're up against."

"I see you're givin' up after we've rode all this way, after we been chased by Indians and everything. You're fixin' to turn around and leave him."

"Sometimes you get dealt a bad hand. You fold and wait for a better deal." Clyde cut his gaze back to Rusty. "So this time the pot is yours. But the game ain't over."

"It's no game to me, Clyde." Rusty looked regretfully at Buddy. "I never wanted to shoot your brother. He forced it on me."

Clyde did not acknowledge that he had heard. "Thanks for the farm, Shannon. It's a good one."

"Don't be likin' it too much. One way or another I'll get it back."

"Come visit any time. We'll be lookin' for you." Clyde jerked his head at his brother and the deputy. They went to their horses.

Watching them mount, Rusty said, "I didn't expect them to give up that easy."

Tanner said, "They ain't given up. You'll be seein' them again."

Rusty did not want to think about that. "This horse is

tired and sweaty. I'm goin' to water him and brush him down." He led the horse to a makeshift corral and pulled the saddle off. He dropped the blanket and bent down to pick it up.

A fence post exploded just above his head. A split second later he heard the loud, flat sound of a rifle.

Tanner shouted, "Get down, Rusty." Tanner steadied his rifle across a fence rail and fired at the retreating Clyde.

Burmeister and his scouts quickly covered Buddy and the deputy with their firearms. Rusty felt points of fire in his face. Clyde's shot had driven splinters into his skin. He reached up and felt the warm stickiness of blood on his fingers.

Bent low in the saddle, Clyde was spurring away, his boots flailing at his horse's ribs, his shirttail standing out behind him. His hat blew off, but he did not slow down.

Tanner watched Clyde's desperate flight with disgust. "Had my sights on him right between the shoulder blades. Gettin' to where I can't shoot worth a damn anymore."

Rusty pulled at a splinter that had pierced his cheek. It burned as if it had been set afire.

Burmeister walked up to Buddy Oldham, his eyes smoldering. "That is some brother you have. He tried to do murder here."

Stubbornly Buddy said, "We got a warrant."

"Take your warrant and go before I get mad. You don't want to see a German get mad. It is a terrible thing, all thunder and lightning."

Buddy glared at the captain, then turned to Rusty, hatred burning in his eyes. He said, "You come south any time you're ready. We'll give you back your farm . . . six feet of it."

Buddy and the deputy left. Watching the deputy dismount to pick up Clyde's lost hat, Tanner said, "Losin' his arm made Buddy mean as poison."

"He's not as dangerous as Clyde."

"Clyde's a coward."

"That's why he's dangerous. He'll get you when you're

not lookin'." He reached up and felt his burning cheek.

Burmeister gave Rusty an anxious study. "You bleed. He hit you?"

"Just splinters. They'll come out." Rusty turned to Tanner. "Thanks, Len. If he'd had time for a second shot he'd've killed me sure."

Tanner shrugged, his gaze on Clyde and the deputy, riding away. "That's what I'm paid so high for."

· 16 ·

The horse tracks were easy for Andy to follow. This far up in their plains stronghold, the raiders had no reason to try to cover them. Their direction gave him a strong clue about the destination. He remembered a place where his band had camped several times, a location that offered water enough and trees for shade and shelter from the wind.

To look less like a white man he had shed his hat, shirt and long underwear, keeping only his trousers and the moccasins. The rest he tied behind the cantle. He remembered the time soon after he fell back into Texan hands that his uncle, Jim Pickard, had come to have a look at him. The uncle had rejected him because he considered him a savage beyond redemption.

He ought to get a look at me now, Andy thought.

The camp was where he expected it to be. As before, he approached the horse herd first, looking for Billy's pony or Vince Purdy's mount. And again he was disappointed.

He rode into camp with all the boldness he could muster, trying not to show any sign of his nagging concern that some of Tonkawa Killer's friends might be here. He saw a few faces he remembered, though they stared at him without recognition. He had grown, and his features had matured since he had been with the Texans. The camp people met him with both curiosity and suspicion, for they were not prepared to see a white-skinned young man come among them of his own accord.

He spoke in the Comanche tongue, and their suspicions began to fade. To a man he remembered having ridden with Steals the Ponies he said, "Do you not remember me? Steals the Ponies is my brother. I was known as Badger Boy."

With recognition came a warm welcome. "Come. Come and eat. There is plenty."

Andy was glad to accept. He had eaten little besides a bit of tough jerky since leaving Martínez. His host plied him with questions about his years among the Texans, about the Texans' strange lifeways. Andy tailored his answers to what he thought the man would want to hear. "They are a strange people," he conceded. "But not all their ways are bad."

When the questions began to lag, he offered his own. "Do you know where I might find Steals the Ponies?"

The Comanche said, "He left here yesterday and went north with his family. They joined some others who came back from a raid against the Texans."

Andy's senses sharpened. "A raid?"

"Yes. I went myself. We took many horses."

Andy thought of Vince Purdy. "And scalps?"

"Only one. An old man we found."

"No one else?"

"We took a small boy. Fights with Bears was the leader. He claimed the boy and the horses. I took second coup on the old man, but I got only this." He lifted a watch that hung around his neck on a leather thong along with his medicine bag. Its case looked like silver.

Vince Purdy's! Andy thought.

He reached out. "May I see it?"

His host lifted the thong from around his neck. "It is of little use. It is but a pretty trinket."

Andy clasped the watch with reverence, as if somehow it contained the spirit of Vince Purdy. In his mind's eye he visualized the kind old gentleman, and his throat tightened. This keepsake would mean much to the Monahans if he lived to return it to them.

He saw that it had run down. Evidently its new owner did not know to wind it. He would not have understood the white man's concept of time anyway. Andy started to wind it but changed his mind. He asked, "What will you do with it?"

"I may give it to my wife's father. He is old and becoming foolish. He likes things that shine."

"Would you trade it to me?"

The man's eyes brightened. Comanches enjoyed the challenge of trading. "What do you have to offer?"

Andy knew he did not have much. "A white-man hat. It will keep the sun from your head in summer and snow from your hair in winter."

"Not enough."

"A white-man shirt. It will help protect you when the cold winds blow."

The Indian shook his head. "My father-in-law would not like those. They do not shine."

Andy considered long before offering, "The saddle, then. The white man's saddle is comfortable. It will not rub sores on your legs." He would regret giving it up, but he could ride bareback. He had done it for years with The People.

Nothing about the saddle was fancy. It was plain, its seat slick from long use. Someone had already ridden it for years before Rusty had acquired it for Andy. The Comanche rubbed his hands over it, his eyes shining with delight. He said, "I wanted the old man's saddle, but Fights with Bears would not give it up. We trade."

Andy wondered if the watch would still run, but he did not wind it. Its ticking might give his host second thoughts. He put it around his neck.

He said, "You mentioned a boy." He trembled a little, fearing the answer. "What became of him?"

"Fights with Bears took him north." The Comanche pointed with his chin. "He has not decided whether to keep him to raise as a slave or to kill him. The boy has caused him much trouble. Fights with Bears is not a man of much patience."

Good for Billy, Andy thought. The more fight he showed, the better his chance of surviving. Andy remembered that when he had first been taken he had been subjected to heavy abuse. He realized later that he was being tested for his prospects as a warrior. Had he not kept fighting back, he might have been killed.

He asked, "Was my brother on the raid with you?"

"No. Fights with Bears was the leader. He and Steals the Ponies do not like one another."

Andy was relieved that his brother had not participated in Vince Purdy's killing and Billy's kidnapping. Yet he would have thought no less of him if he had been a party to the incident. The Comanches were simply following the customs of their grandfathers. Raiding enemies was a natural part of their life, like eating, like breathing. It almost took on the aspects of a game, though ofttimes a deadly one. Living with them, Andy had regarded this as normal. Now, having lived away from them, he could no longer accept it without question, not when it took the lives of good people like Vince Purdy and involved the capture of innocent children like Billy Gifford.

Yet, white men of the North and South had fought one another during four long years for reasons he had never quite fathomed. They had killed strangers, people they had never seen before and who had never done them harm. He could not see a great difference between that and the Comanche way.

Impatience set his skin to prickling. He was eager to move on, to find Steals the Ponies. Perhaps his brother could help him in some way to free Billy. "I must go," he said. "The longer I wait, the farther my brother may travel."

His host tried to get him to stay the night. "With families, they move slowly. You could start with the morning's light and catch them before the sun sleeps again."

Andy had another potential problem to consider. He had not seen everyone in this camp, nor had everyone seen him. A friend of Tonkawa Killer might yet recognize him.

He said, "I can ride far before the sun sleeps."

To replace the saddle, Andy obtained a rawhide rope to loop behind his horse's shoulders. He could tuck his knees beneath it to hold him steady should he encounter rough traveling. Except for his trousers, he left his white-man clothing behind in return for the hospitality. With a stick, his host drew a rough map on the ground. He described the site where he thought the group was likely to camp for at least a few days. The description sounded familiar.

"I believe I remember the place," Andy said.

"May friendly spirits ride with you."

The trail was as plain as a white man's wagon road, beaten out not only by horses but by tepee poles lashed together to form travois. Andy could have followed it at a lope and in the dark, but he did not want to push Long Red. He might have to depend upon the horse's stamina if circumstances called for a hard run.

In the middle of the afternoon he came suddenly upon three Comanche hunters on horseback. Two carried deer carcasses in front of them. They reined up and waited for Andy, suspicion strong in their faces. The one not encumbered held a bow with an arrow fitted into its string.

Nervously Andy greeted them in their own language. Like so many others he had encountered, they wanted to know how a white youth knew the words of The People. He explained as briefly as he could. "I have been away from my people a long time. I am looking for them."

He decided against using his brother's name. Should things go badly, he did not want to bring trouble to Steals the Ponies.

The hunters accepted him with reservations. "Ride with

us," one said. "We will take you to our camp. Perhaps there you will find your family."

Nearing the encampment, they passed by the horse herd. This time Andy was not disappointed. He recognized Billy's pony and Purdy's horse standing together near the outer edge, like two old acquaintances thrown unwillingly among strangers.

One of the hunters said, "We hope you find what you are looking for."

Andy already had. He saw a woman cooking meat over an open fire in front of a tepee. She was Steals the Ponies's wife. Seeing no other woman with her, he assumed she was still the only one. Two children, a boy and a girl, played nearby.

He approached slowly, not wanting to startle her. She looked up at him without recognition. He said, "Do you not know me?"

Her face was blank. "I do not believe so."

"I am Badger Boy."

She almost turned over the meat pot. She embraced him, then stood back for a better look. "I can see now, but you are much changed. You were a boy. Now you are a man."

"I have come to see my brother."

"He scouts for buffalo. He should be here soon."

The boy and girl had stopped their play to stare at him in curiosity. He asked, "These are yours?"

"Yes. Before winter there will be another." She looked away, then pointed. "He comes. Say nothing. See if he recognizes you."

Andy's heartbeat quickened. The passage of years had not changed the way his brother sat on his horse. Andy could have recognized him from far away. Steals the Ponies did not seem to notice the visitor at first. He dismounted, obviously tired, and tied his horse behind the tepee. He carried his medicine shield inside, for it was a sacred thing to be protected from harm.

Coming back outside, he spoke to his wife. "I am hungry."

"The meat is soon ready. Look. Someone has come to see you."

Steals the Ponies stared blankly a moment, then his eyes brightened and the weariness fell away. "Badger Boy!" He embraced his brother with such strength that Andy almost lost his breath. "But Badger Boy is no longer a fit name. You are not a boy."

"Among the Texans I am known as Andy."

Steals the Ponies spoke the name but found it not to his liking. "It means nothing. We must find you a new name, something better."

His delight began to fade, and concern crowded in. "You should not be here. Have you forgotten why you left us, why you had to go back and live with the Texans?"

"I have not forgotten. I remember the one who was killed." He avoided speaking the name. "I had hoped none of his friends are in this camp."

"They come and they go. One is here. Do you remember Fights with Bears?"

Andy had been hearing the name but could not recall the look of the man. His brother nodded toward the tepee. "We will go inside. We would not want him to see you."

"You believe he would still want me dead?"

"His wives are sisters of the one who was killed."

After entering, Andy waited until his brother sat, leaning against a back rest, then he seated himself.

Steals the Ponies said, "When you left, we agreed you should never come back. Why are you here again?"

"I have come looking for a boy. He is the son of people who have been good to me. I am told he was taken by Fights with Bears. I have come to take him back to his family."

Trouble pinched his brother's eyes. "You have come far and risked your life for nothing. You want too much. Fights with Bears has claimed the boy for his own. He will not give him up."

Andy remembered the proposal James and Evan had made to Martínez. "Perhaps he would trade for horses."

"He already has many horses. If you brought him more he would probably take them, kill you and keep the boy. He listens to bad spirits, that one."

Andy did not know what else to propose for trade. He did not know how much money the Monahans might have. It was unlikely Fights with Bears had much concept of money's value anyway. Comanches understood goods, something they could hold in their hands, something they could use. Coins were of value only for ornamentation, and paper money was worth nothing at all.

"What can I do?" he asked.

"Go back to the Texans. You belong among them now. Forget about the boy. Tell them he is dead."

"His family are my friends. They weep for him."

"If they are young they can have other children."

"It would not be the same. Texans love their children just as The People do."

"Fights with Bears would not even talk to you."

"Then I will steal the boy in the night."

Steals the Ponies stared at Andy in disbelief. "Your Texas friends are too far away. He would catch you and kill you. He might be angry enough to kill the boy."

"I have traveled many days to find Billy. Now that I know where he is, I cannot turn away from him."

"You must. Or are you so willing to die for the Texans?"

Andy considered a long time before suggesting, "What if I offered to trade myself for him?"

"Fights with Bears would kill you and keep the boy. Why would you suggest such a foolish thing?"

"Because it is my fault the boy was taken." He explained about his failure to warn of the raiding party he had encountered prior to Billy's capture.

Steals the Ponies was incredulous. "You would trade your life for this boy? It would not be reasonable, even if Fights with Bears were a man of his word and would let the boy go. But of course he will not."

"I will not go back without Billy. I could not face those who have given me a home. I would be ashamed."

"You cannot stay here. There are others besides Fights with Bears who would gladly kill you." Steals the Ponies's expression became grave. "Even if they did not, you would not want to share the future of our people."

"What do you mean by that?"

"I have had a vision. It came to me one night, clear as in daylight. I saw our prairies without buffalo. Where the buffalo should have been, I saw the blue-coat soldiers. They were as many as the buffalo. We were helpless and hungry and cold." He shivered. "They herded us like the white man's cattle to a terrible place where we did not want to go."

"The reservation?"

"I think so. Many of our people are already there. It is the wish of the Texans and the soldiers that we all go there or that we die."

Andy argued, "The blue coats have done little against The People since the white man's war ended. The Texans cry for help, but the soldiers do not listen."

"They will, and soon. The vision was very strong. For your own good, your place is among the Texans. You do not belong among The People anymore. If Fights with Bears and his friends do not kill you, the soldiers may. They will not see you as a white man. They will see you as one of us."

The bleakness of Steals the Ponies's vision left Andy depressed. He wanted to believe that his brother had simply experienced a bad dream. Yet during his years with the Comanches he had heard many stories about visions that came to pass. The People had strong faith in them. He could not dismiss this one lightly.

He said, "Perhaps the vision was a warning of what *might* happen. Were you not shown a way to avoid it?"

"The soldiers were too many. Their guns were too powerful."

"If the vision was true, there is no future here for Billy either. I must take him back to his own. It is a matter of honor."

Andy's brother sat in silence a long time, his face an expressionless mask. But Andy imagined he could see the mind hard at work behind half closed eyes. He could sense the internal struggle. At last Steals the Ponies spoke. "You talk of your honor. If I helped you do this thing, I would lose my own honor. I would betray my people."

"Not all the people. Just Fights with Bears. You said you do not like him."

Steals the Ponies went silent again for a time, thinking. Finally he said, "There might be a way, but the spirits must be with you. You could die if they are not."

Eagerly Andy asked, "What is it?"

"I have not thought it all through. We will talk of it later. Now I must move your horse so Fights with Bears will not see him and wonder."

"I do not want to place you in danger. This is a thing I should do by myself."

"Fights with Bears would not kill me, and I would not kill him. We are bound together by the blood of The People. But you are not of our blood, and neither is the boy. He would kill you both. So I will help you."

Steals the Ponies was gone awhile. His wife was in and out of the tepee several times. Andy could sense that she was curious, but she asked no questions. The two children came inside and stared silently at Andy without approaching too closely. He wanted to tell them he was their uncle, but he decided against it. They might tell other children later, and word might find its way to Fights with Bears. He would know that Steals the Ponies was somehow involved in Billy's liberation . . . if it worked.

When his brother returned, Andy asked, "What do we do now?"

"We rest. We wait. We can do nothing until Fights with Bears and his family are asleep."

"Do you know for certain where Billy is?"

"He is in their lodge. They keep him tied because he tries to run away. I wonder about his intelligence. Even if he were to escape and not be found, by himself he would soon starve. The boy does not reason well."

"He has the stubborn will of the Monahans." Andy did not know how to explain the fierce independence of the family who had suffered so much because they stood by their unpopular convictions. He said, "They have much in common with the Comanches."

That was explanation enough for Steals the Ponies. "Sleep now. You will have little time for it later. You have far to travel."

So much was running through Andy's mind that he did not expect to sleep at all. However, when his brother shook his shoulder gently to awaken him, he was surprised to see that it was dark outside.

His brother said, "It will soon be time. You must eat now."

Andy did not feel like eating. He burned with excitement over what was coming. Steals the Ponies said, "You will need strength. Eat."

Andy forced himself to down the leftover meat from the previous evening.

Steals the Ponies said, "I have been to the lodge of Fights with Bears. Not everything is as we would want it to be. One of the children is sick."

"Billy?"

"One of the others. But when a child is sick, its mother does not sleep well. It will be difficult for me to crawl into the lodge without arousing the family."

If caught, Steals the Ponies would be expelled from the band at the very least. He and his family would be outcasts. Andy said, "That is not for you to do. It is for me."

"I am pleased to see that you have much courage. I would be more pleased if I saw that you were also blessed with much judgment."

Andy asked, "Do you know where the boy will be sleeping?"

"I have seen him tied to a lodge pole." Steals the Ponies picked up a stick and drew a circle in the sand to represent the interior of a tepee. He pointed out the front flap, then moved the point of the stick around the perimeter and stabbed it into the ground. "This is where I have seen him. I suspect the other children are placed around him at night to make it difficult for him to escape."

"Once I have freed him, what then?"

"I will have two horses for you. The sorrel on which you came and another for the boy."

"What about his pony?"

"It will not travel fast enough. I have other use for the pony and the tracks it makes."

Andy did not understand. His brother explained, "I will take another horse and lead the pony southward. That is the direction Fights with Bears would expect. I will leave a clear trail. When I have misled him far enough, my trail will disappear. I will circle back to camp while he is still looking for my tracks."

"But south is where I need to go with the boy."

"Not at first. You will ride eastward in the creek where you will not leave a trail. You must travel far before you leave the creek."

"That would put us into the settlements a long way east of where the boy's family lives."

"But east from where Fights with Bears will be looking for you."

Andy could see flaws in his brother's plan, but it was better than anything he had been able to think up. It had all the marks of the trickster, the coyote.

Much depended upon Andy's being able to get the boy out of the tepee without arousing the family. Beyond that, much depended upon being able to fool Fights with Bears.

He said, "I hope he is not very smart."

"He has been in many battles. Not one has he lost."

• **17** •

The moon provided light enough for Andy to see that the tepee skins were rolled up a foot or so from the bottom to allow fresh air to pass through. He would be able to crawl in where he chose rather than have to enter through the front flap and feel his way around. He looked behind him but could not see Steals the Ponies. He had the comfort of faith that his brother was back there somewhere, holding two pairs of horses.

From inside he could hear loud snoring. He guessed it came from Fights with Bears. That was gratifying. But not so welcome were the sounds of a child's cough and a woman's calming whisper. Andy lay on his stomach at the tepee's edge, listening, his skin prickling with impatience.

He waited until some time had passed since the last cough. He began to drag himself forward slowly, trying to make no sound. Somewhere a dog barked, and he froze. The child whimpered, causing him to wait again, half in and half out of the lodge.

As his eyes adjusted to the interior's poor light, he was able to see the sleepers. The largest he took to be Fights with Bears, lying on his back, snoring again after having lain on his side for a while. Next to him lay one of his wives. Andy sought out the second wife. She lay among the children. He assumed that the sick child was one of hers.

It took him some time to be sure which of the other dark lumps was Billy. He was not quite in the place Steals the Ponies had indicated in his rough dirt sketch. Billy's hands were tied above his head, a leather thong binding them to a tepee pole. He lay with his feet together. Andy suspected they were also bound.

He began backing out of the tepee but bumped against one of the other children. The child grunted and raised up on one elbow. Andy lay still, barely daring to breathe, until the child settled down and resumed sleep. Then he crawled free of the tepee, backwards, and inched his way around to the pole where Billy was tied.

Billy stirred restlessly. He appeared to be asleep, but Andy knew he could not be comfortable with his hands lashed above his head. If startled, he was likely to cry out and awaken the family. Andy dragged himself inside the tepee just far enough to reach Billy. Gripping his knife in a cold-sweaty hand, he cut the thong attached to the pole. His hands suddenly free, Billy brought them down in reflex and opened his eyes in surprise.

Andy clamped a hand over Billy's mouth before the boy could do more than grunt. Billy stared wildly at him and for a few seconds fought to pull free.

"Shhh," Andy hissed, softly as he could.

Billy calmed. Andy removed the hand and crooked his finger, silently beckoning. He began backing out of the tepee. Hands and feet still tied, Billy wriggled after him.

The sick child coughed and cried out. Instantly its mother was awake, speaking gently. She dipped a cloth into a bowl of water and laid it across the fevered face. Andy froze again and motioned for Billy to do the same.

Fights with Bears gave a loud grunt and pushed himself up on one arm. He demanded, "Can you not keep that girl quiet? I want to sleep."

The child's mother did not take the comment in good

grace. She answered with a sharp retort. Andy feared the
two would become too angry with one another to go back
to sleep. But the man grunted something unintelligible and
lay back down. In a few minutes the child became quiet,
and its mother stretched out beside it.

Andy feared she was not asleep. She might not sleep the
rest of the night. He could not afford to wait too long. After
a few minutes he began crawling again, inches at a time.
Billy came along after him. It seemed an hour before the
boy was out of the tepee. Andy cut the leather thong that
bound Billy's hands, then the one that tied his feet.

Billy recognized him in the dim light of the half moon.
"Andy!"

Andy shushed him again and beckoned for him to follow.
Billy was awkward on his feet. He fell to hands and knees.
Being tied had cut his circulation and numbed his arms and
legs. Andy lifted the boy up and carried him in the direction
where Steals the Ponies would be waiting. Billy clung desperately to his neck.

Andy's brother stood in the edge of the creek, holding
four horses. He appeared much relieved. "It took you a long
time," he said. "I feared you had entered the wrong lodge."

Billy reacted with fear to Steals the Ponies. Andy whispered, "Don't be afraid. This is my brother."

Billy did not understand that. Andy would explain it to
him later, when they were far from here.

Steals the Ponies said, "Put the boy on this horse. He is
one of best I have. I hope he can ride without a saddle."

"He can. He will."

Billy recognized his own pony and asked why he could
not ride it. That was something else Andy would have to
explain later. For the moment he said only, "This is your
horse now." He mounted Long Red.

Steals the Ponies swung up onto a third horse. He had a
leather rope around the neck of Billy's pony. "Remember,"
he admonished, "follow the creek eastward. If the spirits
are with us, it will be daylight before Fights with Bears

knows the boy is gone. I will see that the pony leaves good, clear tracks for him to follow."

Andy felt as if he would choke. The breach between him and The People, already broad, would be irretrievably unbridgeable after this.

He grasped his brother's arm. "You have done a brave thing for me."

"But it is the last thing I can ever do for you. With what you do tonight, you have chosen the white man's road. You are no longer Comanche."

"It is a hard thing to know that I may never see you again."

Steals the Ponies's voice was grave. "Perhaps we will see each other in another world, less troubled than this one. Now go. Do not look back."

Andy did look back, once. He saw Steals the Ponies ride up out of the creek, leading Billy's pony. Moving southward, he was quickly lost from sight.

Billy asked, "Why do we ride in the water?"

"So we don't leave tracks."

"Your brother leaves tracks."

"So they will follow him, not us."

"Are you takin' me home, Andy?"

"That's my intention."

"They killed Granddaddy Vince."

"I know."

"He had a watch. It looked like the one you're wearin' around your neck."

"I'm takin' it home too. Now, let's don't talk for a while. Let's just ride."

It seemed beyond reason to ride eastward when all his instincts tried to pull him south, but he recognized his brother's wisdom. Fights with Bears would expect the escapees to flee southward. The false trail created by Steals the Ponies would bear him out.

Andy recognized that his brother was running some risk,

but he felt that Steals the Ponies was wily enough to avoid being caught. At some point he would see to it that his trail came to an end. He would circle back to camp and be the picture of innocence when Fights with Bears finally returned empty-handed. By that time Andy and Billy should be beyond reach.

Daylight gave Andy his first clear look at the boy. Billy's back showed quirt marks. His face was bruised and swollen.

"Treated you pretty mean, didn't they?" he said.

"They wanted me to cry, and I did, a little. Pretty soon I found out that when I cried they hurt me more, especially that big ugly one. Never could figure out what his name was."

"It'd take you a week to learn his Comanche name. In English you'd call him Fights with Bears."

"He's the one killed Granddaddy Vince. We didn't know where they came from. All at once they were there. After that ugly one killed Granddaddy, I thought he was fixin' to kill me too. But he whipped me and tied me to my pony."

"Figured on makin' a slave out of you, or maybe a warrior if you showed enough fight."

"Is that what happened to you?"

Andy searched his memory. "Pretty much. It was a long time ago."

"You didn't have anybody to come after you and take you back?"

"They tried, but they didn't know where I'd be. I had some notion where I might find you."

"I'm glad. I don't want to live with the Indians. I just want to go home to Mama and Daddy."

"That's where I'm takin' you."

The creek gradually narrowed, its flow shallow and sluggish. Andy suspected by midmorning that it had about run its course. After several hours of traveling in a generally easterly direction he thought it should be safe to turn south. Even assuming the unlikely proposition that Fights with

Bears had seen through the ploy, Andy figured he and Billy had a long lead.

He came to a bend where gravel had accumulated in times of high water. "Here's where we'll quit the water. We won't leave much of a track."

Billy said, "I'm hungry."

Andy handed over a bit of pemmican his sister-in-law had given him. "It may not taste like your mother's cookin', but the hungrier you are the better it gets."

Riding up out of the creek, Andy stopped for a long look around. He did not expect pursuit, but it would be dangerous to take too much for granted. Billy responded in kind to his concern.

"They after us?"

"I don't see a thing, not a buffalo, not even a prairie chicken."

"I wish we had us a prairie chicken right now."

"Eat what I gave you."

He had to fight down a temptation to run the horses. Instinct told him to put as much distance behind them as possible, but they had a long way to go. It would not be done in a day, or even two. The horses had to be spared if they were to go all the way.

Once Andy saw half a dozen horsemen on the horizon. His pulse raced. He dropped down the side of a low hill and quickly dismounted. "Get down, Billy. Maybe they didn't see us."

"Indians? You think they're after us?"

"Probably a huntin' party, after buffalo. But they might settle for us."

"If they're Comanche, can't you talk to them?"

"They might not be Comanche. And if they are, they may be friends of Fights with Bears."

In a little while the riders were gone. Andy found himself sweating more than the afternoon sun would justify. He said, "Some people claim this country is empty. But they never rode across it hopin' not to see anybody."

At dusk Andy saw the light of a fire directly in his path.

"We'd better wait for night, then go around," he said. "No tellin' who that might be."

Billy asked worriedly, "You think they're lookin' for us?"

"Not likely. But in the dark it's hard to tell who your friends are."

They rested the horses until the stars were out. Andy and Billy passed closely enough to smell the smoke of the campfire and of meat roasting over it. Billy said, "I sure am hungry."

Andy was too, but he had learned long ago to ignore hunger when other considerations pressed harder. "We'll get a-plenty to eat at the Monahan farm."

"That's still a long ways off."

Andy heard laughter from the camp, and a voice raised in a shout. He brought Long Red to a stop and listened. He was almost certain he heard some words in English.

"Billy, those may be white men."

"Let's go see."

"Not too fast. We'll work our way up close and make sure." Andy was uneasy. It did not seem reasonable to encounter white men up here in what was essentially a Comanche stronghold. Perhaps they were soldiers, making an extended scout. Or they could be frontier guards like Captain Burmeister's ranger detachment.

He dismounted and led Long Red but motioned for Billy to stay mounted. Billy's horse was too tall and Billy's legs too short for him to mount without help. They halted fifty yards from the firelight. Listening intently, Andy discerned that the men were indeed speaking English.

By himself he might have moved on, hungry or not. But the boy had had little to eat all day except a bit of pemmican, which he had forced down. "Billy, we're goin' to take a chance. Let me do the talkin'."

He led the two horses to within twenty yards of the fire. He shouted, "Hello the camp!"

Instantly several men jumped away from the campfire's reflected light. Someone shouted back, "Who's out there?"

"Just two of us. We're white."

"Show yourselves, but come in slow."

Andy could not see the weapons aimed at him, but he could feel them. He led the horses as near the fire as they would go. He raised both hands.

A voice demanded from the darkness, "Where's your guns?"

"All I've got is a rifle." He raised it so the speaker could see.

A man emerged from the night, into the flickering light. He carried a pistol aimed at Andy. "You talk white enough, but you both look Indian to me."

Andy said, "There's a reason. We got away from a Comanche camp." He looked toward meat roasting over the fire. "The boy is awful hungry. That's why we came in."

The man's suspicions were not yet satisfied. "You got names?"

"He's Billy Gifford. Comanches stole him from his folks a little while back. Mine's Andy Pickard. They took me when I wasn't no bigger than he is."

The man lowered the pistol. "Lift the boy down. You-all help yourselves to some buffalo haunch."

Other men emerged from the darkness. Andy saw six altogether. They were a ragged bunch. If there was a comb or a razor in camp, it must have lain undisturbed for days in the bottom of a saddlebag. One man wore what remained of a Union Army coat. Another wore patched Confederate gray trousers. If nothing else, the outfit appeared to be politically neutral.

The one in gray complained, "Jake, we come to trade with the Comanches. They won't take it kindly, us helpin' these runaways."

Andy said, "They don't need to know about it. Me and Billy sure ain't goin' to tell them."

The complainer said, "Indians got ways of knowin' everything. Claim spirits come and whisper the news in their ear."

Andy started to deny it but could not. Despite his years

in the white man's world and many earnest sermons by Preacher Webb, he had not become convinced that such spirits did not exist. He was almost certain he had felt their presence in certain sacred places.

Nothing about this place struck him as sacred, however. He said, "I doubt there's any spirits watchin' us here."

Jake said, "We've got nothin' against you boys. But you have to understand, we're out here to try and strike a trade with the Indians. We can't afford to stir them up."

"Then just let us have a little somethin' to eat, please sir, and we'll be on our way. Nobody'll ever know we was here."

The trader considered. "No, you're here, and you'd just as well stay all night with us. No tellin' what you might stumble into out in the dark."

Andy was so intent on eating, and on watching Billy wolf down a big chunk of roast, that he paid little attention to the appearance of the camp. But as his appetite began to be satisfied, he looked around. He realized there were no wagons. A string of pack mules was tied to a rope picket line beyond the firelight. The packs lay on the ground in the middle of camp. From what he could see, they contained mostly bottles and jugs.

Whiskey runners, he realized.

The Comancheros had used liquor mainly as a come-along to help them dispose of their trade goods. With these men, liquor *was* the trade goods.

Jake plied him with questions about himself and Billy. He seemed particularly interested when Andy told him about the offer James and Evan had made to the Comanchero about ransoming the boy with horses. The man's eagerness made Andy uneasy. He wished he had not talked so much.

His stomach full, Billy's exhaustion caught up with him. He fell asleep and slumped over onto the ground. From one of the packs Jake brought a blanket and spread it. "The boy's wore out. I expect you are too. You'd best get yourself some sleep."

Andy was tired, but he was suspicious too. He lay beside Billy on the blanket but tried to fight off weariness. He could hear several traders huddling with Jake near the fire, talking in low tones. He heard just enough to sharpen his suspicions, then to stir fear.

Jake suggested that they should take the boys home and demand that the Monahan family give them as many horses as had been proposed to the Comanchero. The smuggler in gray argued if they took the boys back to the band from whom they had escaped, the Indians should be grateful enough to take the whole cargo of whiskey off their hands at an even higher price in horses.

Jake seemed not to have thought of that. "Adcock, you got a good head on your shoulders."

Andy felt chilled at the thought of going back to Fights with Bears. He doubted that Steals the Ponies, tied down by Comanche tradition, could do much to help him or Billy.

The traders made considerable use of their own merchandise in premature celebration of the profit they were to realize. One finished off a bottle and tossed it into the fire. Almost immediately the bottle exploded with a flash of bright flame.

"You damned fool," Adcock yelled, "you could've put somebody's eye out."

The answer was a rough curse. The two men fell into a violent quarrel until Jake put a stop to it. "No more throwin' bottles into the fire, and no more of this damned fightin'. Else I'll knock somebody in the head."

The two fell back, mumbling dire but empty threats until they descended into a blind stupor.

The other traders were not so besotted that they forgot their plan. They made their beds in a protective rough circle around Andy and Billy. Andy was sure this was not to guard them from outside danger but to prevent them from escaping. Any desire for sleep fell away as he contemplated the dark prospect of falling into the hostile hands of Fights with Bears.

He had purposely avoided encountering Indians, but a

false sense of security had brought him willingly into the camp of white men treacherous enough to sell out him and Billy for a price. He dwelt bitterly on the irony of his bad judgment.

He waited until the sounds of even breathing indicated that the men were asleep. He raised up slowly, intending to make his way to the picket line. He would retrieve his and Billy's horses, then come back for Billy.

Jake spoke roughly, "Better do it in your britches, boy. Out in the dark, somebody's apt to blow a hole in you."

Alarmed, then frustrated, Andy muttered, "Wasn't goin' nowhere."

Billy stirred just enough to turn over on the blanket. Andy lay back down beside him, his stomach knotting with worry. His eyes remained open. He tried to think of a way that might allow him to get Billy out of this camp. If they could just reach their horses, they would not have to worry about saddling up. Neither had a saddle. They had been traveling bareback.

He thought about the explosion of the empty bottle. In the dim light of the smoldering campfire he could see the traders' packs of goods. He wondered what would happen to full whiskey bottles or jugs if they fell into the coals. He had had no experience with liquor. It might burn. On the other hand, like water it might simply put the fire out.

If it did burn, it should cause enough excitement to create a momentary diversion. After all, some people called it fire water.

He crawled to the edge of the blanket to see if he would be challenged as before. He was not. Jake seemed to have gone to sleep. Andy crawled a few inches more and paused, expecting someone to stop him. No one did.

He wriggled up against one of the packs which the men had opened earlier and from which they had imbibed freely. He could barely see, but his probing hands found several jugs. They seemed to be of clay. He got his arms around three of them and carefully crawled back, setting them on the ground within reach of the fire. He returned for more.

Before carrying three additional jugs away he uncorked those that remained. The whiskey softly gurgled out onto the canvas.

He waited, listening for an indication that he had disturbed anyone. Then he placed the jugs in the fire and crawled back to the blanket. He pulled the edge of it up and over himself and Billy as a shield against flying pieces of clay in event the jugs reacted as the bottle had.

A cork blew free with a sound like a small-caliber gunshot. Enough whiskey spouted out behind it to ignite a large bluish flame. The jug exploded with a loud pop, the flames blazing high. One by one the other jugs began to blow.

The camp came awake as if a thunderbolt had struck. Confused men shouted and cursed, trying to scramble away from flames that lighted up the night. Coals and firebrands flew in all directions. One landed on the canvas where Andy had spilled several jugs of whiskey. A second blaze flared up, almost as large as the first.

Andy grabbed Billy, who seemed too groggy to grasp what was happening. For the moment the traders were too involved in trying to escape the fires to pay any attention. He ran for the picket line. There the horses and mules reared and kicked, panicked by the noise and the flashes of fire.

Andy plopped Billy up on top of his horse and freed the reins from the picket rope. He untied his own reins and swung up onto Long Red. He wished he could cut the picket line and free the rest of the horses to run away, but Jake had confiscated his knife as well as his rifle. He had neither the time nor the inclination to try to retrieve them.

"Let's see how fast these horses can run," he said.

Billy was still bewildered. He had no inkling of the danger they had been in. But he followed Andy's lead.

"What started all the fire back there?" he wanted to know.

Andy said, "Maybe lightnin'."

"Shouldn't we ought to stay and help put it out?"

"They got all the help they need." Andy looked at the sky to be sure he was traveling in the right direction. He made a little correction and said, "You're doin' just fine, Billy. First thing you know, you'll be home."

For two days Captain Burmeister's rangers had followed the whiskey runners. Rusty and Len Tanner rode in front as trackers, though any man in the group could have read the trail as easily. The contrabanders seemed to have had no concern about being followed. They had no reason to suspect that a sharp-eyed settler had tipped the rangers about their passage.

The farmer had lost family members to raiding Indians. He had told Burmeister, "If there hadn't been half a dozen of them I'd've lit into them runners myself. They don't give a damn about the trouble they cause. They'll get some Indians drunk and cheat them. That'll make the Indians mad, and they'll come raidin' honest folks."

Burmeister had promised, "We will stop them if we catch them before they pass out of Texas."

"How will you know where the border line is at?"

Burmeister's gray mustache had wiggled. "We won't."

The settler had ridden along the first day but felt he had to drop out and return to protect his family. "If you catch them," he said, "bring them back to my farm. We'll throw the biggest barbecue you ever seen. And if you're lookin' for a place to hang them runners, I've got a grove of live-oak trees that ain't bein' used for nothin' but shade."

Burmeister had promised to remember the offer.

Tanner was a little bothered. "The thought of hangin' always kind of chokes me up," he told Rusty. "The captain wouldn't really do that, would he?"

Rusty shook his head. "I don't think the law calls for hangin' whiskey smugglers. They'll just get room and board awhile at the state penitentiary."

"Not too much room, I hope, and not much board."

Most of this second day Tanner had said so little that Rusty had begun to be concerned about him. Ordinarily Tanner seldom gave his jaw much rest. If a bird flew in front of him he would speculate for half an hour on what kind it was, what it ate and what its mating habits were.

Rusty asked him, "You feelin' all right?"

"Nothin' wrong with me. It's you I been worried about."

"Why me?"

"Because you ain't said nothin' about Andy. Yesterday and today I ain't heard you mention his name."

"What can I say that I haven't already said? God only knows where he is or what he's doin'." Rusty bit down on the words and did not finish speaking all of his thought. If he's not been killed already . . .

Tanner said, "After we catch up to these runners, maybe me and you ought to take leave and go huntin' him."

"You have any idea how much country we might have to cover? We could ride 'til our whiskers got tangled in our stirrups and still never find him."

Rusty wished Tanner would drop the subject.

But Tanner always had another word, or several. "Better than waitin', wonderin'. Think about it anyway."

Rusty *had* been thinking about it. He simply saw no solution. The two of them, searching aimlessly across an impossibly broad, open land neither of them knew . . . If the Indians didn't get them, hunger and thirst would.

Tanner went into another long, unaccustomed silence. He broke it suddenly. "Looky yonder." He pulled on his reins. "Way up there. Is that buffalo, or is it horses?"

Rusty squinted against the sun's glare on the waving brown grass. "Looks to me like two horses. Can't tell whether they're comin' or goin'."

Tanner studied them a minute. "I believe they're comin' this way. Must be Indians."

"Or a couple of those whiskey runners comin' back." Rusty pulled his horse around. "We better tell the captain."

Burmeister had halted his detail and was waiting. Rusty told him, "We see two horseback riders comin' this way. Our guess is that they're Indians."

"Two of them only?"

"They could be scoutin' for a larger bunch."

Rusty could see momentary conflict in Burmeister's eyes. This mission had been intended to overtake whiskey runners, but stopping incursion by Indian raiders was of greater importance. Burmeister pointed to a shallow ravine carved by runoff water after rare hard rains. "We hide. We wait."

The men followed him.

Rusty and Tanner crawled up over the edge and lay on their bellies so they could see. Rusty caught an occasional glimpse of the riders as they came over a rise, then lost them as they dropped to lower ground. "Still comin' toward us," he said.

Tanner nodded. "Sure look like Indians to me. A little one and a big one." He brought up his rifle but did not aim.

Rusty said, "Let's not be quick to shoot. If they're scoutin', there's no tellin' how far out front they are and how big of a bunch may be followin' after them."

Sweat seeped from beneath Rusty's hat band and ran down to burn his eyes. He wiped away what he could and blinked away the rest. "Does somethin' about that bigger one look familiar to you, Len?"

"He sets his horse like Andy."

Rusty looked again, then gave a glad shout. "It *is* Andy, and he's got Billy with him!" He turned and yelled at the men in the ravine, "It's our boys. Don't anybody shoot."

Rusty scrambled to his feet. The two riders stopped abruptly and seemed about to turn back. Tanner said, "They don't know who we are." He took off his hat and waved it. "Andy! Billy! It's us."

The two riders hesitated a little longer, then seemed satisfied. They set their horses into a long trot. Andy jumped to the ground and ran to throw his arms around Rusty. Tears of relief rolled down his face, leaving tracks in the dust. Tanner reached up, lifted Billy from his horse's back and hugged him.

"Young'un," he declared, "we was afraid we'd never see you again."

"Andy found me," Billy said. "Where's Mama? Where's Daddy?"

Rusty hugged him when Tanner got through. "They're at home. We'll be takin' you to them."

Both boys were scratched as if they had ridden through brush. Billy was badly sunburned, his lips blistered and swollen. Tanner handed him a canteen. The boy drank so desperately that Tanner had to take the water back from him. "Easy, Billy. Not all at once."

Andy watched Burmeister and the rangers ride up out of the ravine. He turned and glanced worriedly at the trail over which he and Billy had come. "We're bein' chased. Last time I saw them was maybe half an hour ago."

"Comanches?"

"No, whiskey merchants. They figured on tradin' me and Billy back to the Indians for a lot of horses. We got away from them, but they must still figure we're worth somethin'. They've been on our trail."

Burmeister came up in time to hear the last of it. He asked only one question. "How many are they?"

"Six, if none of them got trampled in the excitement."

"There was excitement?"

"I managed to put some of their whiskey jugs into the fire. Caused a hell of a commotion. I never knew the stuff would burn like that."

Burmeister said, "That is good to consider if ever you are tempted to drink it." He turned back to the task at hand.

"You and the boy could help us capture those *verdammten*. Do you object if we make of you bait?"

Andy frowned. "I'll do whatever you want me to, but leave Billy out of it. He's wore out. He's had too many scares already for a boy his age."

Burmeister accepted. "We want them to think you are too tired to go on. When they come close we will move up and . . ." He made a quick motion as if catching a bug in his hand.

Andy said, "I won't have to play at bein' tired. I'm wore to a frazzle."

Rusty felt himself swelling with pride. "Andy, for bringin' Billy back, the Monahans would let you live on their farm the rest of your life and never do a lick of work."

"All I want is for them to forgive me. And then I'd like to forgive myself."

Tanner interrupted. "It's hard to tell through the heat waves, but I think I see somethin' to the north."

Burmeister signaled the rangers to drop back out of sight. Rusty admonished Andy, "Be careful. If they act like they're fixin' to shoot, you scoot down into the ravine."

"They ain't goin' to shoot me. They'd rather sell me and watch a Comanche do it."

Rusty retreated but stayed in a shallow part of the ravine so he could see over the edge. He had checked his rifle a couple of times before he had identified Andy and Billy. He checked it again.

The riders gradually materialized out of the dancing heat. He counted four. Andy had said there were six. That gave the rangers excellent odds.

The longer Rusty watched them, the more his anger built. The idea of their being depraved enough to sell two boys to the Indians . . . he almost hoped they would put up a fight. He felt that he could kill all four without a twinge of conscience.

The riders were two hundred yards away, then one hundred. Rusty whispered, "Andy, come on down from there."

Andy sat hunched as if exhausted, as if he did not care

whether he was caught or not. He waited until the men were fifty yards away before he acknowledged them. He stood his ground until they were within twenty yards. Then he put his mount into a hard trot down into the ravine.

Burmeister shouted an order. "Go get them boogers."

The rangers swarmed out of the ravine, encircling the whiskey runners before they had a chance to react. One dressed in Confederate gray foolishly fired at Burmeister but missed. A ranger shot him out of the saddle. The other men raised their hands.

One demanded, "What in the hell is this?"

Burmeister said, "What the hell it is, you are under arrest for running whiskey."

"We got no whiskey on us."

Rusty said, "But you did have. We've got two witnesses that say so."

Andy rode up out of the ravine. He said, "Howdy, Jake. How did you like the fireworks?"

Jake muttered, "You damned hoodoo. I ought to've cut your throat the minute you rode into camp."

"But then you couldn't have sold me to the Indians."

Burmeister said to the smuggler leader, "You were six men. Now you are four. Where are the other two?"

Jake did not answer.

Andy guessed, "They likely stayed to watch what was left of the whiskey while these came after me and Billy."

Tanner dismounted and examined the fallen man. Burmeister leaned from his saddle. "He is dead?"

Tanner nodded. "He showed damned poor judgment for a man who wasn't no better shot."

Andy had no sympathy. "He's the one who first said they ought to trade me and Billy for horses."

Burmeister said, "The weather is warm. He will not keep well." He turned to the smuggler named Jake. "He was your man. You will bury him here."

Jake scowled. "I don't see no shovel."

Burmeister pointed to a bend in the ravine where runoff

water had deposited a layer of stones. "Rocks will cover him finely enough."

The burying went slowly because the three smugglers had to carry the stones an armload at a time to the top of the ravine. Their shirts were soon soaked with sweat.

Rusty asked the captain, "Ought we to go back and find them other two?"

"We have these. Indians will get the rest perhaps. Better we get the little boy home to his family."

Tanner agreed. "I want to be there and see the look on his mama's face."

Rusty thought of Geneva's despair and the futility he had felt in any effort to comfort her. The reunion would be a joyous moment for the Monahans. He knew he would stand back and watch in lonely silence. He was not part of the family, not that one or any other.

The afternoon was wearing down when Burmeister judged the grave to be covered well enough. He asked Jake, "Do you wish to say words over your friend?"

Jake's hands were rough and bleeding from handling the stones. He grunted. "Ain't no use. He can't hear them."

Burmeister removed his hat. "But the Lord can, so I will speak to Him." He looked up. "Lord, we send Thy way this day a lowly sinner who lost his way. Thou may send him to Heaven or to Hell, it is for Thee to judge. We are done with him. Amen." He turned. "Let us be gone from this place."

They were a couple of miles from the Monahan farm when James and Macy burst suddenly and unexpectedly from a grove of trees. Half the rangers raised guns before they recognized that the riders presented no threat.

James spurred up, face flushed with excitement. "You found Billy!" He reached out and threw both arms around the surprised boy. His voice was jubilant. "There'll be a big celebration tonight."

Burmeister said, "And time for a bit of prayer, I would hope."

James nodded vigorously. "Preacher Webb will see to that. I swear, it was lookin' like we'd have to bury half the family, startin' with Billy's mama. How'd you-all get him back?"

Rusty said, "Andy found him."

James turned toward Andy. "I reckon it takes an Indian to know where to look. No offense meant."

Rusty said, "The way you came bustin' out of the timber, we could've shot you."

James's excitement diminished. "We didn't know at first but what you-all might be Indians. We been out lookin' for sign."

Burmeister asked, "You have seen Indians?"

"One, for sure. He showed up yesterday evenin', watchin' the houses. We've seen him two or three times, but when we go out lookin' for him we can't find him. We figure he's scoutin' us for a war party."

Andy swallowed hard, his expression grim. "Fights with Bears. He knew where he found Billy. He knew we'd bring him back here. Most likely he's waitin' to try and grab him again."

Rusty doubted. "He ought to know Billy's goin' to be guarded extra heavy. He could steal some other boy a lot easier."

"Fights with Bears had him and lost him. That done hurt to his pride. He doesn't want to settle for some other boy. He wants Billy back."

James declared, "Well, he ain't goin' to get him, not as long as there's a Monahan breathin'."

James seemed for the first time to notice the three prisoners, their hands tied to their saddles.

Tanner explained the circumstances. He said, "Maybe the Comanches would settle for a few scalps instead of Billy. Here's three they can have."

The smuggler Jake reacted with fear. "You wouldn't do that to a white man. Would you?"

Tanner kept a straight face. "You were fixin' to let them have two white boys."

Approaching the corrals, Rusty saw many horses penned there. He assumed that James and the others had gathered as many as they could find and brought them here where they could be kept under guard. He saw several of the Monahans' neighbors gathered at the barn. It appeared that much of the community had come together for mutual protection.

Josie was the first family member to see the procession coming. She stood in front of the main house, shading her eyes. She turned and shouted something, then ran to the house in which Geneva and Evan lived. In a moment Geneva rushed out the door, holding her little girl in her arms. Josie took the girl from her so Geneva could run toward her son.

"Billy! Billy!" she cried.

Billy slid down from his horse. It was a long way to the ground, and he went to his knees. He was instantly on his feet and running to meet his mother.

Dust had gotten into Rusty's eyes and made them burn. He looked away.

In a minute the Monahans were all gathered around Billy. Clemmie hugged him, then he was passed to Josie and Alice and Preacher Webb. The boy's father had been in the corral among the horses. He vaulted over a fence and went running to grab his son.

Face shining with tears, Clemmie walked forward to meet Rusty and Burmeister and the others. "Men," she said, her voice near breaking, "there ain't words enough . . ."

Burmeister bowed without leaving the saddle. "Madam, it is to this young man that all thanks should go." He nodded toward Andy. "He found him and brought him out."

Clemmie looked up. "Get down off of that horse, Andy Pickard." Her tone of voice was commanding.

Sheepishly Andy complied, looking as if he dreaded a whipping. Clemmie threw her arms around him and embraced him so tightly Rusty half expected to hear Andy's ribs crack. For a small woman, she had always been amazingly strong.

"God bless you, Andy," she declared.

He stammered, "I'm . . . I'm sorry about your daddy."

"It was God's doin', not yours or mine. We can't fault the Lord for doin' His will."

Haltingly Andy said, "I got his watch back for you."

He slipped the loop over his head and handed her the silver timepiece. Reverently she pressed it to her cheek. "Bless you, Andy." She cleared her throat and turned toward the larger group of horsemen. "You-all must be tired and thirsty and hungry. Come on up to the house. We'll fix you a celebration supper."

Burmeister dismounted and touched the brim of his hat. "In a while, madam. First we must see to the horses."

Geneva released Billy only long enough for the other family members to hug him again, then she clasped him as if she never intended to let him go. She leaned her head against her husband's shoulder and cried.

Rusty wanted to go to her but could not. Instead, Josie came and put her arms around him. "It's a happy day you've brought us, Rusty."

He found it hard to speak. "It was Andy's doin'."

"Billy told us a little. If it hadn't been for you and the rangers, Andy and Billy might not've gotten home. I don't know how Geneva could've lived. It's a bitter thing to lose family."

"I can imagine."

"You've been a member of this family for a long time, Rusty, whether you've realized it or not. And so will Andy be from now on. It takes more than just blood to make a family. It takes love."

She tiptoed to kiss him on his bewhiskered cheek. Warmth rushed into his face.

He said, "Maybe you shouldn't do that out here in the sight of God and everybody."

"I'll do it again, Rusty Shannon, whenever I want to. But I'll wait 'til you get rid of those whiskers."

Preacher Webb led the family and everyone else within hearing in a prayer of thanksgiving for Billy's deliverance. "Lord, we thank Thee mightily for the deliverance of this child who was lost. And we beseech Thy blessings on the lad who brought him back to us, for in some ways he is also a lost soul, seeking his way."

Andy appeared overwhelmed. Rusty tried to ease his discomfort. "I know you've been blamin' yourself, but nobody else feels that way. You heard what Clemmie said."

"You don't suppose she just said that to make me feel better?"

"Clemmie Monahan never says anything she doesn't mean."

Andy had long since lost his shirt. Josie fetched him one that belonged to James. Bearing patches on the elbows, it draped around him like a tent. The sleeves extended almost to the tips of his fingers. "At least it covers you up decent," she said.

When she was gone Andy rolled the sleeves up past his wrists. Ruefully he said, "I don't guess folks will ever get used to the Indian side of me."

Rusty said, "Main thing is that *you* know who you are."

"But I don't. I felt out of place when I was up there amongst the Comanches. I feel out of place here. Maybe I don't fit anywhere."

Though he was offered any bed in the house, Andy chose to sleep on the ground in the rangers' camp near the barn. Rusty knew he felt suffocated by all the attention from the Monahans and their neighbors who had gathered in anticipation of an Indian raid. The rangers at least did not fawn over him.

Rusty was awakened by a shout of alarm. The sun was just beginning to rise. A night guard shouted again. "Everybody up. Indians comin'!"

Rusty cast off his blanket and grabbed for his boots, the only thing he had taken off the night before. He grasped his rifle and jumped to his feet. The night guard pointed.

In the dawn's rosy glow Rusty saw more than a dozen

Comanches standing their horses in a rough line. A single warrior moved out twenty yards in front of the others. He gestured with a bow and shouted words Rusty did not understand. He asked, "Andy, do you know what he's sayin'?"

Andy listened, his face grim. He sucked in a deep breath and slowly let it go. "He's makin' a challenge."

"A challenge?"

"That's Fights with Bears. He's the one who had Billy."

"Well, he's not gettin' him back. Every last man here would die before they take that boy again."

Andy shook his head. "He's not askin' for Billy. He's askin' for me."

"You?"

"I shamed him. I stole Billy right out from under him while he was asleep. It's a matter of pride."

"You ain't goin' out there to him."

Andy picked up the rifle he had recovered from the smugglers. He checked the load. "If I don't they'll charge down on this place."

"We've got men and guns enough to whip them."

"But what'll it cost? I've got people on both sides. I don't want to see anybody dead."

"That Indian wants to see *you* dead."

"Maybe he'll settle for somethin' less." Andy walked toward the lone warrior, the rifle cradled in his arms.

Rusty shouted, "For God's sake come back here."

Andy kept walking. He focused his main attention on Fights with Bears, but he tried to watch the line of Comanches to the rear as well. If they decided to rush him he would have no chance. But Bears was Andy's immediate concern. The rest were likely to take their cue from him. Bears had no firearm that Andy could see. He held a lance and had a bow and a quiver of arrows slung over his shoulder.

Andy had the advantage. His rifle was loaded and cocked. He stopped twenty feet short of the horseman. He felt cold sweat on his forehead and hoped Bears could not see it. He said, "I am the one you asked for."

Bears looked at the rifle. "You have come armed."

"You are armed too." The lance had a sharp-looking flint point, fashioned for killing buffalo. Bears could drive it all the way through Andy's body if he so chose.

Bears's eyes were fierce. "You stole the boy that belonged to me."

"He never did belong to you. He belongs to his mother and father."

"I won him in battle."

"It was no battle. You killed a helpless old man and took the boy. They had no chance."

"No matter. He was mine. You stole him from me. You owe me something."

"A fight?" Andy raised the muzzle of the rifle an inch. "I could kill you before you could move."

"My warriors would kill you before you drew another breath."

"And there are enough white men at this place to kill them all. Who would be the winner? Not your warriors. Not you or me."

Bears tried to show defiance, but his eyes reflected frustration. "You have a good fighting spirit. I would take you in place of the boy."

"I would never be accepted. I have killed one of The People. I am told that the one who died was a brother to your wives. They would gladly hack me to pieces."

Bears's mouth twisted as he contemplated the impasse. "It is a matter of honor. I must satisfy my honor."

"Perhaps you would like to have my scalp."

That surprised and puzzled the Comanche.

Andy said, "Here, I will give it to you." Laying down his rifle, he drew his knife. He reached up for one of his braids, cut it off and tossed it. Bears almost dropped his lance in grabbing for it. Andy cut off the other and threw it. Bears missed it but picked it up from the ground with the point of his lance.

Andy retrieved his rifle. "You can have a scalp dance over those."

For a moment Bears seemed perplexed. Then he raised the braids high over his head and gave a loud, victorious whoop. The warriors behind him took up the cry. Bears rode slowly forward, lowering the lance.

The rifle felt slick in Andy's sweaty hands. He pointed its muzzle at Bears, his finger on the trigger. One twitch and the Comanche would be dead. The battle would be on.

Bears touched a flat side of the lance point against Andy's arm. Then he wheeled his horse around and set it into a long trot back toward the waiting warriors. As he passed them, shouting and holding the braids high, they turned and followed him away.

Andy had held his breath. Lungs burning, he gasped for air and allowed himself to wipe a sleeve across his forehead. The cuff came down over his hand.

Rusty hurried out to his side. "You all right?"

"I'm not bleedin', if that's what you mean."

"I thought he meant to kill you."

"He knew I'd take him with me. He didn't want me *that* bad. So he accepted a piece of my scalp and counted coup. That was enough to patch up his pride."

"He's liable to keep tryin' to get you."

"I doubt it. Him and his wives will make medicine with those braids. They'll try to cast spells and send dark spirits after me. But I think that'll be all of it."

The Indians were quickly fading from sight. Rusty looked relieved. "You afraid of dark spirits?"

"I wish I could say I'm not, but there's still a part of me that wonders."

"Don't worry. We'll sic Preacher Webb onto them."

· 19 ·

By the next day the neighbors were dispersing back to their own homes, feeling that at least for a time the Indian threat was over. A courier arrived looking for Captain Burmeister. He handed the officer an envelope. "You're hard to find," he said. "Been huntin' you for a week."

"I have been busy for a week, and much more." Burmeister tore the edge from the envelope and unfolded the letter, frowning as he read. Finished, he called his rangers around him. "It is from the governor's office that I have received this. The money is gone. We are to disband."

Tanner commented, "I didn't figure we'd get paid anyhow."

Rusty asked, "What'll you do now, Captain?"

"The letter says there is other work for me. I am to become a judge."

"That's better than ridin' all over hell and gone chasin' Indians and whiskey runners."

"Perhaps." The captain folded the letter and put it in his shirt pocket. "I am no longer so young. But I liked it, to be a ranger again even for just a little while. What will you do, Private Shannon?"

"Go back home. I've some unfinished business there."

"You will be subject to arrest if you go there."

"I'm subject to arrest anywhere. Even here, if the Oldham brothers take a notion to come for me again, or to send
somebody. I can't go on forever with a warrant hangin'
over my head. I want to get things straightened out, whatever it takes."

Burmeister said, "All I can give you is a wish for good
luck. I have not even the money to pay you for the time
you have served."

"I knew that when I joined up. It's always been that way
with the rangers. One day of side meat and a month of
sowbelly."

Burmeister nodded agreement. "If a character witness
you need, send for me. I will gladly serve."

Rusty knew Burmeister's record as a Union officer during the war would give his word extra weight in a reconstruction court. Especially if he were a judge. "I'd be much
obliged."

Josie grasped both of Rusty's hands when he told her.
She said, "You have friends here who would never let the
state police take you away. Stay. The government is bound
to change sooner or later."

"I can't keep leanin' on my friends. I've got to find some
way to settle this. I have to try to get back what's mine."

"I've told you before, it doesn't matter to me whether
you have anything or not."

"It matters to me. I've got to set things right."

"Even if it means goin' to jail?"

"Even that."

She leaned her head against his chest. "All right," she
said reluctantly. "I'll keep on waitin'."

Holding her hands, he stepped back to look at her. "Josie,
you know I get strong feelin's when I'm with you. For a
long time I wasn't sure if they were really for you or if
they were for somebody else."

"You mean Geneva?"

He did not answer. He did not have to.

She said, "She's got a life of her own, a husband and two little ones. She's out of your reach. But I'm not. I'm here. All you have to do is ask me."

"I know. But I don't have a right to ask you so long as I've got nothin' to offer."

"I don't need anything. I'd live in a tent. I'd live in a dugout if it was with you. It wouldn't bother me."

"It would bother *me*. I couldn't do it."

She looked up at him, eyes glistening. "Then go. Do what you have to. I'll be here whenever you come back."

Something was different about Andy. Rusty puzzled over it a minute, then realized what it was.

"What did you do to your hair?" he asked.

Andy said, "Alice cut it for me. It looked ragged with the braids hacked off."

"You don't look much like a Comanche anymore."

Soberly Andy said, "My brother saw a vision. It told him the old ways are almost gone. He said I have to walk the white man's road whether I want to or not."

"Think you can?"

"He didn't say I'd like it. He said I don't have a choice."

Rusty made a sweeping motion with his arm. "You like this place and the Monahans, don't you?"

"They're good people. But I don't want to stay here while you and Len go back home."

"There's no tellin' what we may run into."

"But it's home—at least the nearest thing to home that I have."

"I may end up in jail."

"Me and Tanner will bust you out."

Rusty smiled. "Aidin' and abettin' a fugitive is what caused all this trouble in the first place."

"So I ought to be gettin' pretty good at it."

* * *

Rusty ached to see the farm where he had spent the larger part of his life, but he knew he must defer that visit until he learned how things stood with him and reconstruction law. His first destination, then, was the Tom Blessing farm.

He and Andy and Tanner tried to be vigilant, but their vigilance was compromised by the excitement of nearing home. Consequently they almost ran into an armed band of riders. Just in time they dropped into a dry creek bed and dismounted to avoid being seen.

"Soldiers?" Rusty asked.

Andy's eyesight was the keenest. He said, "No, they ain't wearin' uniforms."

Tanner said, "State police. They got the look of high authority and meanness. Maybe they're huntin' for you, Rusty."

"I wouldn't think so. The Oldhams don't know but what I'm still at the Monahans'. But that bunch is sure on the hunt for somebody."

Tanner grimaced. "I'd hate to be the one they're after. They look serious enough to shoot him on sight."

Rusty added, "Then claim he tried to get away."

The three remained in the creek bed until the posse passed out of sight. Later they cautiously dismounted in timber and watched the Tom Blessing place for a while before showing themselves. No one was working in the fields. The only sign of life Rusty saw was a thin rise of smoke from the cabin's chimney.

He said, "No sign of trouble, and I don't want to stay here 'til dark." He mounted and moved his horse out into the open. Andy and Tanner followed.

A dog announced their coming. Tom Blessing's wife came to the edge of the dog run and held her hand over her eyes. When Rusty hesitated fifty yards out, she shouted, "It's all right. Come on in."

Rusty dismounted and took off his hat. "Kind of spooked us a little, not seein' Tom or Shanty or anybody."

She said, "They're over at Shanty's place. Our boys too. They're puttin' up a new cabin for him."

"Takin' a chance, aren't they? Some of the hotheads around here will burn it down like before."

"Not likely. Tom and our boys paid a visit to Fowler Gaskin and everybody else they thought might have such notions. Put the fear of God into them. Ain't heard a word out of Fowler since, nor anybody else."

"What about Jeremiah Brackett and his son, Farley?"

"Farley's got himself in real bad trouble. He's run the law ragged tryin' to catch him, so they've been campin' on his daddy's doorstep. The old man's got too much grief on his plate to bedevil Shanty or anybody else."

Rusty and the others watered their horses. He told Mrs. Blessing, "We'll ride on over to Shanty's. I need to talk to Tom."

She warned, "Keep a sharp eye out for the Oldhams and their state police. They came back mighty sore over not bein' able to arrest you. Tom says Buddy's gone a little crazy."

"He always did seem about three aces shy of a full deck. I'll watch out for him."

Shanty's crop of corn had been cut and set up in shocks across the field. His dog came trotting out to meet the visitors. Hearing him bark, Shanty put aside an ax with which he had been trimming a log. He stared a moment until he was sure, then hobbled toward Rusty. Beyond him Rusty could see that the cabin walls were almost finished.

"Mr. Rusty," Shanty shouted, "welcome home. And you, Mr. Tanner, and Andy."

Rusty stepped down and grasped Shanty's hand. "It's good to see you. You been gettin' along all right?"

"Fine as frog hair. I wisht you'd look at the cabin the Blessings are helpin' me build. It'll be bigger than the old one was."

"I'm glad, Shanty."

"It'll feel good to stay at my own place and take care of my own land, just me and my old dog. Hope it don't rain before we get done."

Rusty saw no sign of a rain cloud. "Doesn't appear likely."

Shanty's enthusiasm gave way to concern. "You looked as much dead as alive last time we seen you."

"I've healed up pretty good. Don't have a lot of strength in that shoulder, but it'll get better."

"Them Oldhams don't mean to just wound you in the shoulder next time. They'll aim for your heart."

Tom Blessing strode out to greet Rusty and the others. He still had a crushing handshake. "Been expectin' you," he said, "even though I hoped you wouldn't come. Things have turned off real mean around here."

"I thought they already were."

"They've got worse. The Oldhams and a bunch of state police made a wild sashay after Farley Brackett. He shot one of them dead and wounded two more before he got away."

"I don't suppose Buddy or Clyde were hit."

"No such luck. Now there's hell to pay. Governor Davis is threatenin' martial law."

"Maybe they're too busy to be worryin' about me."

"The Oldhams ain't forgot you. They've added some new charges. Fleein' to avoid prosecution, refusal to submit to arrest. Also attempted murder. They claim you fired on Clyde up at the Monahan place."

Tanner protested, "That was me, not Rusty."

"Doesn't matter. They say it was Rusty, and the carpet-bag judge we've got will take their word for it. He's hell on any old rebel that gets brought before his bench."

Rusty said, "I've thought some about givin' myself up. Not to the Oldhams but to the court."

"You'd better get over that notion. The judge would turn you over to the Oldhams anyway. Remember what they did to you the last time."

Rusty rubbed his shoulder. "What can I do?"

"Smart thing would be to quit this part of the country and not show yourself again 'til the government changes.

It will, when all the old Texans finally get a chance to vote."

"But Clyde Oldham stole my farm. I want it back."

"Be patient. The land ain't goin' anywhere."

Rusty, Tanner and Andy pitched in to help with the cabin raising. They finished the walls a while before sundown. Tom Blessing stepped back to gaze on the work, smiling in satisfaction. "Me and the boys all got our chores to see after before dark. We'll start on the roof in the mornin'."

Shanty bowed to all of them in the subservient manner cultivated during long years of slavery. "I'm much obliged to all of you." He stood beside Rusty as the Blessings rode away. He said, "I ain't got no money, but I've got somethin' better. I've got friends."

Rusty nodded. "That's somethin' you couldn't buy if you had all the money in the world. But I'm afraid you've still got some enemies too."

"Been a long time since they bothered me. Mr. Tom and his boys put the Indian sign on them, and lately the state police been chasin' them around some too. They ain't had time to mess with old Shanty." He walked to an outdoor fire pit and stirred the coals until they glowed, then added small pieces of dry wood to coax a flame. "You-all are goin' to stay the night here, ain't you?"

Rusty said, "I'm anxious to take a look at my own place."

Shanty warned, "You'll be safer stayin'. Them police don't mess around here, but the Oldhams'll expect you to show up at your farm sooner or later."

Rusty reconsidered. "We'll impose on your hospitality, then. But it'd be a good idea if we sleep a little ways out yonder, just in case."

Shanty said, "That old dog of mine'll warn you if anybody comes snoopin' around. He don't let nothin' bigger than a rabbit come close without he raises a ruckus."

Andy had told Rusty about the night Fowler Gaskin broke into the smokehouse without arousing the dog. But he said, "He's a good one, all right."

Shanty said, "Hope you-all like catfish. I caught me a big one down in that deep hole."

Tanner grinned. "Sounds like a feast to me."

They sat around the campfire after a supper of catfish and cornbread. Rusty recounted Andy's rescue of Billy. Shanty enlarged on what Tom Blessing had told about Farley Brackett's scrap with the state police. "They thought they had him, but it was the other way around. Folks say Clyde Oldham turned tail and run like a scalded dog. Buddy stayed 'til he was out of cartridges. Got to give him credit for guts. He's just shy on sense."

Shanty punched at the fire. "Ain't hardly nobody likes the Oldhams except a few people in the courthouse. They help one another steal everything that ain't nailed down tight."

Tanner said, "There'll be a big comeuppance someday."

Eventually Shanty yawned. The day's work had been hard. He said, "Tonight I'm goin' to sleep in my own house."

Tanner pointed out, "It's got no roof yet."

"Don't matter. It's got walls, so I'll be sleepin' indoors."

Rusty was up long before daylight. He roused Andy and Tanner from their blankets. "We don't want to ride up to the farm in broad daylight. Let's go while it's still dark."

He knew where the Oldhams had posted guards in the timber along the river to watch his farm when they had been looking for him before. He thought he might find some of them there, but a careful search turned up no one. He said, "If it was a good place for them to watch from, I reckon it'll do for us. Let's wait here a spell and see if there's any sign of life."

He watched the chimney in particular. If anyone was staying in the cabin, there should soon be smoke. But none appeared.

As the sun came up and spilled strong morning light across the farm, he could see the field and the garden. He winced in disappointment. "There's weeds out there tall as the corn. And that corn ought to've already been cut. It's dryin' up."

Tanner pointed out, "Clyde and Buddy didn't take this place because they wanted to farm it. They took it to spite you."

After an hour he still saw no sign that anyone was in or around the cabin. Andy volunteered, "I'll go see for sure. Nobody's lookin' for me."

Tanner said, "Even if they was, they wouldn't know you. You don't look Indian anymore with your hair cut."

Andy rode up to the cabin, circling it first, then entering. Shortly he reappeared and waved for Rusty and Tanner to come on. He waited for them at the dog run. "Rusty," he said, "you won't like what you see. It's a boar's nest in there."

Rusty knew Tom Blessing had hauled away everything that could be moved so the Oldhams would not get it. Someone had brought in a broken-backed table and a couple of wooden boxes that evidently served in place of chairs. Two iron pots and a tin bucket sat on the cold hearth, smelling of spoiled meat, grease, and congealed beans. Coffee grounds had been spilled across the floor between the hearth and the table. Two tin plates held remnants of the last meal someone had eaten here. A piece of cornbread had molded almost to the color of gray ash.

Tanner said, "Somebody's mother sure didn't teach them much."

Rusty replied, "Looks like the time I was gone to the rangers and Fowler Gaskin moved in. Took lye soap and lots of water to get the stink out."

Andy said, "We can throw all this stuff away and at least sweep out a little." He looked for a broom but did not find one.

Rusty said, "Never mind. It'd just tell the Oldhams that somebody had been here. They'd figure it was me." He felt resentful, remembering how hard Mother Dora had worked to keep the cabin clean. "Let's shut the door behind us and leave things the way they are. I've got a visit to make."

Tanner said, "There ain't nobody left to see."

Rusty did not answer him. He rode to the small rock-fenced plot that served as the Shannon family cemetery. Tanner and Andy trailed. Stepping down from the saddle, Rusty handed the reins to Andy and opened the wooden gate. He stopped before the stone markers and took off his hat. For a long time he stood, staring, remembering.

Andy's voice broke into his consciousness. "Rusty, there's a rider comin' this way. We'd better be movin' down to the timber."

Rusty tried to see him but could not. Andy's eyes were sharper than his own. He hoped they were sharper than those of the oncoming horseman. Turning again to the stones, he said, "Daddy Mike, Mother Dora, they've stole this place from us for now. But I swear to you we'll get it back."

From their place of concealment Rusty and the others watched the horseman ride up to the cabin and draw a bucket of water from the well. After a fast drink he moved on. Andy was the first to identify him. "Farley Brackett."

Tanner said, "He's sure pushin' on them bridle reins."

Andy pointed. "He's got reason. Looky yonder."

Half a dozen horsemen followed along in Brackett's tracks. Rusty asked, "Do they look like soldiers?"

Andy squinted. "State police would be my guess. They're after Farley."

Tanner observed, "Don't look like they're really wantin' to get close to him. They're probably thinkin' about the last time they did it."

Andy said, "The Oldham brothers must be with them. I see a man with just one arm."

Rusty pulled the skin at the corners of his eyes to sharpen his vision. "That's Buddy, all right, and Clyde just behind him."

Tanner said, "Sounds like Clyde. If there's to be any shootin', he'll be behind somebody." He looked down at his rifle but did not reach for it. "I believe I could pick off both of them from here. Nobody would ever know who done it."

Rusty replied, "Somebody else would take up the warrant they put out against me. And I need them alive if I'm ever to get my farm back. Dead men don't sign deeds."

Tanner shrugged. "If Farley had any brains, he'd be half-way to California by now instead of wearin' out posses around here. And that's what you ought to do, Rusty, get away 'til Texas has a new government."

"No tellin' how long that'll be."

They remained hidden in the timber by the river until dusk, then made their way back to Shanty's farm. The dog greeted them two hundred yards from the cabin and barked at them the rest of the way in.

Rusty did not want to cause anxiety to Shanty. He shouted, "It's just us. We're comin' in."

The rising moon revealed that the roof had been added during the day and partially shingled. Rusty felt a fleeting guilt for not having remained here to help with the work.

Shanty emerged from the darkness of the log walls. "You-all come on in. I'll stir up the fire and fix you somethin' to eat."

"We brought venison." Rusty had decided to take a chance and shoot a deer so they would not burden Shanty's food supply. He dismounted and eased the carcass down from Alamo's back.

The dog sniffed eagerly at it. Shanty shooed him away. "You'll get your share by and by. Git!" He carried the deer to a crude bench set beside what would be the front door when the cabin was finished. He fetched a butcher knife and cut a generous portion of backstrap.

He asked Rusty, "Get a look at your farm?"

"Doesn't appear like anybody's done a lick of work. They're lettin' the crops go."

"I know. And after all the sweat we put in plowin' and plantin'. The Lord can't abide slothful ways. He'll sooner or later fix them Oldham boys."

Tanner declared, "But He generally needs some help. That's what I keep tryin' to tell Rusty."

Shanty said, "If the Lord needs help, it'll come. He'll send out a call, and the right man will hear. He's got mysterious ways."

Rusty had been asleep a short time when the dog set up a racket. From out in the darkness someone yelled, "Hello the house!"

Shanty's voice answered from one of the open windows that as yet had no glass. "Who's out yonder?"

"Farley Brackett. All right if I come in?"

"Come ahead. Ain't no police here."

Rusty sensed reluctance in Shanty's voice. Neither Farley nor his father had shown him any respect.

Farley led his horse up to the dying embers of Shanty's outdoor fire. "You got anything a starved-out man could eat? Them state police been houndin' me so bad I ain't et since the day before yesterday."

Rusty said, "There's still some venison."

Farley whirled in surprise, drawing his pistol. "Who in the hell . . ."

"Rusty Shannon. You don't need the gun."

Farley holstered the weapon. "I come mighty close to shootin' you. Ain't good manners to walk up behind a man in the dark. Bad for the health, too."

"We saw you stop for a drink of water at my place. Saw the posse that was after you."

"They ain't really wantin' to catch me and have an open fight, especially Clyde Oldham. He wants to dry-gulch me where I wouldn't have a chance."

"Why don't you hightail it for Mexico, or maybe Arizona?"

"Been wantin' to, but my pockets are empty. My old daddy has some gettin'-away money waitin' for me, but they keep a guard around his place so that I dassn't try to go in." He turned to Shanty. "That's why I've come to your place. I need a favor from you."

Rusty said crisply, "I don't see where Shanty owes you

any favors. You tried once to run him off of his place."

"I have repented my ways."

Shanty asked, "What's the favor?"

"My old daddy works several nig—fellers like you. I don't think the police would take much notice if another one was to show up there. It's hard to tell you people apart. My daddy could give you the money, and you could fetch it here to me. I'd pay you for your trouble."

Shanty said, "Your old daddy don't have no use for the likes of me. How come you think he'd trust me with his money?"

"I'd write a note for you to give him."

Firmly Rusty said, "Shanty, the Oldhams know who you are and where to find you. If they caught on to what you were up to they might damned well kill you. At least they'd see to it that you never got out of jail."

Andy had stood back, listening, saying nothing. Now he spoke. "Shanty don't need to go. I will."

Rusty turned on him. "Why? Why you?"

"Anything to bedevil them Oldhams." He rubbed the quirt mark on his face. It still burned at times. "They owe me."

Rusty argued, "It'd be just as risky for you as for Shanty. They'd grab you by the collar as soon as you showed up."

"But I wouldn't show up, not to where they could see me. I sneaked into a Comanche tepee and got Billy out without wakin' anybody. I ought to be able to slip into the Brackett house without stirrin' up the police."

Rusty disapproved, but he soon saw he was going to lose the argument. He said, "I'll ride with you, then. I want to be close by in case you need help."

"No. You stay here. All of you stay here. This is a job I'd best do by myself, the coyote way."

A ndy could barely make out the house as a thin cloud
stole most of the limited light from a quarter moon.

Farley Brackett had told him three times, "Don't forget,
my old daddy's bedroom is in the southwest corner. If you
go into the wrong one my mother or my sister are liable to
holler."

Andy had become impatient with the advice. Farley
seemed to consider him slow in the head. He suspected that
Farley was not especially concerned about Andy's safety.
He wanted to get his money as quickly as possible and run.

Farley had said, "I just wisht I could shoot me one more
state policeman before I leave. Clyde Oldham would be my
pick. Or Buddy if I couldn't get Clyde."

Rusty asked, "What is it you like so much about shootin'
police?"

"I don't rightly know. Maybe it's the way they jump
when they're hit. Anyway, they're all Yankees at heart.
Texas could do with a lot less of them."

Andy stopped a hundred yards out and tied the reins to
a tree. He reasoned that the guards would have moved close
to the house at dark. Before he put down his full weight
he tested each step for twigs that might crack or gravel that

might slip underfoot. Shortly he saw a flash of fire as someone lighted a cigarette. Good. He had *that* guard located.

The cloud drifted on, uncovering the moon, though the
light remained dim. Andy moved sideways to put more distance between him and the guard he had spotted. He
stopped abruptly as he caught a movement and heard a
voice.

"Silas, you got any tobacco? I'm plumb out."

The guard he had seen first moved toward the voice.
"Yeah, but be careful when you light it. If the captain sees
it, we'll all catch hell."

"Reminds me of an officer I had in the army. Mad about
somethin' all the time. He's sure got it in for them Oldhams."

"With good reason. We almost had Farley Brackett, 'til
Buddy charged in before we was ready and got his horse
knocked out from under him. Damn, but that Farley's a
crack shot."

"At least Buddy's better than Clyde. Never saw a man
who could disappear so quick when he hears a gun go off."

While the two guards continued their conversation, Andy
circled around them. He was almost to the back of the
house. He worried over a dim patch of moonlight he had
to cross before he could reach the porch. He worked along
carefully in the shadow of a shed, looked hard in all directions, then passed quickly through the stretch of open
ground. He stopped in the darkness of the porch, listening
for any indication that someone had seen him. He could
still hear faintly the guards' conversation. The only other
sound was crickets in the trees.

The back door was open for ventilation, so he need not
worry about noisy hinges. Inside the house, he found himself in a hallway that extended all the way to the open front
door. He saw the dark outline of a guard sitting on the edge
of the front porch.

The floor creaked under his weight, giving him a moment's pause until he saw that the guard was not respond-

ing. He decided that nervousness exaggerated his perception of the noise.

Jeremiah Brackett slept in the southwest corner room, Farley had said. The doors to two other bedrooms opened into the hallway. Bethel and Elnora Brackett slept in those, he reasoned. He had no wish to awaken them. Startled, they might cry out and bring the guards running in.

His eyes grew accustomed to the gloom. He could make out a bureau with a mirror on it and a pitcher and bowl. Brackett's bed was pulled up next to the deep window for fresh air. Brackett snored softly.

Andy touched his shoulder and leaned down to whisper in his ear. "Mr. Brackett. Wake up."

The farmer jerked. His snoring ended abruptly with a choking sound. He raised up from his pillow, looking around wildly.

"No noise, Mr. Brackett," Andy whispered. "There's a guard sittin' on your front porch."

"Who are you?" Brackett demanded hoarsely. "If you're here to rob me you've come to a poor place."

"You remember me. I'm Andy Pickard, from over at Rusty Shannon's."

"The Indian boy? What do you want?"

"I've come on an errand for Farley. He says you've saved some gettin'-away money for him."

Brackett seemed to have awakened fully. He swung his legs out of the bed and set his feet on the floor. "How do I know you're doin' this for Farley? How do I know you're not here to take the money and light out with it?"

Andy reached into his shirt pocket. "Got a letter from him to you. He was aimin' to send Shanty, but I've come instead."

"Shanty? That darkey?" The thought seemed to puzzle Brackett. He unfolded the letter but could not read it in the poor light. He reached toward a lamp.

Andy said, "I wouldn't light that. Might cause the guards to come in and see what's goin' on."

Brackett tried holding the letter close to the window but

still could not read it. "I'll have to take your word. I reckon if you weren't honest, Shannon wouldn't have put up with you for so long."

He pulled a pair of trousers over his bare legs and half buttoned them. "The money's in the parlor, hidden in the back of a drawer."

"I hope you can get it without rousin' up the guard on the porch."

Brackett's weight made the floor squeak more than it had under Andy. Andy stood in the hallway, his back to the wall beside the parlor door, and watched the guard. The slump of the man's shoulders indicated that he might be asleep, but Andy knew he could not count on that.

He heard the desk drawer slide, wood dragging upon wood. It rattled as Brackett reached inside. Andy heard the drawer being closed again, slowly and carefully.

All the caution went for nothing, because Brackett knocked something off of the desk. It crashed on the floor. Andy's heart leaped.

He heard a woman's startled cry from one of the bedrooms. The guard jumped to his feet, pistol in his hand. Mrs. Brackett came into the hallway, carrying a lighted lamp. Andy desperately signaled for her to blow it out, but it was too late. The guard stood in the front door, eyes wide.

Andy recognized Buddy Oldham.

Jeremiah came out of the parlor. Buddy took a quick glance at him and jumped off of the porch. He turned and fired a wild shot into the hallway. He shouted, "Git him, Clyde. It's Farley Brackett!"

Andy realized that in his confusion Buddy had mistaken the father for the son. Both Oldhams fired again. Elnora Brackett gasped and dropped the lamp. It smashed, spreading kerosene on the floor. Flames hungrily followed the flow.

Clyde Oldham shouted, "We got him. Shoot! Shoot!"

A dozen shots exploded from the darkness, smashing into the walls.

Bethel rushed from her bedroom and gasped in horror.

She ran to her mother, twisted on the floor. Andy helped her drag Elnora away from the flames.

Jeremiah hobbled to the door, waving his arms. "Stop firing! You've hit my wife!"

Andy heard the thud of a bullet as it caught Jeremiah in the chest. It was followed by another. The farmer grabbed at the door facing, sighed and fell, his body sliding down the wall.

Andy lay flat on the floor and motioned for Bethel to do the same. He shouted, "Quit firin'. Farley Brackett's not here."

The firing tapered off, then stopped. The two guards who had been in the back yard rushed into the hallway from the far end. They wasted only a few seconds surveying the situation. One went to the front door and called to his companions, "It's over with. We got two people shot in here."

The other guard trotted into the nearest bedroom and returned with a heavy quilt to spread over the flames. He stomped on the quilt until the fire was snuffed out.

Clyde Oldham entered the hallway, trembling with excitement. "We got him. We got him." Buddy followed, pistol in his hand. It was still smoking.

Andy's fear receded. In its place came outrage. "You sorry son of a bitch, you shot Farley's mother and father. Farley ain't here. He never was."

Buddy argued, "But I saw him."

"You saw Jeremiah, and you killed him."

Clyde recognized Andy for the first time. "You're Rusty Shannon's Indian."

Defiantly Andy said, "I'm nobody's Indian."

Someone found another lamp and lighted it. A policeman of severe countenance motioned for the holder to lower it while he looked first at Jeremiah, then at Elnora. She was still alive and moaning. He gave Clyde Oldham a look of loathing.

"All you did here was kill an old man and wound an old woman. I've had as much of your bungling as I can handle, Clyde. You're off the force."

Clyde demanded, "You're firin' me?"

"Damn right. And take your quick-triggered brother with you. I'll be at the courthouse in the morning to pay you off. Then I never want to see either one of you, ever again."

Buddy argued, "But Captain, I was certain—"

"Git, before I take a notion to shoot you myself."

Bethel knelt and took her mother's hand. Elnora squeezed Bethel's fingers. Her eyelids fluttered open. She turned her head painfully and looked toward her husband. Her voice was barely audible. "Is he—"

"Yes, Mama, he's gone."

Elnora closed her eyes against a flow of tears. "I'm sorry. I treated him badly. I wish . . ."

She sobbed softly. Bethel laid her arm across her mother and cried.

The police captain growled, "It was so damned unnecessary." He cut his gaze to Andy. "Who are you? I don't remember I ever saw you before."

"Name's Andy Pickard."

"What were you doing here?"

Under the circumstances, lying came easy. "I was lookin' for a job. They asked me to spend the night."

The captain gave him a critical study. "Do you always sleep with your clothes on?"

"Yes sir, most of the time."

The captain shook his head in disdain. "It'll take forty years for this part of the country to become civilized." He looked down at Bethel. "We'll see what we can do about your mother's wound, then carry her to town. Can you get one of your hands to hitch a team to your wagon?"

A black woman hesitantly entered the front door, her husband close behind her. "Lord God," she cried. She rushed to Bethel's side.

Bethel told the man to fetch a team and hitch up the wagon as the police captain had said.

The captain gave directions as two policemen carried Elnora into her room. He asked Bethel, "About your father . . . you want to bury him here or in town?"

"Here," she murmured. "Here's where he belongs."

The captain turned to his men. "Well, don't just stand there. Get that old man up from the floor. Carry him into that room yonder. The least we can do is to lay him out like a Christian."

Andy followed Bethel into the room where the police had carried her mother. She studied Andy as if she were seeing him for the first time. "What *were* you doin' here?"

He made sure none of the rangers could hear him, then explained his mission for Farley. "Your dad was fetchin' some money for him out of the parlor. It's probably in his pocket."

Bethel's voice went hard. "I almost wish they *would* catch him. It was him and his wild ways that caused all this."

"I heard the war turned him thataway."

"A lot of other men went to war without goin' outlaw. Anyway, it won't do any good to give him the money now. He won't leave 'til he's evened the score for this."

"How many more state police has he got to shoot?"

"Two, at least. The Oldhams." Bethel turned to the black woman. "Flora, I want you to go and bring all the hands. We've got a lot to do. We've got to let our neighbors know."

Andy stopped in the door and stared down the hallway toward the darkness of the front yard. "I dread goin' back and tellin' your brother what happened."

"It's mostly his doin'."

Andy saw a dark figure step up onto the porch and enter the hallway into the lamplight. It was Rusty. Andy met him halfway. "You oughtn't to be here," he said urgently. "There's police all over the place."

"I heard the shootin'."

Andy beckoned Rusty into Elnora's room. He said, "You followed me, didn't you?"

"I just said I wouldn't come with you. I didn't promise not to follow you. Wasn't no tellin' what trouble you might get into." He looked with concern at the wounded woman. "What about her husband?"

Andy shook his head. "Buddy Oldham started the shootin'. He saw the father and thought he was Farley." A worrisome thought struck him. "I hope Farley didn't come with you."

"I convinced him to stay at Shanty's. Told him he might bring danger to his folks." Ruefully Rusty added, "He did that without even bein' here."

Andy told Rusty about the captain firing the Oldhams. "Just the same, they've still got charges against you. Better get away from here before somebody recognizes you."

"We'd better both get away from here."

Andy took Bethel's hand. "You goin' to be all right?"

"It'll be a long time before I'm all right. But if you're askin' whether it's all right for you to go, the answer is yes. I've got good folks here to help me, and there'll be neighbors here in the mornin'."

"I'm sorry about all this. It wouldn't have happened if I hadn't come."

"But you came for Farley. It wasn't your fault. Wasn't anybody's fault but Farley's and the Oldhams'."

"I'll come back when I can and see if I can be any help."

"I'd like that, Andy. You'll be welcome." She clasped his hand tightly, then released it.

Andy felt a glow unlike any he had known before. He said quickly, "We better go, Rusty."

Some of the black laborers had begun coming in so that there was traffic on the front porch and in the hallway. Andy and Rusty departed through the back door into the darkness. No one seemed to pay them any attention, probably assuming they were policemen.

They retrieved their horses and started toward Shanty's. Rusty asked, "Did you get Farley's money?"

"No. There wasn't a chance, once the excitement started. He don't deserve it anyway."

Rusty grimaced. "I was hopin' he'd take it and go west, or down to Mexico. I'm afraid now he'll stay around for a chance at the Oldhams."

Andy said hopefully, "Maybe they'll kill one another, and it'll all be over."

"I've got a problem with that. Clyde Oldham took my farm in his name. He's the only one can sign it back over to me."

"He won't ever do it."

"He might, with my gun barrel stuck in his ear."

The coming sunrise was already lacing the skyline clouds with pink and purple when Andy and Rusty rode up to Shanty's place. The dog announced them. Farley Brackett came out from beneath the shed where he had spent the night. Andy had known he was unlikely to sleep in the cabin under the same roof with Shanty. Farley held a pistol in his hand until he was certain no one had come with Andy and Rusty, and no one had followed.

He demanded, "Where's my money?"

Andy felt like hitting him. "I didn't get it."

Farley's face twisted with anger. "Did that damned old man refuse to give it to you?"

Outrage gave a sharp edge to Andy's voice. "That damned old man died *tryin'* to give it to me."

Farley stood slack-jawed. "Died?"

In as few words as possible, Andy told him what had happened. Farley looked as if he had been shot in the stomach. "How bad is my mother hurt? What about my sister?"

"Your mother is probably on the way to town by now. Your sister wasn't hit."

Shanty had heard most of it. He stood silent, eyes sympathetic for a man who had shown him only contempt.

Farley turned his back, pulling himself together. When he turned again, his face was taut with anger and hatred. "What about them Oldhams? They still at our place?"

Andy said, "The captain fired them. Told them he would pay them off in town."

"Town!" Farley dropped his hand to the butt of his pistol. "Whereabouts in town?"

"I don't know. Courthouse, I guess."

Rusty frowned, motioning for Andy to be quiet. But the bag was already open and the cat let out.

Farley started for the corral, where his horse stood waiting for feed. "Then they'll get paid off twice."

Rusty said, "I wish you hadn't told him. Now he's on his way to kill the Oldhams."

"Wouldn't make any difference whether I told him or not. He'd figure it out."

Rusty swung back into the saddle. "We've got to try and get to town ahead of him. Maybe we can find some way to stop this."

"We might delay it, but I doubt we can stop it short of killin' him ourselves. Bethel said he won't leave here 'til he gets his revenge on Clyde and Buddy. I expect she's right."

Rusty said, "Shanty, see if you can keep Farley here a little longer. Offer him coffee, fix him breakfast . . . anything you can do."

"I'll try, Mr. Rusty, but looks to me like he's got the devil ridin' with him. Watch out he don't kill *you* if you get in his way."

Rusty spurred into a lope. Andy managed to bring Long Red up even. He said, "He'll know what you're up to. He'll run that horse to death tryin' to beat us to town."

Andy had reason to fear they might run their own horses to death. Rusty kept pushing hard, frequently looking back over his shoulder. Andy looked back too but could not see Farley.

He said, "Hadn't we better slow down a little? I can feel my horse givin' out."

"He can give out after we've done what we have to."

Andy muttered under his breath, then realized he had been talking Comanche to himself. He understood Rusty's reason for wanting to keep Clyde Oldham alive, but he could not help thinking that the community would be better off without either the Oldhams or Farley Brackett.

The courthouse was new, built of stone, with a cupola and a parapet. The old frame building had served well, but the local reconstruction government had decided that its dignity demanded something better, no matter the cost. The taxpayers were mostly rebels anyway.

Rusty reined up at the low rail fence that surrounded the courthouse square. His horse was lathered and breathing hard. Andy pulled in beside him and tied Long Red to a post. He said, "Maybe you'd better let me go talk to the Oldhams, if I can find them in there. Goin' by what they did last night, they may shoot you and *then* ask what you want."

"No, I want to try and make a bargain with Clyde."

Andy shrugged and followed Rusty up the steps. He had never been inside the new courthouse. Once through the door, he had no idea where the state police office might be. But Rusty knew. He led off down a corridor, Andy on his heels.

Andy remembered the captain from the night before. The officer looked up. He recognized Andy, but he did not seem to know Rusty.

Rusty said, "I'm lookin' for the Oldham brothers."

The captain studied him a moment. "I released them from the service this morning. They are no responsibility of mine."

"But where are they at?"

The captain's eyes narrowed. "Are you some kin of the Bracketts?"

"No, I'm Rusty Shannon. But if I don't find the Oldhams pretty quick, they're fixin' to meet up with a member of the Brackett family."

That got the captain's attention. "You mean Farley?"

"Yes, and if he gets to them first Jeremiah won't be the only man needs buryin'."

The captain said, "The Oldhams were in a surly mood when they left here. I would guess they have gone to one of the liquor establishments around the square to soak their anger in whiskey. What is your interest in them?"

"Clyde Oldham owes me a farm."

"I know about that. And you wish him to remain alive until you get it back?"

"That'd be long enough."

The officer reached for his pistol and belt, hanging on a hat rack beside the door. "I'll take the north side of the square. You take the south. But stand clear if Farley Brackett shows up. He belongs to me."

Rusty and Andy stepped out into the hallway. Rusty stopped so abruptly that Andy bumped into him. A sturdy man with thick gray mustache came out of an office on the other side. Rusty exclaimed, "Captain Burmeister!"

"Private Shannon. And Andy." The old ranger limped across the hall, his hand outstretched.

The police captain stopped, puzzled. "You know these men, Judge Burmeister?"

"Indeed. Many a long mile Private Shannon and I rode together as rangers. And Andy, he did a remarkable thing."

Rusty was still immobilized by surprise. "You're the new judge here? What happened to the other one?"

"He was a stealer. A little one only, but he did not share with the big stealers in Austin. He was fired. What brings you here?"

"Hopin' to stop a killin'. Maybe two of them. You remember the Oldham brothers?"

Burmeister nodded briskly. "But too well. Who are they about to kill?"

"More likely it'll be the other way around if we can't stop it."

"Then go, by all means. My docket is full already with murders." Judge Burmeister waited until Rusty and Andy were near the door before he called and pointed. "My office is here. Come visit sometime."

The police captain collared one of his deputies to help him. They went out another door.

To Andy's recollection, two whiskey shops stood on the street due south of the courthouse. He was considered underage and had not been allowed inside. He followed Rusty into the first one. A quick look around did not reveal the Oldhams. Rusty glanced anxiously up the street. Andy knew he was looking for Farley.

Rusty said, "Let's try this other one."

He headed for another, which Andy knew by reputation. Its sign marked it as LONE STAR GROCERY, with smaller letters proclaiming that it dealt in the finest of tobacco and spiritous liquors, and a billiard table from St. Louis. It was known as a hangout for off-duty state police and others of Union leanings. Most old Confederates avoided it.

Buddy Oldham sat at a table, a full glass and a half-empty bottle in front of him. Clyde Oldham stood with his back turned. He was haranguing half a dozen listeners with an account of how they had been unjustly dismissed from the state police force because of a natural mistake anyone might have made. "The old man was a diehard rebel anyway," he declared. "Ought to've been killed years ago, him and Farley too."

Buddy recognized Rusty and pushed his chair back from the table. He called to his brother. "Clyde."

Clyde was so busy talking that he did not hear the first time. Buddy repeated the call and stood up. "Clyde, looky who just came in."

Clyde turned. He froze a moment, then placed a hand on his pistol. "Rusty Shannon, you are under arrest."

Rusty said, "You've got no authority to arrest anybody. But if you want to try, there's a lot bigger game than me out yonder lookin' for you."

Buddy asked, "And who would that be?"

The startled expression in Clyde's face indicated that he already guessed. He spoke the name fearfully. "Farley Brackett?"

Rusty nodded. "He's on his way. May already be here. I'd advise you boys to go out the back door and not let your shirttails touch you 'til you're in the next county. Maybe two counties over."

Clyde's voice was shaky. "How come you tellin' us?"

"Because I want to keep you alive, at least 'til you sign my farm back to me."

"That'll be a cold day in hell." Clyde jerked his head. "Come on, Buddy." He started for the back door.

Buddy did not follow. Stubbornly he said, "I ain't scared of Farley Brackett. Almost got him a couple of times. Get him now and maybe they'll take us back into the police. Even if they don't, there's a reward on him."

Clyde was halfway to the back door. "I never seen a dead man collect a reward. Come on, Buddy, let's go while we can."

"No. I'm takin' Farley Brackett." Buddy started for the front. Clyde trotted after him and grabbed a handful of Buddy's shirt. Buddy jerked loose and went out the door.

Trembling, Clyde started after him but stopped, still inside the saloon. "Come on, you men," he called. "Buddy don't stand a chance. You got to help him."

Nobody seemed much inclined to move. Rusty said, "He's your brother. You stop him."

Clyde's hands shook as he surveyed the men in the room, some of them state police. "If we work together we can get Brackett this time. We'll split the reward, even money for everybody."

Nobody moved.

Clyde drew his pistol and shuffled uncertainly out the door. Rusty and Andy followed.

Andy asked Rusty, "Ain't you goin' to stop them?"

Rusty answered gravely, "It's gone out of our hands. The only thing that'll stop Buddy now is a bullet."

Buddy stood in the center of the street, pistol in hand, waiting. Farley was riding toward him. Other men, sensing what was building, hurried out of the way. As Farley dismounted and dropped his reins, Buddy shouted, "Farley Brackett, you are under arrest in the name of the law!"

Brackett did not reply. He walked toward Buddy. Buddy shouted at him to stop, but Farley kept coming. Buddy raised the pistol and fired.

Farley did not even flinch. He drew his revolver and put

two shots into Buddy's chest. Buddy buckled forward and fell on his face. He twitched a couple of times and was still.

Clyde made a noise that was almost a scream. The hand that held the pistol shook uncontrollably. He tried to raise the weapon, but he could not lift it. It was as if it weighed a hundred pounds.

Farley strode past Buddy and bore down on Clyde. Clyde cried out, "No!" His whole body was shaking. The pistol fell from his hand, and he sank to his knees.

"For God's sake, don't kill me."

"You wounded my mother. You killed my old daddy," Farley shouted at him. "Now pick up that pistol and die like a man."

Clyde hunched over, sobbing. "Oh God. Don't." He twisted around, trying to find Rusty. "Shannon, help me. Don't let him do it."

Andy did not know whether to pity the man or walk over and spit on him. He looked at Rusty, seeking Rusty's reaction.

Rusty walked forward to stand beside Clyde. "Farley, you've killed Buddy. One ought to be enough. I need Clyde to stay alive."

Farley hesitated, then leveled his pistol almost in Clyde's face. "I need him dead worse than you need him alive."

Rusty stepped between the two men. "I said one is enough. You'd better get on your horse and ride. There's a bunch of state police comin' around the courthouse."

Farley did not appear to believe him until he heard the captain shout. He gave Clyde a poisonous look. "All right, Shannon. But whatever you need him for, you better take care of it quick, because I'll be back."

He ran to his horse. He spurred out between two buildings and was gone. The captain called for his men to get their horses, but it would take them a few minutes.

A few minutes was all Farley Brackett needed.

Rusty reached down and took hold of Clyde's collar. "Get up from there. You're goin' over to the courthouse with me and sign some papers."

Clyde had quit sobbing. He resisted Rusty's strong pull. "I ain't signin' nothin'."

"You will. I know where Farley's goin'. Mess with me and I'll take you to him."

Andy knew that was a bluff, but he kept a straight face. Rusty too could play the trickster.

Reluctantly Clyde got up onto wobbly legs. "You wouldn't do that. You wouldn't turn a man over to somebody like Farley."

"I will if you don't dot every i and cross every t just like Judge Burmeister tells you."

It took about an hour for the judge to write out the deed and for all parties to sign it. Clyde's signature was shaky but legal. Done, Rusty said, "Judge, after I get the place cleaned up, I'd like you to come out and see it. We'll barbecue a hog."

"That would make me glad, Private Shannon. Glad indeed."

Rusty and Andy escorted Clyde to his horse. Clyde was still in shock, his gaze roaming up and down the street as if he expected Farley Brackett to come charging back any minute. He asked, "What we goin' to do about Buddy?"

Rusty said, "The county will take care of the buryin'. If I was you I'd leave before Farley shows up again and buries you. I wouldn't stop runnin' 'til I got to Louisiana. Maybe even Mississippi."

Farley had ridden westward. Clyde reined his horse eastward and put him into a lope. Andy doubted that he would slow down until the horse was exhausted. He said, "I hope we've seen the last of him. And Farley too."

Rusty said, "You never know."

Up the street a wagon arrived, driven by a black farm hand. Bethel Brackett sat beside him. Rusty watched them. "Looks like they're headed for the doctor's. I expect they've got Mrs. Brackett in the wagon."

"That's the way I figure it."

Rusty made a thin smile. "That Bethel's a nice-lookin'

girl but a little light in weight. Maybe you'd better go see if you can be any help to her."

Andy nodded. "I think I'll do that." He trotted up the street.

Rusty held the deed tightly in his hand. Watching Andy speak to the girl, he was reminded of Josie Monahan. Soon as he caught up doing what was needful around the farm, he would write Josie a letter.

He might even take it to her himself.

• EPILOGUE •

By the December election of 1873, the disenfranchised Confederate veterans had regained the right to vote. Two to one, they chose Richard Coke over the longtime reconstruction governor, Edmund J. Davis, a basically honest man who had been given too much power for his own good or the good of the people of Texas. Davis for a time rejected the results and maintained that the election was unconstitutional. As the inauguration date approached in January, 1874, Davis held out, refusing to relinquish his office. For several days armed groups from both sides jockeyed for position in and around the state capital, threatening but never quite coming to violence.

Barricaded in the capitol building, Davis twice telegraphed President Ulysses S. Grant, begging for military force to keep him in office. Grant refused, advising him to give up the struggle. Davis did, finally, and a new era dawned in Texas.

A new constitution was written, guaranteeing that no governor ever again would have dictatorial powers. The Texas Rangers were reorganized, stronger and more efficient than ever before.